THE CHAINED

LAST OF THE GARGOYLES BOOK 1

FoxTales Press

DANI HOOTS

The Chained
Last of the Gargoyles, #1
© 2018 Dani Hoots
Content Edits by Chantelle Aimée Osman of a Twist of Karma
Entertainment
Line Edits by Justin Boyer and Hilary Kamien
Cover Design Copyright © 2020 by Biserka Designs
Formatting by Dani Hoots
All rights reserved.

This is a work of fiction. All characters and events portrayed in this novel are
fictitious and are products of the author's imagination. Any resemblance to actual
events, locales, or persons, living or dead, is entirely coincidental.

ISBN: 978-1-942023-55-5

CHAPTER 1

Chaos ran through the streets of Paris once again. It had been such a long time since Gwen had witnessed such a revolt, and such bloodshed. People were in a panic throughout the city—smashing windows, fighting neighbors, stealing what was not rightly theirs. She wondered how many of them were still human, or if a lesser demon possessed them. Only time would tell.

War had begun. Gwen had sensed it a few years back as tension rose higher and higher in many of the more developed countries, or at least what humans thought were developed. Humans were fools as they did not know how truly uncivilized they were compared to the Heavens. Then again, she could never go back to Heaven because of her past choices, so maybe she was the bigger fool.

Taking one more look around, Gwen stuffed an old knife she had been waiting to use for exactly this moment into her backpack and hurried off toward her black 1940 BMW R75 motorbike that waited outside on the curb. Luckily it hadn't been damaged in the riot that was going through the city. As she pulled on her helmet, Gwen took a deep breath, her eyes flashing yellow. The smell of blood saturated the air so completely she could taste it. Shaking the desire to feast out of her head, as she couldn't afford to take any part in the violence that erupted around her, Gwen sped down the street. Motorcycle regulations in France had gotten stricter by the year, but with a riot like this happening, no one would bother doling out any harsh penalties to a person breaking a few minor traffic rules.

As Gwen drove, she watched as crazed men flocked the area with lighters and crowbars in hand. Humans broke into shops that merchants had deserted in this time of crisis, and shattered glass in every direction. Security blocked off roads, and the police shouted at Gwen as she rode past the barriers without a care. They did not understand how much force it would take to truly stop her—a demon who had a mission to finish.

Her mission, which was one she had been trying to complete for the past seventy or so years, was to get a one-on-one talk with a Gargoyle, the one named Erik to be specific. There were only three Gargoyles left, which may or may not have been because of her, but she had no choice at this point. She couldn't turn back from her mission now—not when she had risked so much to get here.

Gwen knew where Erik would be, as his kind always went to the same place before a battle—the church. It wasn't the best place for her to enter, but she could manage it. She knew she would be at a disadvantage but she hoped that might allow her to gain even an ounce of his trust.

She knew which church he would be at too—the Saint Clotilda, a cathedral she had seen him attend more than once. Approaching the Cathedral on her motorbike, Gwen got a whiff of a particular scent. It was an aftershave, one that she didn't believe had been around for a good half of a century. Musky with no hint of sweetness, just like his soul, if he even had one. She cursed under her breath. Jürgen, one of the demon generals she once stood beside. That was before she betrayed them all and ruined their chances of opening the Gates of Hell. Not that they still couldn't do that, but more that she ruined their chance to do it a little over seventy years ago.

And she knew he would not be happy about seeing her here of all places, and would send her to Hell where Lucifer *Himself* would punish her for her disobedience.

She twisted back the throttle.

The tall, double spires and the rose-like stained glass of the cathedral loomed before her. Drifting to a halt, Gwen jumped off her bike and ran up the steps into the church.

"Erik!" Gwen called out as she entered the nave.

Except for a few candles here and there, only the light filtering in through the colorful windows lit the main area of the cathedral. Rows and rows of pews surrounded her, casting even more shadows. Gwen never cared for dark cathedrals, or light ones for that matter. They were aesthetically pleasing, but the reminder of being on trial in Heaven, having her wings ripped out of her back, and a chain pulling her down to Earth wasn't something she enjoyed experiencing over again.

A tall, brown-haired man had his back to her as he lit the last of the candles at the altar—a ritual his Holy kind did before every battle. It was some kind of prayer for the souls that would be lost, if she wasn't mistaken, from all the times she had spied on him. She considered it a waste of time, but she knew Erik wouldn't leave before he had completed it, no matter what was chasing him.

"About time you showed up." He turned to her and smiled as if war wasn't being waged all around the city. "I was beginning to think you didn't have the courage to approach me."

His eyes were honest, something she wasn't used to. He had a young face which showed no signs of the weariness associated with someone who had experienced years of warfare. Some would say the same about her. If Gwen didn't know him as well as she did, she wouldn't consider him a threat. But she knew better.

Gwen hurried up to him, hands shaking. She needed to get out of this cathedral. *Fast.* The energy was already affecting her body. *Was she really this weak*, she thought to herself. She tried to bring her attention away from herself and saw that Erik had fully lit the altar now, candles flickering. While dipping his hands into a bowl of water, she noted that he had made sure no drops were accidentally flung out at her. It was Holy water, after all, and it would burn her worse than the fire. So he didn't want to hurt her, at least for now.

"I've been trying to catch up to you for the past seventy years," Gwen kept her eyes on his hands, just in case he did decide to fling water on her, so she would be prepared to dodge it. She knew how badly that stuff burned—like hell. She would know. "This is the first time you've let me say a word to you, at least in these circumstances."

"I figured after this long you must have something important to say." He eyed her as he blew out the match.

The scent of the burnt wood filled her nostrils. The smell always gave her a sense of calm, contrary to the chaos just outside the cathedral. She shook off the feeling, knowing she couldn't afford to waste her time with such emotions. There was another battle beginning.

"And you meeting me here in a cathedral makes me think this isn't a trap, which your kind likes to try every so often. There are so many things I can use in here to hurt you..." He gestured to the crosses, holy water, and candles that surrounded them.

Gwen glanced around. He was right about that. "I'm not here to set you up," she added, even though he had just agreed with her.

"I still wonder, though, why I should believe a demon

like you?"

She ran her fingers through her short, scarlet hair. "Look, I don't have enough time to explain all of this. One of the Twelve is nearby and we should really be getting out of here. I know a Holy being like you has no reason to believe me, especially after what I have done to your kind... and to you. But please, for this moment, trust me. I want to help."

Erik examined her for a second longer, then nodded. "Fine. I'm heading to London this afternoon. Come with me and we can finish this little chat. Then I'll decide if I can trust you or not."

"London?" she asked, surprised he would leave so early in the game. It took a lot to drive Erik's kind from a city. "What about Paris?"

He shook his head as his eyes drifted toward the city. "We have lost París, I got here too late. There are too many possessed to restore balance. We need to leave before we won't be able to."

His tone made her fear what was in store for them once they stepped outside of the church together. She knew it would only be a matter of time before they figured out what she would do. "How do you know London is the next target?"

"After fighting with you Twelve and your minions for the past two-thousand years, you become a bit predictable." He gestured toward the exit. "After you."

Gwen rushed out of the cathedral, shuddering, thankful to finally get out of there. The place gave her the creeps. She stepped down to where her bike waited.

Erik raised his eyebrow as she handed him a spare helmet. "This is your ride? A little outdated, isn't it?"

"I love this bike." Gwen admired her bike's metallic beauty as she let her hand slide against the bars. "I've had it since the second world war. You have no idea how many scrapes it has gotten me out of."

"I think I might." He flipped the helmet in his hand as he started to put it on. "Let me drive, I'd rather know where I'm going than hope you aren't taking me to that little friend of yours that's after us."

"If it makes you feel better." She gestured to him to get on the bike before her. "Just don't hurt my baby."

He climbed on with a little smirk and she followed suit, wrapping her arms around him. She felt his tight muscles but doubted he ever worked out. Neither of them had to do anything to keep up their physical strength, at least in appearance. She, after all, had to feed on blood to keep from dying, while Erik probably didn't need anything to keep his body at a hundred percent on Earth. Sure, he might eat mortal food, but it would have had nothing to do with needs, more just to fit in.

The Heavenly aura that Erik gave off made her a little uneasy. She could barely remember having the same aura once, many centuries ago. It was before being condemned, heavenly wings ripped out of her back, and chained down to this world full of pain and suffering. Though at least she had deserved to be sent to this land. She made the choice in the Holy War. Erik, on the other hand, had to endure this world to fight in the battle between Heaven and Hell.

There wasn't a point in time where she didn't want to destroy a Gargoyle until now. It took a lot of restraint not to give in to the temptation at that moment, as she was weaker than she would like to admit. Gargoyle blood surpassed that of any human—almost like a high that was hard to come down from. It was a high she hadn't relished in for years. She had fought and killed many of the twelve Gargoyles God had sent down to fight those who stood with Lucifer.

Gwen held on tight as Erik revved the engine and started down the street. The riots hadn't spread into this area just yet, but she knew it would only be a matter of time. Erik made his way south down the narrow streets, passing rows of shops of all kinds along the way. Gwen took a deep breath and closed her eyes. One of the Twelve still followed—Gwen could smell him, the scent of a demon differing greatly from that of any human, even a possessed one. She and Erik had to get out of there quickly.

"He's following us," Gwen shouted into Erik's ear. She didn't know if he actually heard her, but knew he understood her worry.

Gwen took in another breath. Not only could she smell the demon following, but she could also smell that old German cologne he always wore. She knew it was Jürgen —one of the remaining five of the Twelve Admirals of Lucifer. Old habits die hard, but who was she to criticize? She bet that he even still had his goatee mustache. The thoughts of him made her shudder. She didn't want Jürgen to find her, not when she had betrayed their kind and now had her arms wrapped around the enemy. Their enemy.

Snaking through the crowds of people and cars, Gwen realized how far France had really fallen. She could sense minions, humans that had been killed while possessed by a lesser demon, around them flooding the streets. It had happened so fast. It surprised her that the trains to other countries were still running. Then she remembered who had control: The Twelve.

Gwen cursed under her breath. Jürgen had gained on them. He was only a few car lengths back now, driving a more modern motorcycle, a black Suzuki GSX-S1000F ABS. Just as she started to say something to Erik, she heard shots. Gwen glanced behind her. Jürgen was shooting at them with some kind of handgun. Gwen couldn't tell what it was from such a distance. He never played fair.

He kept shooting. Gwen remembered he'd always preferred a .45, so she figured he had a maximum of eight bullets in his gun. Hopefully, that was all he had. He could change magazines, but usually he carried extra weapons instead of extra magazines. So sixteen odd bullets, between two weapons, would be the best estimate.

Speeding up, Erik twisted past citizens and tourists, in order to escape the incoming bullets. People were running every which way due to the sound. She wondered how many of them would survive this war.

Erik did his best to dodge the bullets, but Jürgen wasn't one to miss all of his shots. Gwen flinched as a bullet hit her back. Biting her lip, she tried to hold in the yelp of pain. Yes, definitely a .45. Blood soaked the back of her jacket. He would pay for that. She loved that damned jacket.

Gwen held on as Erik drifted into a turn. The Eiffel Tower stood in the distance before them, guarding the city like a sentinel. She felt another bite in her back. Gwen cursed out loud this time. She didn't like being used as part of Jürgen's target practice. She knew he would probably have a good laugh about it later. Oh, how she hated him...

A bus pulled out in front of them. Erik swerved the bike into the park, barely missing the bus. People dove out of the way, making Erik almost flip the bike over in an effort to dodge. Jürgen still followed behind them, immune to the fact the street was full of people scrambling out of the way. He had the skill to make it through as well.

Gwen glanced behind her and was unsurprised to find three more on motorcycles had joined the chase. From their scent, she could tell they were all Jürgen's minions.

It could never be easy, Gwen thought, *how could it?*

"Great, who called in the cavalry?" Gwen mumbled to herself as they opened fire in their direction.

Bullets rained across the park, clipping trees and railings. Gwen saw a few humans hit in the crossfire. There was nothing she could do, and honestly, would she even try to help them? What were a couple of deaths in the name of stopping many from dying? It was a thought she had been pondering for quite some time now.

Two more bullets dug into her back. Today was really not her day. But, to be honest, was any day really her day?

Getting the motorcycle back onto the street, Erik steered around the roundabout. Gwen knew Jürgen was just warning her with the shots of what was to come. He wouldn't risk actually capturing her, thankfully. He just wanted to make a point and cause her pain. Mostly the latter. He always liked doing that, even before she left to stop the demons from reigning on Earth. But it still scared her—the thoughts of what he wanted to do.

Erik skidded through a red light, almost colliding with a car. Gwen closed her eyes until she felt the bike regain its steadiness. The impact wouldn't kill her, but the pain would be a great inconvenience. Not to mention that it might push her over the edge.

Jürgen still followed, making his way through the pile-up. He hadn't given up on the chase yet.

Knowing what they must do to get rid of Jürgen, Gwen motioned toward an entrance to the Paris Metro. Erik nodded, understanding what she wanted him to do. Holding on as tight as she could, Gwen braced herself as Erik took the bike down the stairs and into the station. More people screamed as Erik raced down the station platform, trying to lose Jürgen in the chaos. Jürgen followed them down, which surprised Gwen. She didn't think he would keep following after all of this. He must have been really pissed off at her.

Taking the turn to the platform for line 6, Erik cranked

on the gas just as the train roared into the station. Gwen realized he would try to beat the train before it blocked the exit out. *There was no way they would make it*, Gwen thought. She knew, however, if they came through unscathed, then Jürgen wouldn't be able to pursue them.

Gwen screamed as the motorcycle jumped off of the platform and into the tunnel leading outside. Screeching brakes echoed through the tunnel behind them. They had done it. Glancing behind them, she didn't see any trace of Jürgen or the minions, just the lights from the subway.

Erik took the bike off of the tracks at the next station. Slowing the motorcycle back down to a reasonable speed, Gwen let her body relax. It had been a while since she raced through the streets like that in any city, though the last few times it had been for fun. This time, she felt, it was more about surviving to live another day.

Gwen knew she had to get rid of the bloodstained clothes she had on. Pointing toward an alleyway, she motioned for Erik to stop. He did as she asked.

As he stopped the bike, Gwen jumped off, stumbling a bit due to the rush of adrenaline rushing through her from both the ride and her wounds.

Erik took off his helmet. "I'm surprised you screamed. I didn't think you feared pain so much."

"I don't. I screamed because I didn't want you to destroy my bike." Gwen pulled off her bloodied jacket and opened the dumpster.

Erik's eyes widened as he saw the amount of blood still dripping off the jacket. "Are you okay?"

"I'm fine. I just need to get out of these clothes or they'll be able to smell me no matter where I am in the city." Reluctantly, she tossed the jacket into the dumpster.

"Here," Erik unbuttoned his shirt to get to his undershirt, which he gave her. "You can wear this."

Gwen pulled off her shirt without hesitation. Erik quickly looked away, still holding his shirt out for her.

She grabbed the outstretched shirt from Eric's hands and pulled it on, laughing at his reaction. "You're too modest, Erik."

"Leave it to a demon to not understand the importance of modesty." He watched as she threw the rest of the bloody clothes in the dumpster. The shirt was a bit on the baggy side, but Gwen didn't mind. She tied the loose end in a knot around her waist.

"Oh, I understand it all too well." She smiled and gestured to the bike. "Shall we?"

CHAPTER 2

James woke to the tune of *Before You Accuse Me*, an Eric Clapton classic, playing loudly from his ringing cell phone. He opened his eyes. Checking the time, he fumbled out of bed, half-asleep, reaching toward the phone. The clock at his bedside showed it was only a quarter to four in the morning. Why he kept the phone in his bedroom, and over on his dresser, he didn't know. He supposed it was in case someone important called—not that such a thing ever happened. It was all just for supposed safety measures.

He picked up the phone, jamming the talk button with his thumb. "This better be damn important, do you have any idea what time it is over here?"

James heard a slight growl on the other end of the line.

"Sorry to wake you, I just thought you would want to know who I ran into."

It was Jürgen, one of the Twelve Admirals that served Lucifer alongside him. James rubbed the sleep out of his eyes, letting the sentence sink in. "If this is some kind of joke, I am *not* in the mood."

"It's not a joke. I saw her with my own eyes - Guinevere. She was with one of them. Helping him, I think."

James felt the hair on his neck rise. She wouldn't help them. She couldn't. She was his Gwen. "What do you mean *you think*?"

"All right, I know she is. She was riding with him on that bike of hers."

"Bike? She still has that thing?"

"Yup, it's in pretty good shape too, surprisingly."

James couldn't believe she had kept it, after all this time. He used to ride with her on that outdated contraption everywhere. Now she rode on it with the enemy. James squeezed his fist. She had really done it. She had betrayed him. Taking a deep breath, James remembered Jürgen still waited for his response on the other end of the line. "What did you do to her?"

"Just gave her a little warning." James could hear his smirk.

"What kind of warning?"

"I just shot her a couple times, that's all."

James slammed his fist on the dresser. She was his alone to deal with in any way he saw fit. "How many times have I told you. She. Is. *Mine*."

"I couldn't let her get away with what she did, I'm not like you. My feelings don't cloud my judgment. She deserves to be punished. This war between Heaven and Hell would have been over if it weren't for her and you know it."

The war. The word felt as if it was their life now. A never-ending war had been waged between good and evil for millennia. Every time they got closer to the finish line, the harder everything seemed to get. It didn't help when Gwen had betrayed them by destroying their chance at killing the last three Heavenly beings by shooting their minion they had used to control WWII. Then everything fell apart, and they had to start all over. James would deal with her soon though.

"What exactly happened?" James sighed.

Jürgen went through the details of the chase. James felt his muscles clench as he told of her stunt in the Metro station. James could just imagine it. She had always liked to make a dramatic exit.

"You almost killed her?" James said once Jürgen was done telling the story.

"I didn't make her jump in front of that train."

James tried to control his temper, but all of it started to become a bit much for him. "You shouldn't have chased her in the first place!"

"Oh, because you have done such a great job dealing with her so far."

He ignored the comment. "Where is she now?"

"Heading to London I presume, as am I. I tried following her scent after I shot her since her blood was fresh, but she had already dumped her clothes. I'm keeping her jacket as a souvenir. I want to remember the satisfaction of the moment I shot her. Anyway, it would be in your best interest to come as soon as you can."

"Oh, you can count on that. The minions here should be able to handle things on their own now. Besides, I'm not going to leave you in the same city as her. I will catch the next available flight over."

"Good. I have already prepared for the battle in London. We will have to act fast in order to win this one. Everything is in place except for a few minor details."

"Don't start anything until I am there."

"I won't. Of course we will have to deal with Gwen first. We will need a plan."

"I'll work on it before I get there."

"Just remember she is a master at playing games."

That was the understatement of the century. James needed more than just simple preparation. He needed a full battle plan. "You don't have to remind me."

"Yes, I do. She got past you last time."

He ran his hands through his short dark hair. He knew he messed up last time, he didn't need everyone mentioning it over and over again. "As I've said before, you need not remind me."

"We will see about that. Oh, and James?"

"What?"

"Should you tell Seth, or should I?" Jürgen let the question linger. He only asked to piss James off even more.

James pinched the bridge of his nose. He didn't want

to think about Seth at that moment. As their leader for this round of the war, he was in charge of the tactical decisions. James knew he would order for her execution the moment he found out. No, he wouldn't let him find out.

"Let us wait a bit before we tell him, at least until I talk to her. Okay?" he hoped Jürgen would agree.

"Your choice." The phone started beeping. End of call.

James threw the phone and shoved everything off his dresser out of frustration. He couldn't believe the shit Gwen had gotten herself into this time. James rubbed his face with his rough hands. She had changed after they began the war with Germany as their pawn. Without any prior warning, she began feeling for the humans and destroyed the Twelve's best chance of winning the war. None of the demons had hearts—they deprived themselves of caring for the humans, causing destruction wherever they went. Yet, for some reason, Gwen decided that humans were worth being tortured in Hell for the rest of eternity for, and sabotaged their plan to take down the remaining three Gargoyles. And now she was riding her bike—*their bike*—through the city of Paris with one of them. He didn't know what had changed her mind, but he would find out soon enough.

James looked at the clock again. It hadn't even struck four yet. It wasn't the best time to hear that his girl had truly betrayed him after all these years. He already felt irritable, now he was full-on furious.

Deciding a little cool water may help cool his anger, James went into the tiny closet that was supposedly a bathroom and turned on the faucet. He splashed the water on his face. It didn't help. He punched the mirror above it, with the force of all the anger stemming from any thought of Gwen's betrayal. The mirror shattered.

"Damn her," he whispered as he licked the blood from the cuts on his fist and pulled out the shards of glass sticking out from the wounds. The wound healed in an instant though, as it did for all the Twelve demons. The length of time since he had last fed on blood determined the potency of his healing. He, for example, healed fast with so many meals walking around this part of Washington DC. Though the blood bond he had made with Gwen caused him to be a little weaker than others, as he hadn't seen her in a while and couldn't feed on her blood to replenish his strength.

There was nothing he could do now about Gwen—not until arrived in London. Pulling on his black pants and buttoning up his matching shirt, James figured he would head to the office where his minions awaited him. He wouldn't be able to fall back asleep with this information about his love rolling around in his head.

Grabbing his keys, James ventured down the streets of Washington D.C. Not many humans littered the streets at this hour, as they did during the day and early night. He preferred it that way. That meant there would be fewer witnesses around observing his suspect actions.

A man came at him from the opposite direction. James saw it as the perfect opportunity to get out his anger and frustration. Seizing the man by the collar, he shoved him into the alleyway and covered his mouth as he screamed.

James sank his fangs into the man's throat. The man tried to struggle to free himself, but the effort was well wasted. Human strength didn't compare to that of a demon's preternatural abilities.

Letting go, James wiped the blood off of his mouth and the lifeless body fell to his feet. The man wore a suit. He figured he must have worked for the government, as most did in the city. Glancing around, he made sure no one saw anything and started back towards his destination.

James never cared for Washington D.C. He could name plenty of cities he'd rather be in. It didn't have all the history and culture as others did, or at least not much that was still intact. The city was still young, trying to establish its roots. It had nothing compared to London or Rome.

He couldn't wait to get out of there. He missed the great *food* that Europe provided, and the restaurants as well. They didn't need food, not in the same way that humans did, but every once in a while, they liked to indulge in such pleasures to blend into their human surroundings in a more seamless manner. And some cooks weren't half bad.

Hurrying up the steps of the building his minions had gained access to, James didn't show his ID. He didn't need to as he was their master. James passed through the hall, catching sight of the minions as they worked. They planned, schemed, and caused trouble for any who opposed their conquest. They worked diligently, even though they were easily replaceable, as they were just humans killed by one of the Twelve, then possessed by a lesser demon from Hell, one that couldn't fully create a body on its own in the mortal world.

"Good morning, sir," one greeted him as he passed. This minion had a suit on and slicked back brown hair, looking like any other business man in the city. James nodded to him but didn't return the greeting. He wasn't in the mood for such formalities.

Arriving to his own office, he grabbed his laptop and searched for the next available flight to London. He found an open seat later that evening at six, and it would arrive in London the next morning. It was a seven-hour flight he didn't want to take, but he had no other choice. He had to see what trouble Gwen had gotten herself into.

James clicked the flight he wanted and a window popped up. It asked him if he wanted to book a hotel. He answered no. Another window popped up. James felt his eyes twitch. It wanted to know if he wanted to rent a car, as well.

"Who rents a car in London?" he mumbled as he clicked no. Another annoying window popped up. James slammed his hand on his desk in exasperation.

"No, I don't want a return flight, I clicked one-way for a reason!" he yelled at the computer as if it could hear him. Just because it was cheaper to have a return flight didn't mean he wanted one.

Finally getting through the mandatory scheduling questions, the website asked for his birthdate. James pulled out his wallet and checked his driver's license. The date showed him at almost forty. He needed to get a new ID soon. They usually cycled through identities fast. He had been on this mission too long to have reached that age on a license.

Once he entered all the information the airline needed, James leaned back in his chair and rubbed his face with his hands. After all the things they had done together, the horror they brought onto this world, the lives they had taken, the wars they had made, he had now discovered that she was off gallivanting around with the enemy. No, he would not allow it—he would not let her make a fool of him.

None of the demons knew the exact reason why she had disappeared after her little freak-out in Germany. She just got up and left one day, destroying everything they had accomplished in one fatal blow. Since then, they had to build back up from the bottom. No matter, they could do it all over again. They've done it before, and time was not an important factor. James just had to make sure she wouldn't destroy it all over again. That, he admitted to himself, would take much effort on his part. He was the only one who could stop her from bringing this downward spiral to further disaster. James was the only one who truly loved her and wanted to spare her the inevitable shame of the decision she was making.

Shaking off any further thoughts of her, James went back to his work, finishing things that needed to get done before he left. Any brooding thoughts would have to wait until the lengthy plane ride, where he would have all the time in the world to ponder things.

CHAPTER 3

Collin ran his sword directly into the heart of the creature that stood before him. It still reached for him, trying to tear him apart as it drew its last breath, its face twisted, almost unrecognizable as once being human. Collin was glad for that though, as it would have been harder to kill if it resembled one of his own.

"Bloody minions." He let the thing die as he pulled his sword out. It squirmed until at last it quit moving. One down, two more to go. Hearing footsteps coming toward him, Collin spun around and sliced the next one through the stomach. Blood sprayed out of its mouth and onto Collin. Another shirt ruined.

The last minion wouldn't be as easy to take down. It had sat and watched as its two partners died. Collin wondered if it thought about vengeance or if it just responded to orders. It really didn't matter, he just wanted the creatures dead.

Its skin clung to its body, misshaped in areas where the creature inside moved. Its eyes were always dark, fangs dripping with blood, voice sounding nightmarish as it muttered inaudible words under its breath. Latin, he presumed, just like in the movies. It amazed Collin how they could change from looking like normal humans to turning into nightmarish, disfigured creatures with the craving for human flesh in their mouths.

The minion lunged, claw-like hand extended. Leaning back, Collin dodged its hand as it swiped at his face. Damned thing almost got him. It kept attacking, driving Collin back. There was no opening for Collin to do anything but defend himself, until finally, there was a split-second opening and Collin swung at the fiend. The minion's head rolled onto the pavement, as the rest of its body collapsed onto the ground. Collin took a deep breath. After death, the bodies turned back to looking more human. But it wasn't human, he told himself, it was a minion. It had to die.

Collin dragged all three bodies to the bank of the Thames and threw them into the dark water where they would become just another of the unidentified floating bodies that thronged the deeper depths of the river. Whispers of gang activity had heightened over the past few years as some bodies had risen from the depths and made their way back to the shore. Collin wondered what would happen if they knew the truth that among the mortal bodies being thrown in the river already included some deceptively human-looking minion corpses.

Sitting down to rest, Collin watched as the last body sank into the river. How he got into this situation, he really didn't know. Five years ago, he had met a girl named Gwen. And sometime after meeting her, two men approached him with an offer to help them fight some sort of war between good and evil. Gwen, or at least the two men said, happened to be a demon, but those he helped now weren't demons. Rather, they were beings from Heaven, which is what Collin called them. They never gave their real names, always saying words which no one from this world could ever know or recognize.

He often thought about the night his world had changed—when he found the girl he loved, drinking the blood of another demon. Everything after that became a blur. Collin wanted to know what happened to her, but they would never tell him. Now, he spent his nights with Hugo, one of those beings that had come to him after Gwen's disappearance, hunting minions that terrorized cities. It wasn't the best job in the world, but it had to be done.

Collin heard the sound of glass crunching under a boot, and he quickly turned to find a minion jumping straight at him, its fangs exposed and eyes narrowed. Drool dripped from its bloodthirsty lips. Collin tried to get out of the way, but he knew he wouldn't be quick enough to avoid the thing coming at him. Just as the minion's hot breath touched his skin, it stopped and collapsed. Hugo stood emotionless behind it with a sword dripping in blood.

"Everything alright?" Hugo asked.

"Yeah." Collin stood up, feeling stupid for being caught off guard. "Must have missed one. Did you get yours?"

"I got both of the others." He wiped the blood off his sword on the minion's shirt.

Hugo's brown hair was crusted in blood, his clothes similarly decorated. Collin didn't understand how at both his pub and during the day, Hugo could appear to be the most carefree person, always with a smile on his face or laughing at life. But during the night, he turned into a completely different person. His face always looked serious and he never caught a sliver of a smile on his lips. Not to mention, an almost... perfect... aura surrounded him. Such pure air hovered over him, even as he was covered in blood.

"I will get rid of this one. You can head back to the pub. Get some rest before you have to open." Hugo kept his eyes down at the minion.

Looking out toward the rising sun, Collin realized morning had already approached. He would get only a few hours of sleep, before his assistant manager Hywel would come and help him prepare for the day. There never seemed to be enough hours in either the day or the night.

"Sometimes I wonder what's the point..."

Hugo looked at him for a moment then turned his attention back down to the dead minion, lying at his feet. "You know as well as I do that your job helps us finds these guys. People gossip most when they are intoxicated."

He was right, they did find these minions through rumors at the bar, but they could have easily found them without that. Minions weren't the hardest to find. "Yeah, yeah, I know. See you later tonight then?"

"Same time."

"Aye. Good morning then I suppose." Collin nodded as he left him behind. He would have to get out of the streets before the early birds started heading for work.

They hadn't ventured that far from his pub, which made him happy. They had run a little longer than normal that night. Time became relative when it didn't matter anymore, especially when in the thick of action. Usually they would get done before dawn, which made it easy for him to go back to the pub in the shadows of night, unnoticed. With the sun just about to come up, it made it that much harder not to get noticed by someone he might know in the area.

He passed brick building after brick building in the area that was all part of Chelsea. Famous for their football team, he personally was more of a fan of Manchester City, but he never revealed that to any of his customers. He didn't need to start a fight, especially when the two teams played against each other. There were enough of those already. Though his assistant manager, Hywel, knew he rooted for Manchester City and they took bets on who would win, the loser getting to stay late and clean up the mess the fans left behind. Hywel won more times than not.

Collin's pub stood just on the outskirts of the city, almost encroaching upon the edge of South Kensington. Hidden deep in the alleyways, people had to know about it to find it. That way fewer tourists would visit and more locals would love it. And locals were more likely to gossip.

He could always spot an American tourist though, when they did come in. They didn't understand European pubs. They always stood at the door for a moment, as if waiting for someone to seat them. Finally, they would take a seat before realizing they had to order at the bar. Collin and Hywel would also bet on how long it would take them. They played a lot of games like that. Though, at least Americans tipped. Sometimes...

Collin could see the sign now hanging from the pub's front, marked with the name "Lancelot's Pub." It had been an inside joke between him and Gwen, but he had thought the name was clever, so he kept it even though it reminded him of her.

He learned to live with the fact that he may never see Gwen again, although it ate him up inside. Collin had thought she could be the one, and then she left in a hurry. No explanation. No excuses. Just got up and left.

That's when Hugo showed up and he had been destroying minions ever since.

Pulling out his keys, he unlocked the door and stepped inside. The only light that filled the space was the fresh light of the dawning sky pouring into the pub, along with a small amount of light spilling from his upstairs bedroom. He locked the door behind him and took a sigh of relief. His work was done for the day, or at least for a couple of hours.

Setting his sword on the bar, Collin decided to postpone its cleaning until after he got a little sleep. Sleep had become sparse these days as more minions seemed to be pouring into the city. He had no idea from where they came from, or even what was the cause of their increased numbers. Hugo had said the start of a war always involved the growth of minion activity, but he didn't explain any further. A gut instinct, but the more he thought about the future, the more he feared everything was about to change.

Collin collapsed onto his mattress and stared at his wall. The room didn't have any knick-knacks, color, or any personality of any kind. He didn't see the point, not when he could be forced to leave at any time. The only thing that stood out in the room was that one wall had marks all over it. Grabbing a pen, he leaned over and ticked three more notches. He had begun to run out of room for tally marks. He didn't know if that made him feel good about himself, or if he had seen more than he wanted to admit.

Chucking the pen back onto the floor, Collin closed his eyes to find only blood waiting for him in his dreams.

CHAPTER 4

"You don't really think they will let you take that bike on the train, do you?" Erik raised his eyebrows as he watched Gwen lift her bike up the steps and into Gare du Nord, the station that led to London. It must have looked odd to see such a petite girl carrying a motorcycle without any effort, but Erik knew the truth of why she was capable of such an impressive physical feat. He knew of all the things she had done throughout the centuries, and this was really nothing compared to those things.

"I'm not leaving it behind—not after all these years."

Erik couldn't believe the level of her attachment to this trinket. They were creatures, once angelic, who roamed the earth for centuries, yet she acted like a child who refused to give up her favorite toy.

"And how are you going to get that past security?" He didn't particularly want to know the answer to that question, but curiosity got the better of him. People began to stare and murmur as they walked by.

"You could use your Jedi mind trick on the workers and make them think it's just a regular bicycle or something."

Erik stopped and tilted his head. He didn't know if he heard her correctly, he thought she had just said Jedi mind trick. "My what?"

"Your Jedi mind trick. You know, wave your hand like this and say 'this is not the bike you are looking for.'" Gwen waved her hand in front of his face. "Haven't you seen Star Wars?"

He couldn't believe his ears. A demon, an *Admiral* demon no less, just made a pop culture reference. A reference that wasn't used to taunt them. Then again, he, having been sent down from Heaven itself, knew exactly what she was talking about. "Yes, I have. Hugo really wanted to see it when it came out."

"Then why are you looking at me like that?" She looked at him with such innocent eyes.

Erik didn't know how to respond. She was different— different than he had ever seen her act. He had run into her before, several times in fact, but never this close to talk in any civilized, conversational way. Either she had changed tremendously, or all of this was just an act with no clear motive guiding it. He didn't know which theory was more absurd to believe.

"Just didn't think you would make a movie reference."

She grinned as if the comment amused her. "It looked interesting back when it came out so I snuck into the movie theatre. What? Is a creature like me not supposed to have fun?"

"Yes, but your type of fun usually refers to plundering defenseless villages and such. Not watching science fiction dramas."

"You would be surprised what my kind finds entertaining."

"Actually, I don't want to hear what your kind finds entertaining." Not that he didn't know already. He had dealt with their destruction for centuries now—all the bloodshed.

"Fair enough. Now, could you please get my bike onboard?" She gave him a look a girl would give to her boyfriend to buy her something cute and fuzzy.

Erik sighed. She would never give up—her persistence had always made her that much more powerful. "Fine, but once we board, you need to tell me everything. I've brought you this far, it's your turn to hold up your end of the bargain."

Gwen nodded in agreement. Erik pulled out the two tickets he had purchased ahead of time. He had known she would come with him. He saw Gwen notice the tickets but didn't say anything.

As they approached the train, a security guard held out his hand to stop them. "You aren't supposed to..."

Erik established eye contact. "It's fine. It's just a bicycle."

Any person would have just given Erik a strange look for believing a motorcycle was just a bicycle, but Erik had his 'special talent' as Gwen had pointed out. With eye contact, his kind could get humans to do anything they wanted, which came in handy when battling against the Twelve. They could erase anyone's mind who had witnessed something supernatural in a second. Or make them leave the area.

"Alright, move along." The man motioned toward the train. Erik let out a short sigh. He couldn't believe he actually said 'move along.'

"Thank you." Erik passed him and they boarded the train. The workers started blowing their whistles. The train was about to depart.

"You didn't wave your hand. Looks so much cooler when you wave your hand," Gwen commented as she placed the motorcycle in the bike rack. People stared, but didn't say a word.

"I'm not a Jedi," Erik said with a slightly annoyed tone.

She shrugged. "I'm just saying it looks cooler. But wouldn't it be pretty fun to be a Jedi? The lightsabers and powers."

Erik gave her a suspicious look as they took their seats. "You're a creature from hell with powers of your own. Why would you want to be a Jedi? Besides, you would be more like a Sith member."

"Ah, but a member of the Sith can turn back into a Jedi. I cannot do that."

"But you want to," Erik added. He presumed that was

why she sat before him, she wanted her good status back —that she wanted to return to Heaven and not suffer for an eternity in Hell, as was punishment for turning her back on God.

"I don't make it a habit of wanting things that I cannot have. Only leads to disappointment, and I hate being disappointed."

At least she wasn't lying to herself. Erik appreciated that. But that didn't answer what he wanted to know. "Then why are you here?"

She sighed as she watched the train begin to pass building after building, making its way out of the city. Not many passengers sat near them, which Erik was thankful for, considering the nature of their discussion

.Gwen started her story, "as you may recall, some higher beings and I fell down to this world after a certain fight in Heaven. The Twelve Admirals were assigned by Lucifer to roam Earth, causing any destruction we could. A simple task, but a fun one nevertheless.

"We created many legends and myths throughout different cities and cultures. Then His Son came down to Earth and we saw it as our chance to overthrow Him. Our New Order, in a way. But everything we threw at Him, He had no problem in counteracting..." Gwen stopped as all the memories came rushing back to her. Erik heard stories of all that went on at that time, but he didn't get to witness any of it for himself. He and his fellow comrades didn't come in until later.

"Then it happened. We killed Him, at least that was what we thought. Humanity had lost hope in everything and the Gates to the Underworld had been opened. Spirits of the underworld spread across the world for three days."

"But then He came back," Erik interjected.

Gwen nodded, recalling the event. "Indeed, He did and our victory turned into a severe loss. He put everything that escaped back into that dark tomb of hell. Then He left, giving all of Earth reason to believe in Him again while we were stuck back where we started. Humans are much easier to deal with when they don't have hope."

Erik watched as Gwen's lips held back a thin smile. She still craved those human weaknesses, it was apparent on her face.

"So the rest of your kind was put back in its place." Erik kept the story going. He didn't like the look Gwen had.

Gwen blinked then nodded. "Precisely. But we knew a door once opened could be opened again."

Not many in Heaven saw that coming, Erik remembered. It had always been a legend that such a thing could happen. The door to the underworld was supposed to be closed shut forever after that. But then the demons figured out a way, so that's when Erik and his colleagues were sent down to stop them. "Which is where we come in."

"Yes. You twelve, the heavenly beings with no name, were sent down to Earth to stop us. Twelve Good Admirals against Twelve Evil Admirals I guess, eh? Only through killing you can we reopen the gate and let the mass of beings come out of the deep pits of hell and take control of this world once more." She bit her lip. "And here we are. Two thousand years later. Still fighting a war that never seemed to come to an end. Until now."

"That's a nice history lesson, but what does that have to do with you changing your mind?"

"In order to stop us you have to destroy each and every one of us. Once that happens ,we will be with the others, forever rotting in the darkness."

"So you don't want me to kill you?" Erik questioned slowly, knowing he could never agree to keep her alive in the end. Just because he was letting her take this journey with him didn't mean he was going to keep her alive when it came down to it.

She shook her head. "No, you have to kill me."

"I'm still not seeing what you gain then. Why are you here?"

"I know we won't win this. We lost before and we will lose again. I have done countless things that I regret. Things that I should suffer for and I'm okay with paying that price. All I want is to end on a good note, helping someone instead of trying to cause destruction."

Erik listened to her confession. He realized she didn't know what happened after she left the demons. She didn't realize her kind had the lead now in this war. "Then you think you will have a clearer conscience for the rest of eternity?"

"Exactly. That's all I'm asking." She leaned forward and grabbed his hand. "Help me become a better creature. Help me achieve that."

He couldn't believe what he was hearing. A demon asking him tfor help o become a better being. A creature that lived in the darkness wanting to see one last glimpse of light before being sent back into the dark, as if her conscience affected her somehow. The only problem was that her kind didn't have a conscience, or at least, weren't supposed to. So all of this made no sense to him. There had to be more to it.

"How come it wasn't until recently that you wanted this? Why not before?" he inquired.

She shrugged. "We have lost seven of our Admirals thus far, sent back to Hell where they will never leave unless we succeed and open the doors. When each ane of them was killed, part of me felt as if I too was killed. Over and over again this happened, losing my friends and family, and the more I thought about it, the more I realized that even if we open the doors, will it really be enough? We havdbeen fighting for so long, I began to have doubts."

"It had been bothering me for quite a while so by the time my control over the second world war had come, I panicked. I saw how many human lives I had destroyed and I couldn't stand it any longer. The toll had been too great and it was all my fault. So I stopped that hold we had and I have been running away from my kind ever since."

Which explained why the other demon shot her. "And following me?"

"Yes." She smiled. "You are one hell of a person to follow, you know that?"

"I do." He had to be in order to stay alive on Earth this long. Otherwise, he would have been eaten alive long ago. She would have made sure of that, when she was part of their ranks.

"Anyway…" Gwen looked down at her hands and fiddled with her fingers. "That is all I ask. Just let me help you. The next battle in the war is here and I have a feeling it will be the last."

Erik agreed. This battle felt different from the rest. It felt as if everything depended on it. This would determine who controlled the earth.

"How do I know you aren't lying to me? How do I know this isn't a setup?"

"If you thought this was a setup, you would have killed me by now. It wouldn't take much effort on your part, not in the state I'm in."

Now that she had mentioned it, Erik noticed her sweating. Her hands shook in her lap and she closed her eyes, taking in deep breaths.

"Your curiosity has gotten the better of you after all these years," she added.

Erik smiled at her comment. He had never seen a demon like her. But that wasn't why he kept her alive. That wasn't why he let her come this close. He needed her to finish something she started five years earlier. She just didn't know that yet, and hopefully wouldn't until he wanted her to. Erik took a look at her twitching body. Something had happened to her in Paris and she didn't want to tell him anything about it. Deciding to let her keep it in until they reached London, Erik shut his eyes and let the sound of the train fill his mind.

CHAPTER 5

Gwen opened her eyes to find scenes of the English countryside rolling by the train windows. It had been a while since she had seen the gorgeous hills of green grass and trees lining the horizon. Gwen could even see the Shard in the distance. She had missed London dearly, although it had only been a few years since she last visited.

Shifting in her chair to get a better look of the approaching city, she grimaced. Jürgen's bullets were still in her, scratching the surface of a couple vital organs —mainly her heart. Every time she moved, she caused more internal bleeding and her body kept trying to heal it. It was an endless cycle, resulting in a slow loss of energy. She hated the person who invented firearms;

they had been a nuisance to her ever since their creation. She had lost track of how many times she had been shot.

Gwen really didn't have the time nor the resources to pry the bullets out either. She could try to dig them out with her nails, but she knew they were just outside her reach, unless she wanted to go through her heart to get them, which she didn't feel up to doing at this moment. One slipup and she could kill herself by pulling out her own heart, which would be a pretty embarrassing way to go. She would have to get someone else to take them out for her. Possibly Erik, when they got to London. Gwen glanced at him. He had his eyes closed, but she figured he wasn't asleep. He wouldn't just leave himself defenseless around her.

She had told him why she had left her colleagues. She just didn't want to suffer for eternity. It was the only thing about herself she could control—her conscience. Otherwise, she would have to deal with all the consequential regret that came with the typical actions of a demon, and she couldn't handle it. Now, she just wanted to help them, to make herself feel better about all the lives she had destroyed over the years. To forgive herself. Forgiveness. The only thing she wanted more than anything in the entire world. Ever since she fell from Heaven, it was the only thing forever out of her reach and it ate at her each and every day.

"What's wrong?" Erik interrupted her train of thought. She wondered how long he had been watching her.

"It's nothing." Gwen shifted again, trying to find the most comfortable position to sit, which seemed impossible with all the anxiety racing through her mind. "We're almost to London. What's the plan?"

"I'll contact my group and we'll go from there."

"What will you tell them? I find it hard to believe they would welcome me open-armed, maybe like just armed."

Erik ran his hands through his light brown hair. "I haven't figured that part out."

"Well..." Gwen quickly thought of everything that could go wrong, mostly all ending in her death. "Can't wait..."

Erik didn't say anything else as their train came into St. Pancras Station. All lines from France used to go through Waterloo, but the French got mad about England rubbing their defeat in their faces and England had to change stations. Gwen had always found the French and British people's petty bickering entertaining. Such little things in life brought the best pleasures, especially when she had been alive for so long.

Gwen grabbed her bike and hauled it off the train, garnering a few quizzical stares from passengers leaving the train along with them. They didn't know how someone could have snuck a motorcycle onto the train and in the station itself. A few people tried to question her about it, but Erik intervened. If the Twelve could influence humans like that, they would have won long ago.

Although they had other ways, Gwen smiled to herself.

She watched as Erik walked forward with a resolute stride. He had confidence in everything he did. The same confidence she used to have in her former life. "I'm jealous of you, you know that?"

Erik glanced at her through the corner of his eyes, curious what she meant by that statement. "Because I'm not damned?"

Gwen shook her head. "No, because you can get people to listen to you just by eye contact."

"You just have to bite them to turn them into your minions, destroying the human soul that was inside."

"Yes, but that is a hassle and if others see, they scream and run in panic, then we have to hunt and chase them down and there's all that struggling," she sighed, thinking about how many times she had experienced the problem. "It's a mess."

Erik laughed. "And here, I thought your kind liked all the screaming and the blood."

"We do, but it's not the most helpful thing in the long run. Lots of planning, lots of time spent figuring out who we need to turn and why. What governments to take over, how it will help us and the like. That is why it has been so long since the Twelve have tried anything. But now they started this new war, and that is why you have to let me talk to you about something else important."

Erik raised his eyebrow. "Are you trying to say I need you?"

"Yes, I am." She didn't want to seem cocky, but with her help, they would be able to locate other demons and minions a lot faster.

"And why is that?"

"How many of you are left?" A question that had been

lingering on her mind for the past seventy-odd years. She had lost count of those left after she ran off. She didn't have any way of knowing.

Erik stopped. "So I was right, you don't know?"

She shrugged. "I've been alone for quite some time now."

He waited a second longer before answering her question. "Three."

Gwen felt her heart skip a beat. That couldn't be possible. "Three of you?!" So two had been killed in her absence by her fellow demons.

Four little gargoyles found themselves in a tree, hang one up, and then there were three.

Erik motioned for her to quiet down. People began to give them curious looks, more than they had gotten with the bike. "Yes. We lost two after you left the war in Germany."

"Do you know how many of the Twelve demons are left?" She knew James still roamed the earth. And Jürgen. But the rest she didn't know.

"Including you? Still five."

They hadn't lost anyone since Germany. Gwen figured as much. "So you do need me then."

"In a way, yes."

They stepped out of the station. The busy streets of London were cluttered with people, trying to get to where they needed to go. None knew of the things in store for them, considering the invisible warfare raging all around. Everyone went on with their days, without any recognition that this was the silence before the storm.

Setting her motorcycle down on the street, Erik took the driver's seat. Even though she missed cruising the streets of London alone, he knew where they needed to go, so he was to drive once again. Gwen took a deep breath and climbed on the back of her motorbike, recognizing a handful of scents in the area coming from people she didn't wish to encounter anytime soon.

Erik zipped through London's crowded streets.

As they passed Regent's Park, Gwen smiled, recalling memories she had of King Henry VIII. She had always considered him an interesting lad, causing so much disruption between England and the Church. His daughter Mary sparked even more interest for her. Strong and diligent, the Queen of England ruled like no other. It had been a pleasure for Gwen to watch, but that time had passed and she found herself, centuries later, still cursed to crawl in the dust.

Familiar buildings flashed by, making Gwen realize they had arrived in South Kensington, a small portion of Greater London. This area, she recalled, had great food and more importantly was a place they could easily hide for the time being. People were always coming in and out of the area, so no one would notice them.

Reaching their destination, Gwen examined the building that stood before her as she climbed off her bike.

"Quaint." Gwen knew they didn't go all out when looking for housing, but this flat didn't even seem to be big enough for a couple of roommates. Maybe if they got along nicely, such a tiny place would be endurable.

The door opened to reveal a taller man, whose face and body she recognized right away. His eyes darkened as they met hers. He was the last person she wanted to try to convince she had changed. Gwen ducked as his fist came straight at her.

"Hugo stop!" Erik placed his hand in front of him as he lunged toward her.

Hugo jabbed his finger at her. "She is one of them, Erik, one of the Twelve!"

Gwen raised her hand and waved. "Hello Gargoyle." It was a term she loved using, ever since the Catholic Church started decorating their cathedrals with Gargoyles. Like the grotesque figures, they protected the church and everything in it, and the demons always found them to be vile creatures like in all the stories.

"Vampire!" he lashed back. Another term she loved, mostly because she and a couple others had started the myth in Transylvania.

She cocked an eyebrow. "That's an insult?"

Hugo clenched his fist. "Erik, why is this demon in my presence? And *not* dead?"

"Calm down, Hugo. Let me explain." Erik stepped inside the flat. Gwen stayed out on the doorstep. She needed to be invited in and she didn't want to get that close to Hugo.

"Calm down? She's a demon!" Hugo tried to lash out at her again, but Erik held him back.

"I know, I know. Just hold off on killing her for a second. Let's talk inside, all right?" Erik said.

Hugo shook his head. "I'm not letting her in here!"

"Just invite her in, she is trying to help us."

Hugo looked at Erik as if he had gone crazy. "No, if I invite her in then she can *always* come in. We'd have to move. You have any idea how long it took us to set this place up—how much salt I had to buy? I had to put the salt down in a particular way, so it wouldn't get swept up or easily scuffed away. You know how hard that is to do in this city? I lined the entire inside of this flat with it. To keep fiends like her out of here!"

Gwen took a couple of deep breaths. He was right, it was hard to sense him and he stood right in front of her. James wouldn't be able to find her, at least when she was in there. The moment she stepped out of the area, he would then have no issues tracking her down.

"Hugo, look at her. She's weak. You have nothing to fear right now."

Gwen looked the other way as Hugo examined her. Even though she didn't want to admit it, she felt weaker than she had ever felt in a long time. Throughout countless struggles and fights she fought in the years, she had never been so depleted as her new journey on the 'road to redemption.' All of it had been her fault, of course, but they didn't know that. They didn't know the true reason behind her weakness. She only hoped James would forgive her.

Hugo turned back to Erik. "You realize we will have to abandon this battle, don't you? This changes everything. She knows where we are and she will kill us all."

"She's not going to tell anyone anything. She is here to

help us."

Hugo threw his hands up in the air. "Help us? You have to be kidding! How many traps of hers are you going to fall into, Erik? You are lucky you aren't dead by her hands yet. Are you forgetting who she is? Are you forgetting all that she has done?"

"Well maybe if you would listen for a moment I could explain everything." Erik's voice started to rise.

The two kept arguing while she just stood there outside the flat. Gwen watched as pedestrians started to stare. She knew it would get worse in a few more moments. Her energy was rapidly decreasing due to the bullets that still lay against her heart. Jürgen had a good aim. In any normal circumstance, she could go days, maybe even weeks with such injuries, but not today. Not when she had gone this long without a drop of James' blood.

Her body started to shiver uncontrollably and everything began to turn into a blur. Coughing into her hand, she looked down to find it covered in a dark liquid. Her body couldn't handle the strain anymore. Gwen fell to the ground unconscious.

CHAPTER 6

Another dart hit the sixty-point mark. James leaned back in his chair and thought about his next move. He could drag Gwen away from the Gargoyles and make her remember who, *and what*, she really served—the darkness, until the end of time itself. He never minded her carelessness before, mostly because it always ended up fine for them. Not this time. This time, she could cost them the war and he had to fix that before they lost it all.

James threw another dart, missing the bullseye by a hair. He was off his game—he had been since Gwen had left, leaving him behind to pick up the pieces from the fallout of her strange decision to turn away from their ranks.

Gwen would anticipate him coming, James could

count on that. He needed to figure out a plan she couldn't sneak past, as she always tended to do. She had become sly over the years, which made her all the more irresistible to him. James threw another dart. Bullseye.

He needed to pass the time before getting on the plane that night to London. The minions had most everything under control, so he didn't really need to do anything else. Instead, he decided to play a harmless game such as darts, though he had used darts in many non-harmless ways over the years. This time he wanted to clear his mind and figure out the best way to go about the game Gwen and he had going. Their little game of hide-and-go-seek.

"Sir." A voice startled James. Deep in thought, he didn't realize anyone had entered his office. James swiveled around in his chair to find one of his minions at his door.

James set the darts down. "What is it?"

"We need to run a few things by you before you depart."

James sighed. The major problem they have always had with minions had been their need to be told exactly what to do, word-for-word, sometimes painfully slow and repetitive instructions. They had to be told every detail or else they wouldn't understand. He hated it. He wished for a more "no questions asked" philosophy and immediate obedience from any of his followers. He never got those, though, and instead got these brainless minions that had trouble with even simple instructions.

"Fine." James stood up. "What do you need?"

"To run a few things by you."

He clenched his fist, trying to hold off the urge to punch the minion for being that dense. "And what are they?"

"Oh, follow me." The minion turned and waited for him. James paused for a moment. He didn't know why he couldn't tell him from where he was.

The minion led him down the hallway. Then James sensed it. A demon, one of the Twelve. He just got off the phone that morning with Jürgen, which only left two others. None told him they would visit, so whoever waited for him wanted to catch him off guard. That left only one person.

Entering the meeting area, three minions awaited alone with the one demon James didn't want to see at that moment.

"Seth." James tried to put on a friendly smile, but knew he failed miserably in that instant. "I didn't think I would be seeing you anytime soon."

Seth traced his finger on the indents that freckled the table, some of which came from James' outbursts. "I thought I would see how you were doing. This is your first mission alone after all, at least since Germany, other than that little one you had in London. Without my permission, if I might add. Then again, have you ever worked on your own? Or did you always rely on that partner of yours?"

Seth was trying to push his buttons, but James wouldn't allow himself to react in the way Seth desired him to react. He wouldn't let him have that satisfaction.

"I didn't rely on her, we just worked well together. And I am just about to leave, actually."

"Leave?" Seth stopped tracing the table and looked up at him. He knew James had overworked this area. He just wanted to torment him for caring about Gwen. Seth was in charge of this battle after all, he could call all the shots. "Getting lonely, I suppose. Although I don't recall telling you that you could leave."

James took a deep breath, trying to calm himself. He hated the way Seth never got to the point right away. "You don't need me here anymore so I figured I'd go help Jürgen."

"And you weren't going to run that by me?" Seth leaned back in his chair.

Like he would tell Seth either way. Seth had become the biggest control freak in the history of everything. James hated that it was his turn in the lead role for this war. "Didn't think you would mind. You know, more safety in numbers and all that."

"You mean more safety against the Gargoyles, or against a different target?"

James' heart skipped a beat. Seth knew, but he didn't know how. "Target? What do you mean?"

Seth stood up and slammed his fist on the table. "What do I mean?! I mean that little bitch of yours that seems to show up at the most inconvenient moments."

"How did you..."

"You really think I wouldn't find out about her? That you could just waltz to London without me knowing?"

Just as James thought. Control freak. "I had hoped I

could deal with it under the radar. That way you wouldn't be bothered and you wouldn't bother me."

"You mean like five years ago? Didn't you deal with her then?"

"Not... exactly."

Seth ran his hands through his brown curly slicked-back hair. "Then, explain to me, what did you do? Because if I recall, you didn't bring her back here like you said you would."

"I tried to talk to her and..." James tried to pick his words carefully. "She ended up catching me by surprise..."

"So she tried to kill you and yet you still want to try to help her?"

"She didn't try to kill me, she was just trying to get away. She was scared of what might happen if I caught her."

"She stabbed you with the triduanum and left you to die."

James had to admit, that part of it all hurt the most. In order to survive the knife wound, he had to drink the blood of a demon. Luckily, he found Jürgen in time.

Seth went on. "And now you want to go after her again?"

James didn't even consider that a question. She meant the world to him. Both this one and the one he gave up to be with her. "This is our only chance. We need her to finish this. If I can turn her back to our side of things, we can win this battle and end the war against Heaven. We will be able to open the doors to Hell once more."

Seth stood and came up to him. "Are you saying that because you really believe it, or because you don't want to have to kill her?"

James didn't let Seth intimidate him. "I won't need to kill her."

"I thought so." Seth leaned against the table.

"Look." James pointed at himself. "I need her whether you like it or not."

"Need her? Oh, you mean that little blood bond of yours. Such a weakness, James, you two should have never committed such an act."

James shook his head. He would never regret the choices he made, even if it meant suffering like he did now, especially since she was the reason he left Heaven. "Why are you weaseling your way into matters that aren't your concern?"

"Just curious."

"That's such a bastardly thing to do. You know how I feel about her and you know to what depths I would go for her."

"Really?" Seth straightened back up and circled him, whispering into his ear. "What if I were to tell you that I wouldn't let you go after her? That I will just let Jürgen and Darrell deal with her."

James knew Seth was bluffing, he just wanted to get a reaction from him. "I would say screw you and do it anyway. You aren't my master, you were just chosen by us to lead this battle. I can do whatever I want. All this would be easier if you just let me do what I have to do. Besides, Jürgen won't go against me and Darrell wouldn't hurt her either."

He felt Seth's breath against his ear. "Well maybe I'll just go after her myself."

James let out a sharp laugh. "Good luck with that. She can't be underestimated."

"If she's in the same state as you are, I think I could take her down in a snap. Just need a few minions and I'd be able to corner her. It would be over before she knew it."

James turned and smiled bitterly. "Then I would kill you."

"You are pretty keen on her, aren't you?" Seth stepped in front of him, keeping his eyes on him. "Even after how she betrayed you and left you to suffer the aftereffects of being separated for so long."

He didn't need to be reminded that her betrayal ate at him every day, since the second world war. But he knew she had to have a reason for all of this. She always had reasons for doing everything she did. "There is something going on and I'm the only one who can talk to her. She will listen to me. Either you let me go or I will have to defy you, which, personally, I don't mind doing, even if you threaten to hurt me. It's not like you can kill me, you need me, *and her*, to be able to win this."

Placing his hand on James' shoulder, Seth grinned. "My dear James, how much of that bark is really bite? Just take a look at yourself. You are in such a weak state."

"The state I am in is exactly why I need to find her and talk to her."

Seth studied him and turned away. "Do you really

believe she will come back to you, after all this time?"

James didn't have to think about the question. "I do."

"Fine then. You have your wish." Seth stepped into the doorway, peeking back behind his shoulder. "But if you screw this one up, she's mine."

Seth left him standing there in the meeting room. He hated Seth with a passion. Every time they talked, he wanted to kill something. James slammed his fist into one of the minions that stood nearby and ripped out his heart. He didn't need to go to that extreme to kill him, but it felt more satisfying. The blood dripped down, flowing off his hands. He found such beauty in the deep redness it possessed. Red was love. Red was lust. Red was the color that reminded him of her fiery spirit.

He let go of the body, lifeless, as if he considered a minion to have a life at all. They were more like brainless drones doing whatever they asked. They had no more soul than they did when they were mere humans. The other three didn't budge as he tossed the heart down next to the body.

James licked the blood off his hands as he left the room. "Clean that mess up. I'll be in my office."

CHAPTER 7

Darkness. Blood. Death. All of it swarming around and around, echoing throughout eternity. Trapped forever, none of it would ever be forgotten. None of it would escape this endless cycle that it found itself in. It would never escape. Nothing would ever escape.

Collin saw countless bodies all around him, drowning in their own blood. He had never seen so much blood, even going after minions. Dark shadows lingered over the bodies, as if taunting them one last time before their death. Devilish grins appeared on the shadows as their laughs rang through the deep nothingness that surrounded him. He tried to shut his eyes, but none of it would go away. It would never go away.

He caught sight of one shadow, different from all the

others. It stood alone, kneeling down next to one of the bodies. Collin approached it. He could hear its soft whimper. The shadow touched the blood with its long, claw-like finger, as if afraid of what it was exactly—what it truly represented.

The shadow began to turn away from the body.

Collin's eyes shot open. He tried to catch his breath as he gasped for air that didn't seem to be there. He flipped his legs off of the bed and ruffled his hair with his hands. His heart raced. Another nightmare of all the things he had witnessed.

Something about these dreams made him feel different. They felt real, as if it had happened in the past. They felt like memories he never knew about. In them, he'd never felt so alone. It was like an utter emptiness, as if everything that had happened was all for nothing and he didn't matter anymore. Nothing mattered anymore.

Shaking off any lingering thoughts of the dream, Collin stood up and stretched. He had to clear the evidence of the previous night before Hywel showed up. He didn't need him asking questions about what he does in his spare time. Again.

Feeling a slight crustiness on his clothes, Collin looked down, and realized he hadn't changed before going to bed.

"Feck." He spun back to his bed to find his sheets also covered in blood. He would have to change them. Again. Collin decided he would put it off until later that night.

He looked back down at his clothes. They were beyond washing now. He would never get the stains out.

The blood reminded him of the dream again, which caused him to release an audible moan. He didn't want to recall it. He wanted it to disappear along with all the others.

Tossing his clothes in the little trash can in his bathroom, Collin stepped into the shower and rinsed off the remaining blood that clung to his body. The warm water felt good against his skin. No matter how many times he washed it away, the feeling of being dirty and marked by what or whom he killed never left his mind. He knew just what Lady Macbeth felt—*Out damned spot! Out I say!* He lost count of how many times he wanted to run down the streets screaming that like a madman.

Collin stepped out of the shower, feeling better now that he had gotten all the blood off of his body. He checked the clock. To his amazement, he found that he had been in there for thirty minutes. Time flew by when you didn't want it to. Hywel could show up at any minute now, along with the rest of the workers in the pub.

"Shit, the sword." He quickly pulled on a shirt as he stumbled down the stairs. It still waited to be cleaned and hung up behind the bar, as it was on most days. He quickly rinsed it off and placed it in its spot.

It added to the Arthurian decor of the place. Armor, maces, shields hung throughout the pub. He found most of it on Etsy. It was truly such a great website. He came across the sword one day when the Renaissance faire came to town and thought it a good addition, plus he had easy access to it if he ever needed it for a nightly round of vanquishing some devilish minions.

Collin heard the door click as Hywel unlocked it. He strode inside.

Hywel was a funny man. His blonde hair was always a shaggy mess and his face was never clean-shaven. He wore a kilt more often than not. Today's was blue. Collin trusted him though, and that was the most important thing.

"*Bore da, fy ffrind.*" Hywel smiled as he entered the pub. Always in a good mood, Collin enjoyed working the long hours at the pub with him.

"*Bore da.*" Collin returned. He didn't understand much Welsh, but he was pretty sure it meant good morning, or at least he hoped that was what it meant.

He set a bag of items on the counter. Collin assumed they were extra clothes, which meant he got up late and needed to use his shower.

"How's your morning been?" he beamed.

Collin wanted to say exhausting, but that would logically lend itself to 'why?' type interrogations, and he couldn't explain that exactly. So he lied. "Good, yours?"

Hywel scratched at the back of his head, as if thinking how to put his answer. "Short."

He knew it. "How's that?"

"I woke up about five minutes ago. Had to rush down here. Didn't even have time to take a bloody shower."

Bloody shower. The irony.

Collin pointed up the stairs. "Go take a shower."

"I knew you would understand." Hywel hurried up the stairs into the bathroom.

Laughing to himself, Collin started getting the pub ready for the day. He swore the list of things to do got longer with each day that passed. He presumed that was the curse of owning your own pub—the obligation of having to do everything yourself.

For years, he had wanted to own his own pub. He loved the atmosphere, and hearing tales people told whether they were true or not. So he worked as hard as he could until one day he got enough money and he bought this joint. All of it seemed perfect, until he met Gwen.

She caught his eye the moment she walked into his bar. Red hair, acted like she owned the world. No man could resist her charms. And they didn't. She never paid for a drink, at least none that he had seen. He even gave her a couple on the house. Then, after a while, they started talking more. And more. Very soon, they started getting close and everything he once knew changed. Now, the place didn't matter to him as much as it used to.

It wasn't until after she left that he properly named the pub "Lancelot's." It seemed fitting to him, being in love with a woman named Guinevere and all. He also figured if she ever came back, she would be able to find him easier, or something. He didn't know anymore. He just missed her, even though he knew the truth of what she was.

Collin heard the door to the bathroom open.

"Did you cut yourself shaving or something?" Hywel yelled down to the pub area.

Collin had forgotten about the trash filled with his grimy clothes. There was always something. "Uh, yeah. Had to change."

"Are you okay? It looks like it was quite a lot of blood. Do you need to go to the hospital?" His voice sounded sincere.

"No, I'm fine, just hurry up, you've got things to do!" Collin called back up.

"Will do!"

The door shut again. Collin shook his head. That man would believe anything told to him, or at least to an extent. This was why Collin had been getting lazy about covering his tracks of his other life, the one that involved hunting minions with the support of angelic beings. He found it sounded crazy even in his own head.

No one other than Hugo knew about his nightly ventures. Collin told none of his friends, relatives, nor workers about his nightly excursions to the battlefield. None of them would ever understand. Besides, he didn't talk to his family anymore. He had run away from home once he turned seventeen. He didn't have many friends either. The only friend he considered himself to have was working for him. There never seemed to be time for him to socialize, other than with customers and Hugo, but that never went far beyond the usual "So, what's been up with you, lately?"

Grabbing a couple sacks of garbage, Collin hauled them outside. That's where it hit him, like a wave as he opened the door. A sense, almost like a smell. Sweet and lovely. It was Gwen.

He took a look around. People walked by, but none of them were her. He was sure she was there. He'd never felt that anywhere else.

Shaking it off as a weird case of his own mind playing tricks on him again, he tossed the trash into the bin and went right back inside.

CHAPTER 8

"Well, that was weird." Hugo looked down at Gwen's prone body that now laid on his doorstep.

Erik went to her side and saw the blood on her hand. Dark demonic blood. She had overworked herself and drained all her energy. "Damn."

"What happened?" Hugo bent down next to him.

"We got shot at before we left Paris. I knew she got hit a couple times, but I didn't realize she was injured this badly." He kicked the salt that encircled the home.

"Erik..." Hugo began, but knew it was no use, the seal was now broken. He shook his head. "That was only a couple hours ago, how is she this depleted already?"

"Because she hasn't fed in five years."

"How do you know that?"

"Because she has been tracking me for the past seventy years." He turned his attention back to Gwen. "Now, please. Invite her in."

Hugo let out a sigh, debating if he should listen. "Do you really trust her?"

"Enough to have traveled this far with her. That should be enough for you."

Hugh studied Erik a moment longer, then gestured him inside. "Fine. She can come in."

Erik picked her up and carried her into the flat. He hurried into the kitchen and placed her on the table. Grabbing a knife, he sliced his palm open. Blood poured out of the wound.

He gestured to Hugo. "Open her mouth."

"You have to be kidding me..." Hugo began.

"Just do it!"

Hugo obeyed, understanding that Erik's blood could bring out a darker side in her, bringing out her bloodlust —her true nature. The Twelve had brought forth the term "vampires" through the world, although they were much more than what the myth suggests. They were all once creatures of Heaven, ones that followed Lucifer when he rebelled against God, and were sent down to Hell. That is, except for these Twelve, who were able to haunt the Earth until their own destruction. Erik knew the dangers of what he planned on doing, but nothing else could be done at this point. Erik let the drops of blood fall from his hand and into her mouth.

The moment she tasted blood on her lips, Gwen's eyes shot open. Just as he feared, her eyes shined yellow. Her true eyes. Her demonic eyes. The lust for the blood that he had given her made the demonic side of her emerge. Gwen jolted up and grabbed him by his collar and shoved him into the wall. Erik didn't resist. He felt her hot breath against his neck as her thirst of blood rushed throughout her body. Hugo started for her.

Erik shook his head. "No, don't stop her. I need to see if she can wake up from this first."

Hugo reluctantly backed away. Erik took a deep breath as Gwen sunk her fangs into his neck. He felt each and every drop of energy go from his body into hers. As long as Hugo stood nearby, he didn't worry. If she couldn't control herself in the end, he could easily pull her off of him. His energy would be restored in an hour or two. Not a problem.

The pain wasn't much, but the significance of a demon taking the blood of a being like him was. Angelic beings were above them, and whenever a demon got their hands on their blood, they took it without hesitation. It was like a trophy for them, to show that they had won and were superior to the "Gargoyles." Demons needed blood to survive. It was nothing new. Blood was life to them.

It had been a while since a demon had a taste of his blood, but that was under different circumstances. He had barely made it out of that one alive. This time, though, it didn't matter. He wanted her to have his blood, which he never thought would happen. Giving his blood freely to a vampire—to a demon—went against instinct, in a sense.

Erik stroked her back. He couldn't believe she had depleted her energy reserves this badly. She hadn't had human blood for a long time, as he knew she had been living off minions for the past five years. She shouldn't have been this bad. Erik knew something else had a role in her weakness. If any of the others of the Twelve had found her like this, they could have taken her down easily. Then again, he saw the fight she had five years ago with James. She could handle herself if need be.

Gwen suddenly stopped drinking blood from Erik and quickly backed off from him. Confusion dominated her face. She hadn't realized what had happened, what took over her so suddenly. Touching her lips with her fingers, she found them covered in blood. Then, it came back to her.

"I drank your blood," she mumbled. "How..."

"It is all right. You needed energy. No harm done." Erik placed his hand on her shoulder. "You passed my test."

"Test?" She watched as he grabbed a towel and wiped the blood off of his hands and neck. The wounds had already healed themselves, as he was almost immortal. The only way to kill them was by decapitation or by removal of their heart. Neither were a fun way to go.

"You stopped yourself. That was all I needed to know." Erik glanced at Hugo. He still kept his eyes on Gwen, not exactly believing what he saw. A demon with self-control.

She scrunched her nose and brought her hand to her mouth. "What's that smell?"

Hugo didn't skip a beat. "Incense. I'm snuffing it out while you are here so get used to it."

Gwen coughed and gagged as she went to grab a towel. She jerked back, clenching her heart. "It hurts."

Erik rushed to her side. "The bullets?"

"Yes." She coughed up blood into her hands again. "Two of them are lodged into my heart. The other two in my lungs. I need to get them out or my energy will slowly deplete again." She pointed at the knife that Erik had just used. "Dig them out. I can't reach them."

He took the knife. "You trust us with this against your heart?"

"I don't really have a choice now, do I? Can't exactly go to a hospital and ask them to do it. You two are the only ones who can."

Gwen sat down and pulled the back of her shirt up. Pointing with her finger, she showed them where the bullets had embedded themselves.

"Two here, two here. You may want some pliers as well. I don't care what you use, just get them out of me." She nodded to the cabinet. "Unless you have some nice Scotch here, that always helps."

Hugo opened one of the doors and pulled out a bottle of Lagavulin. Gwen smiled. "Oh, bless your heart." She grabbed the bottle and took a swig. "That helps so much." She placed the cloth from her shirt into her mouth to bite down on, ready for the pain to start.

Erik nodded to Hugo. "Get some pliers."

Hugo looked at Gwen a second longer and then hurried to the drawers and pulled out a pair of pliers.

Erik plunged the knife into Gwen's back at the point where she said the bullets would be.

She slammed her hand on the nearby kitchen table. Erik knew she had experienced worse pain throughout the years, but for him to have to slice into her heart had to be causing enormous amounts of pain.

He could easily do it right then and there. Pull out her heart and have one less demon to deal with in this world and help the Gargoyles win the war. But Erik would consider that a cheap shot, especially since she had curiously come to him to help. She apparently wanted to seek some form of penance for everything she had done in her past life. Erik still didn't understand why exactly, but he knew he couldn't kill her just now. Not until she did the one thing he needed her to do. Then, he wouldn't feel any remorse for ending her life.

"Why were you shot at by your own teammate? I mean, I understand why I would want to shoot you." Hugo sat down at the table across from her.

Erik kept digging around her heart. He didn't have to be overly careful, once he got the bullets out, she could heal herself quickly. He also admitted to himself it felt good to cause her pain for everything she had ever done to them-both her and her loathsome lot of "the Twelve."

Gwen's body shook as the knife pierced its way into her heart. Her voice was muffled a bit from the edge of her shirt being in her mouth. "You are really questioning me now, Hugo? I'm a little preoccupied with getting my back treated like a slab of meat."

He shrugged. "Don't see any better time, really."

She started to laugh, but the pain made her body suddenly jerk, and the moment was lost. "You must be enjoying this sight, after all we've been through."

Hugo nodded to Erik. "The only thing I would enjoy more is seeing Erik pull out your heart after this, but I have a feeling he won't."

Gwen went quiet, knowing that he did have her in the exact position to do so. Erik pulled out one of the bullets from her heart. He caught sight of the other and pulled that one out as well. "Where are the other two again?"

Gwen reached around and placed her finger on her back. "There." She moved to the left of it. "And there."

"Okay, hold still."

Gwen moaned as he pierced the knife into her back again. At least this time it wasn't near her heart.

"Who shot you?" Hugo didn't care about the state she was in.

Erik understood that all he wanted was to know why a demon sat across from him and that he could hurt her. He admitted that Hugo's calmness came as a surprise to him. It had taken him over seventy years to get over what she had done to him.

Gwen took a deep breath. "Jürgen Vlad, one of the Twelve. We had a falling out before I left so the whole running away didn't play that well with him. He got mad and shot me for the hell of it." She squeezed her fist as Erik took out another bullet. "He's a pretty good shot too."

Erik recalled the name. Vlad, as in Dracula. Once, he was one of the most feared men in Transylvania.

Countless legends came from the times he drank the blood of his victims. He wouldn't put it past a demon to do such a thing. But the stories of the demon named Vlad and what he has done to all types of beings were far worse than any of those the humans knew, from Bram Stoker's fictionalized account of Vlad's atrocities. Erik didn't realize that was who chased them through Paris. He never saw or tried to figure out just what demons hid behind the scenes in France.

"Vlad, eh?" Hugo knew of him as well. "You Twelve and your names."

"We like keeping names that others give us, yes. A reminder of the legends we lived up to. I suppose a being with no name like yourselves would ever understand."

"Names are part of this world, which, unlike you, we aren't. That is the difference. We aren't bound here by that chain that is around your ankle, nor have we had our wings ripped out of our backs. We are all still in one piece, even after these human bodies are destroyed."

"Why didn't you say anything?" Erik started for the last bullet and decided to change the subject before it got any worse. "Why didn't you let me heal you earlier?"

"Seemed kind of odd, me asking you to stick a knife into my back, given the circumstances and all."

Withdrawing the last bullet, Erik wiped the extraneous blood off of Gwen's back. "All done."

Gwen pulled her shirt back down over her already-healing wounds. "Thank you."

"Now, Erik," Hugo began as he joined them at the

table. "Please explain to me what is going on."

"Well, I can skip introductions since you two have already run into each other more than once."

Hugo held up his hand. "Five times actually. All of which make me really, really want to end her here and now."

Erik eyed Hugo. "She ran away from her colleagues, ending the destruction that was World War II. She ended it there and has been running from them ever since."

"How do you know that this isn't some trick? How do you know she isn't going to call her buddies and end us at any moment?"

Erik took a deep breath. He knew Hugo's anger could break any moment. He didn't need that right now. "Because I have been watching her this entire time. This isn't some plot, Hugo. She has risked everything to come to us."

"But why? What is in it for her?"

"Because I want to be free of this burden of hatred." Gwen stared straight into Hugo's eyes. "I want to be able to forgive myself in the end."

Hugo raised his eyebrow. He probably didn't believe what he was hearing, nor could Erik blame him. "You feel remorse?"

She nodded. "Yes."

"No matter what you do, you can't turn back time. What's the point of feeling sorry when you can never be forgiven?" Hugo said exactly what had been in the back of Erik's mind. What was the point behind all of this? She couldn't go back, she could never go back, yet she felt something. She felt something that none of the demons have ever felt.

Gwen turned and looked out the window at the sky. "The demons will not win the war and I don't want to be rotting in hell for eternity regretting the fact I didn't try to change myself, when I had the chance. If I do this, I can feel a little better about myself."

"You don't think you will win?" Hugo asked.

She turned back to them. "We thought we won before. We didn't. We aren't strong enough, you will always have the upper hand. You will always have our Father on your side."

"And it took two thousand years for all that to sink in?"

"Time's irrelevant, my dear Hugo, you should know that."

Hugo slammed his hand on the table. "Two thousand years of torturing us and hunting us down like animals? That's relevant!"

Gwen leaned back in her chair and smiled. "You were sent to stop us—how did you think we would react?"

He jabbed his finger at her. "Yes, but you yourself were responsible for most of the deaths. You weren't one to let up either. You made them all suffer before killing them."

Erik rubbed his forehead. This was exactly where he didn't want the conversation going. Gwen hadn't been the nicest of demons, which was exactly why he wanted to know what her plan was.

"And because of all my fun and games, some got away." Gwen hinted toward their last encounter.

"You mean like me?" Hugo questioned.

She nodded. "Yes. And you too Erik, so you know that if I trust you enough to let you dig a knife into my heart, I mean to help."

Erik did remember the torture she put him through. The knives, the ropes, shards of metal throughout his body, all of it he played over and over in his mind. But the moment she asked him to dig a knife into her back, he knew she really wanted to help. The only problem was how long she would feel that desire. How long would she seriously want to seek out forgiveness for her past wrongs?

"We know you well enough by now to know that you will go to *any* lengths to kill us. Play with our thoughts and emotions until we trust you, and then BAM." Hugo slammed his fist against the table again. "You will pull out our hearts or rip off our heads."

"Or burn you alive?"

"That too." Hugo took a deep breath and released it slowly. "Erik, I don't know what you're thinking, but I can't let you do this. Even if she really means it, she doesn't deserve it. She doesn't deserve to turn her life around. She doesn't deserve to forgive herself."

Erik knew he was speaking the truth, but more rode on this than they could hope for. "Who are we to judge? Who are we to say that she can't?"

"Well, the fact she is a demon and turned her back on everything she was created for is a starter. They wreak havoc on this land and have destroyed countless countries and nations over the centuries. All because they wanted to…" His eyes met Gwen's. "No reason, just selfish, blood thirsty wrath."

Gwen pulled out an object from her bag. Hugo and Erik gaped at it.

"Is that…" Erik began.

"Yes. The triduanum. It's yours." She placed it on the table. "The spear that pierced Christ's side as he hung on the cross. In three days, he rose, in three days we die. Guess it's a knife now. Found it a few years ago. Figured you would want it back."

Erik couldn't believe what he saw. He didn't think she still had it. He assumed she had destroyed the knife after she used it on James five years before.

Hugo reached for it and studied it. "You are giving us a weapon that can hurt you, even kill you, given the right amount of time?"

She nodded. "I am."

"What's in it for you?"

"Just give me a little trust, Hugo. That's all I ask."

Hugo looked at the weapon a moment longer. "Fine. I'll give you until tomorrow night. See if you can get me to trust you by then."

"Challenge accepted." She turned to Erik. "You told me there were three of you. Where's the other?"

"She's in the United States," Erik explained. "She should be meeting up with us soon."

Hugo stood up. "But for now, Erik and I have some things to talk about, without you listening in. You can stay here. Then later tonight we can head over to Collin's." Hugo left them in the kitchen and strode out.

Gwen turned to Erik and laughed as if she'd found the secret she was looking for. Erik had hoped Hugo wouldn't mention Collin's name. He wished he had said something while she was passed out, but he had been preoccupied.

"So that's it then. That is why I'm here. Collin Gallagher. I won't do it. I don't care if you want me to. I won't put him through that," she warned, as he stepped into the doorway.

He wished she hadn't figured it out so soon, why he needed her. Now he would have to find a new way to get what he wanted. He would have to persuade her any way he could.

CHAPTER 9

Gwen walked in silence behind Erik and Hugo as they made their way to Collin's bar. She remembered the last time she saw Collin, approximately five years ago. It was a time when she thought she could fit in as a human. A time when she was running away from her past and hoped she could simply forget it all. Collin had helped with that.

Then came James. Gwen had let her guard down and he had gotten the better of her for a second. Eventually, she had him pinned against the wall, draining him of his blood and his strength. However, Collin saw the two of them and didn't understand what he was seeing. James put the pieces together soon after. He knew she had feelings for Collin and so he tried to take that all away from her. The result of that came back to haunt her in the here and now, and it was the reason Erik hadn't decided to kill her right off the bat.

She couldn't believe Erik had used the human like this. Gwen thought he trusted her, but really he just wanted her to finish what she started five years ago. She wouldn't do it—she wouldn't cause Collin that kind of pain.

Gwen cursed under her breath, as she got her first glimpse of the pub, named "Lancelot's." He renamed his bloody bar "Lancelot's." It had been a joke between them at the time, of their short-lived rendezvous, that he was her Lancelot, taking her away from her Arthur. James. She told him there was another man, but Collin didn't care. He had tried everything to get her to love him. He even gave her his heart. That was the one thing she never quite understood—the human heart. It was something that she always wanted to experience, and perhaps understand more intimately. Real feelings. But she didn't have a heart. She didn't get to have that type of pleasure —nor did the Gargoyles, as a matter of fact.

Gwen pulled Erik back. "I really don't want to face him."

"You have to. You have to deal with the consequences of your past actions."

"I should have known you would say that."

Erik chuckled.

Taking a look inside, she saw him at the bar. He worked away, as customers ordered their drinks. A smile never left his face. "Does he know?"

Erik shook his head. "No."

Gwen watched Collin for a moment longer, then turned her attention back to Erik. "Didn't have the heart to tell him, did you?"

"It's not my responsibility. Besides, I'm not the one he would want to hear it from."

No, that wasn't true. The reason he didn't want to tell him was because he didn't want to admit that he had been using the human, if one could call him that still. "He will hate me when he finds out."

Erik shrugged as Hugo entered the bar. As Gwen followed him closely, she felt as if she hit an invisible wall. She fell back, hitting the hard cobblestone ground outside the pub's doorway. She rubbed her nose. If she were human, that would have hurt a lot, maybe even have broken her nose. She looked around to find only Erik had noticed just what had happened.

"What the hell?" She got up and tried punching her fist through the barrier. Nothing. "Damn it. He lives here, doesn't he?"

Erik came back to her. "What?"

"I can't go in."

"But it's a public place."

Gwen shook her head. "No. He lives here now. Damn it."

"But he's..."

"He's not turned fully yet, he is still partially human. Rules are rules."

"I will send Collin out here." Erik started to turn back toward the interior of the pub.

She held out her hand, as if she could stop him. She smacked her hand into the barrier. "No, I'll stay out here," she said as she rubbed her hand. "I didn't want to talk to him, anyway. Please don't make me do it."

Erik nodded and entered the bar. Gwen groaned as she sat down on a bench outside and watched as people walked into the bar all willy-nilly, and unaware of any barriers.

Gwen knew Erik was going to send Collin out here, no matter what she said. He would make her face him. She had left him five years before, even after she began to feel something for him, though Gwen wasn't sure exactly what that feeling was. Then she had to do the one thing she never wanted to bestow on him—she had to give him her blood so that he didn't die from the wounds James had given him. This left more complications than she ever wanted to be a part of. Even with all that going through her mind, that wasn't her deepest concern at the moment. Her deepest concern was the figure standing in the shadows.

"Hello Jürgen. What brings you to such a place as this?" Gwen greeted.

Jürgen stepped out of the darkness. "Surprisingly enough, not you."

Gwen smiled. She wondered how long it would take him to notice. Just one little scent. "Whatever do you mean?"

She didn't resist as he quickly flashed to her side and clutched his hand around her throat. "Cut the crap Gwen. What did you do?"

"Just tell James that human didn't deserve to die," she choked out.

"You two-timing..." The door of the bar opened and Jürgen left in an instant. He didn't want to risk being seen by either of the Gargoyles, not at this stage of the game. Gwen rubbed her neck. Jürgen couldn't do anything until James arrived, which made her happy and terrified at the same time. She needed to help the Gargoyles before James tore her away from them.

Collin came out of the pub. Just as she suspected. Gwen didn't turn to look at him as he sat down. She didn't want to face him. They sat in silence for several moments.

"I didn't ever expect to see you again," he finally said, breaking the silence.

Gwen forced herself to turn and look at him. The same blue eyes she had wished she'd never corrupted looked right back at her. These were the eyes that she used to think could see right into her mind and know her most intimate secrets. Though, she supposed, the Gargoyles did tell him all her secrets.

"It isn't exactly my choice to be here," Gwen replied.

"Well that makes me feel special." He smiled as if all of this was just some sort of joke.

She stood up and ran her hands through her hair. "I didn't want to drag you into this. I don't want you to get hurt."

Collin stood up and put his hands on her shoulders. The look he gave her made her regret ever leaving him. "Did you ever stop to think maybe I *want* to be a part of this? That I had a choice in the matter?"

Gwen knew he didn't realize how wrong he really was. "No, you don't. You should run away right now if you know what's best for you."

"And leave a beautiful girl like you all alone? I could never do that."

She shoved his hands away. "I'm not a *girl*, Collin. I'm a demon. I'm a being who doesn't give a damn about human life." She gestured all around her. "A creature from hell that will use every last drop of power I have to bring terror to this land."

He just stared at her. "If that's true then why would you care what I do?"

"Because..." Gwen turned to face the other way. She couldn't bring herself to say it. That she actually had feelings for this human. She clenched her eyes shut.

Collin grabbed her hands and brought her close. "You aren't like the others, Gwen."

She shook her head. "You don't know what I've done. If you saw the true me, you would never say that. You would never look at me with that smile again."

"That's where you're wrong. I knew you for a while and there isn't one doubt in my mind that you are different from them. You may have done things in your past, but you have changed. You can't deny that."

She laughed. "You are so naïve. You haven't seen war."

"Wrong again. I've been helping Hugo since you left. I had to help once I knew what was going on, even though you left me. We've kept the peace in this city— destroying every minion that's come here."

Gwen couldn't believe what she heard. "You have been hunting *minions*?"

"I have. Seeing what you truly were that night opened my eyes to your world, and I wanted to be a part of it, no matter the cost. I'd rather die than sit by and act like nothing's happening."

"Minions are nothing compared to us. The things we have done, the things I have done. You would never be able to sleep again. The images would haunt your dreams forever."

Collin pulled her in closer. She could feel his breath against her skin. "It will all be worth it." He leaned in and kissed her gently.

Surprised, Gwen backed away, touching her lips. She didn't know how he could still feel for her after all she had said. After all he had seen.

"You can't tell me you didn't feel something." He let go of her hands and walked back toward the bar. "I've got to go back to work, see you around."

She stood watching him, unable to speak. As the door was closing behind him, he turned.

"Oh, and by the way, you can come in."

With that, Collin left her standing there. She was surprised he would let her in, after everything he had seen her do, after everything he had learned about her. She would never let one of her kind in, if she had the choice. It wasn't smart, whoever they let in could always get back in. The mortals in this city weren't safe. She didn't want to hurt them anymore, but she admitted to herself that she didn't know what could happen to them and those that she loved beyond this point. She knew how persuasive James could be. That's why she had been running for so long. It wasn't because of the things the demons wanted to do to her, but what he could convince her to do. Gwen was fearful she might get sucked back into being his partner again.

Gwen stared at the door, debating whether or not she should go in. She then realized if she stayed outside she might get attacked by Jürgen. She didn't have to think about it twice, once that thought crossed her mind.

She entered the pub, wincing as she stepped through the doorway. The fear of running into an invisible barrier really stays with a demon, no matter if it has been dismantled or not. Taking a breath once she was in, Gwen gasped. She didn't realize how much he'd kept to the Arthurian theme. Replicas of artifacts and Waterhouse reproductions littered the walls. Gwen had to keep herself from laughing. It was a little over the top.

She smelled it too, blood. Lots of it. She looked up the stairwell. The smell came from somewhere up there. It was probably soiled clothes from all of his fights with minions. Her eyes flashed yellow.

Gwen quickly grabbed a glass of wine that went by her on a tray and took a large gulp. The drink would make the cravings go away, at least for a while. Spotting Erik and Hugo, she made her way towards them.

"You going to pay for that?" Hugo commented as she sat down.

Gwen took a sip of the wine. "With what?" Erik chuckled as he took a drink of his water. "So." She set the glass down. "What do we do now?"

"Well, *we*." Hugo gestured to Erik and Collin. "Usually hunt minions."

"Sounds like fun, I'm game."

"You can sense them, can't you?" Erik inquired as she motioned to the waitress for another glass.

"Of course, what kind of demon would I be if I couldn't?"

CHAPTER 10

James hated airports as much as the next being. You couldn't bring anything even remotely sharp on the plane, not even a pencil. Well, maybe a pencil, but someday he figured he would find its picture on the "do not bring aboard" list. He watched as an elderly lady's thread cutters were taken away from her. He shook his head. *Like she could do anything with those.* Ironically, they sold those same cutters in the store on the other side of security. Humans. They never made sense to him. They never realized what went on around them and never saw the start of an invisible war, which has far-reaching consequences for them depending on who won.

He entered the security checkpoint and pulled out his ticket and passport—forged by his IT boys.

"James Arthur." The security man checked.

"That's me." James grinned.

Getting the nod of approval, the man marked his ticket. James grabbed it back from him and went to put his stuff in the little boxes. He slipped off his shoes and placed them in the box.

"Hey, nice tat," a younger man commented as he took off his shoes. His hair was light and his skin was tanned. He spent way too much time in the sun. "How long have you had it?"

James looked down at his ankle, holding back every thought he wanted to say. "A long, long time." It was the best answer, he decided.

"Still looks good," he dumped his stuff into a bin.

"Thanks, I appreciate the comment."

That was a lie, he hated being reminded of the black chains on his ankle that bound him to the Earth. It made his hatred for plane rides even worse. It hurt like hell. Literally. Every time he went up higher than the chain permitted, which wasn't far, maybe a few stories in a building, the area where the tattoo was located burned intensely. The higher he went, the hotter it burned. The price he had to pay for going across the ocean. He missed the simpler times when humans hadn't mastered flight, and were stuck with the slower, yet more painless experience of sailing on a boat.

"I hope when I get to your age, mine still looks that good," the boy said.

James shot him a look that made the man change security lines. His body wasn't that old. Young people these days. They considered everyone around them to be old.

Gathering his things, James headed toward his gate. He had a little time to kill before his plane was boarding, which meant he could raid the Business Class bar. Alcoholic beverages were the only thing that could keep him sane from the pain that would engulf his ankle. Demons never got drunk in a human sense, but it did make certain pains and feelings go away.

"Glass of scotch. On the rocks." He sat down at the bar.

The bartender pulled out a glass. "Any specific brand?"

"A good one."

The bartender nodded and grabbed a bottle of one of the more expensive brands, a 12-year Ardbeg. He looked like he had been around for a while, not even having to check the labels surrounding him. Pouring it out quickly, he handed it to him. James grabbed it and drank it in one gulp.

He set the glass back down. "Another."

The bartender poured another shot and James handed him some cash, then took the glass to a nicer area of the Business Class lounge. There were leather couches and seats scattered across the room, with a fireplace in the middle. Tables with even more chairs littered the sides of the room.

Taking a seat, he sipped at his drink and closed his eyes, thinking about the long flight ahead. If the scotch worked its magic, at least he could sleep during most of it.

Hearing the sound of someone taking a seat next to him, James looked over to find a young woman with a glass of white wine. Her blonde curls bounced as she moved. He smiled at her to see if she would say anything.

She saw his smile and held out her hand. "I'm Katy, and you are?"

He shook her hand. "James."

"Heading to London as well?" She gave him a once over with her deep brown eyes, a look he got quite often.

He nodded. "I am."

She took a drink of her wine. "Are you from the area or just visiting?"

Good question, James thought. "Hard to say, I've traveled so much in my life."

"Salesman?" She leaned in a little, playfully. "Or are you some kind of secret agent?"

James laughed. "No, I'm an archaeologist."

Her eyes lit up. "So you are like some kind of Indiana Jones then."

The exact response he was looking for. Girls dig Indy. "I like to think those movies are based off of my life," he joked.

"Must be fun to be able to travel a lot." She twirled the last bit of wine that was still in her glass.

"It is. I enjoy all the different cultures I come across." He took a sip of his scotch. "What about you? Visiting, or...?"

"Just visiting. I love London and all of its history.

Usually I come with a friend, but she bailed on me."

"Oh," James leaned in closer. A loner was always a good mark. "That's too bad."

"Yeah, but no worries, I'll probably find someone interesting to talk to on the way over." Katy checked her watch. "Oh, we should get going, we should be boarding soon."

"Well then, after you," he gestured towards the exit of the club. She hurried ahead and before he could grab his coat, he lost her in the crowd.

"Damn," he mumbled as he scratched the back of his head. If he had enough luck, he could have tried to get a seat next to her and would then have an easy drink when he landed. Now he would have to find someone else to fill that void.

The flight was crowded as usual, but that didn't matter to him, he was used to crowds. Usually, they consisted of a screaming mob running away from him, but not this time around. Everyone stayed calm and didn't know they should fear him. Not yet anyway.

As much as he wanted to start some delectable chaos here and now, he knew that would just add to the time between where he was now and seeing Gwen. That's what mattered most to him at the moment. He wanted to see her face, to feel her in his arms. To taste her blood.

Sighing, he realized what he really was thirsting for. Gwen's blood. It had been five years since he had the taste of her blood on his lips and he has longed for it ever since. Nothing came close though, to an angel's blood, fallen or not. While human blood satisfied him enough, the Gargoyle's blood gave power beyond anything else. A minion's blood tasted like yesterday's leftovers. But her blood... It was so much more than just power. It was...

Personal.

The only thing he worried about was trying to catch her. She knew he would make his way to London, and she would no doubt be preparing for it. If she ran, then he would simply have to find her again. If she stayed, then she must have a plan in place on how best to face him, which scared him the most. She liked playing games with him and he would not allow that, not again. More than likely, she would act as if she had come back to him and give any information she had found during their brief reunion to the Gargoyles. He would have to watch her like a hawk to see how exactly she would plan on responding to him, and whether she had her usual slippery tricks up her sleeve as was the case with past encounters.

James grinned to himself. He would play her game. Only problem would be getting Jürgen to comply. Seth had already made it clear that he didn't approve of him going after her, and James figured that the only reason Seth let him go had to do mostly with the promise of having Jürgen's help in finding and dealing with her. The only thing Jürgen wanted to do to Gwen involved her death, or at least torture for a very long time, if not for eternity. James couldn't let him do that to her, he cared for her too much, even after all of this. She wouldn't mind the torture, not after gaining an immunity to all of it. After all, she had a lot of practice.

Jürgen never got over the fact she had betrayed them, and he didn't appreciate letting James take care of it last time. Jürgen thought Gwen made him weak and that she could use him easily. He was wrong. She didn't make him weak, she just surprised him. This time he wouldn't let her do that. He had prepared himself for anything.

Shaking those thoughts out of his mind, James took his seat in business class and closed his eyes. The day had gone by slowly. Thoughts revolving around how he would capture Gwen flowed through his mind. He would take her back and force her to comply with his greedy wishes. One of these wishes, involving knocking any inclination to help the Gargoyles out of her mind and fill it instead with the evil that once was there. It could take a while and much effort on his part, but he didn't mind it. Everything was worth the effort, if it resulted with him being with her again.

"Sir, would you like anything to drink before we take off?" He heard a woman ask. He opened his eyes to find a flight attendant standing next to him.

"Some red wine would be nice," he said. She nodded and quickly retrieved it and brought it back to him.

"Thank you." He gave her his charming smile. At least that's what Gwen called it, making her blush as she helped the next passenger.

"Well, talk about coincidence." A familiar voice interrupted his train of thought.

James looked up to find Katy taking a seat next to him. "Katy, what a surprise. We were seated together after all."

"Yes, what luck." She tossed her hair back and smiled at him. "Now we can get to know each other a little better."

More luck for him than for her. Now he had a fresh drink when he landed. As she turned to adjust her seat, James' eyes flashed yellow. Things were going the way he wanted. He just hoped it would stay that way.

CHAPTER 11

Shooing the last drunk person out of the pub, Collin dismissed Hywel and the other workers for the night. The once joyous and noisy room, filled with conversations and people having a good time, now felt hollow and empty. The only people remaining were Hugo, Erik, and Gwen.

"What about those three?" Hywel nodded to Hugo and the others as he put on his poor excuse for a jacket. Hugo did not want to know how long Hywel had that jacket and whether or not he ever cleaned it. It was riddled with holes, stained with some kind of black liquid, and smelled of cheap cologne, as if he had sprayed it to make it seem cleaner.

Looking over at the others, he found Gwen with

another glass in her hand. He had seen her finish at least five shots of whiskey and a couple of glasses of wine.

"No worries. Have a good night Hywel."

"Hwyl fawr." He waved as he left. The door shut and Collin closed his eyes and rubbed his face with his hand. Now was the time that his real job began, defeating minions.

As he opened his eyes, he found Gwen standing in front of him. He jumped back, startled to find her there. She moved fast apparently, because she had been sitting far away in a corner of the pub just minutes ago.

She raised her glass higher. "Can I have another before we go?"

He gave her a suspicious look. "How many have you had?"

"Does it matter?"

"In a way."

Gwen shrugged. "Just a few. It reeks of blood in here, I presume it's because you have clothes upstairs covered in blood of either your own or some minions… Alcohol makes the cravings go away, to an extent, if you catch my drift."

He understood what she meant, and he did have clothes soaked in blood upstairs. It bothered him that she could sense that even down here. He didn't know that she could sense things like that. Collin grabbed a bottle of wine that had already been opened. "Here, knock yourself out."

"That's white. I want red."

"Why does it… oh never mind." He grabbed a different

bottle and handed it to her. He really didn't want to think about what she had just said.

"Getting wiser." Gwen grabbed the bottle and downed the rest. Collin followed her to the table that Erik and Hugo still waited at. "So, how do you boys go about this?"

"I really don't like her being here," Hugo grumbled. Collin noted Hugo hadn't let his eyes leave her all night.

Erik rubbed his forehead in irritation. "Hugo, we have already discussed this."

"Yeah, Hugo." Gwen smiled playfully. "Knock it off already."

Before Hugo could make a response, or rip Gwen's head off, Collin interrupted, answering Gwen's question. "We either go off of rumors or just search around."

Gwen gave them an incredulous look. "That sounds... efficient."

"It's the best we got," Hugo replied. Collin wondered why he hated her so much, if it was just because of her being a demon, or if they had met once before in the past.

Gwen traced her finger on the top of her glass. "When's the last time you checked Southwark?"

Collin thought back on all the searches they'd done over the years. "Not for a while. Didn't find anything there."

Gwen stood up. "We should check there."

Erik grabbed her wrist before she could head for the door. "Why?"

"Because, at night after the tube shuts down, there are

a lot of wanderers. It's a good place to find lonely people, and it's a good place to hide."

Hugo stood up and grabbed his coat off of the chair. "And you would know this how? I thought you turned good."

Gwen smiled. "I can still notice things, can't I?"

After Hugo and Erik reluctantly agreed to check out Southwark, the four of them headed toward the South Kensington station to catch the last train. The walk, or what felt more like a jog to Collin, over to the station was quiet. Hugo and Erik kept a close eye on Gwen. He watched her too, but not for the same reasons as the others. He wanted to see if there was any hint of her still caring for him. So far, she had ignored him and didn't want to talk about what happened, which to him meant she did care still in some small way. Gwen kept her head faced forward, disregarding the watching eyes she probably knew were on her.

They barely made it in time. The last train had pulled up right when they got to the platform. They jumped on, finding it mostly empty other than one man seated on the other side of the car.

"That was a close one, I didn't want to walk all the way to Southwark." Collin grabbed onto the handrail as the train began to move.

"It wouldn't have taken *that* long." Gwen flashed a smile.

"Yeah, for you," Hugo muttered.

Collin looked back and forth between the two of them. "I don't understand."

"Demons can move incredibly fast, depending on their strength," Erik explained.

"Oh." None of them told him about the powers of the demons, just those of the minions. Collin looked over at the other man that was in the same car as them. He didn't seem to be paying any attention. "That would come in handy."

"Indeed it has." She also glanced over at the man on the other end of the car. She kept her eyes on him, not looking away for a moment, as if in a trance.

"Gwen?" Collin tried to catch her attention. She didn't respond. Erik noted her distraction.

"Gwen." Erik shoved his elbow into her stomach. "Knock it off."

Gwen blinked, coming back to them. "Sorry, haven't been in the underground this late at night. He looked so lonely. It's dangerous to be so alone, you know."

"If you hurt one human, we will kill you." Hugo's voice sent shivers down his spine. Collin looked back at Gwen to find her laughing at what she probably considers an empty threat.

"I won't hurt anyone. I haven't killed anyone in years. Anyone human, at least. Can't you tell?" She held out her hand. It shook slightly. "Been like that for a while now. Won't seem to go away."

"If you were that weak five years ago then how did you beat your..." Collin paused for a moment, not sure what word he should use.

Gwen raised her eyebrow. "You mean my blood partner? That's simple, he's weak too. He's a bit stronger than me since he does drink human blood, but nothing a little flirting can't handle. Gets him every time."

Before Collin could ask about whom she meant, Hugo interrupted. "You're talking about that bastard you always fought with, aren't you?"

Gwen nodded. "I am."

"He was almost as bad as you. He never played fair and gave no mercy. Ever."

"All's fair in love and war. Especially when you have nothing to go back to."

"What happened to him?" Collin decided to get the topic back to the night 5 years ago. "You didn't kill him, at least not that I remembered."

"No I didn't kill him, just knocked him around pretty good. As to where he is now." She shrugged. "Probably got in trouble for going after me alone and then got assigned to another country, or what I would call a battlefront as he would be trying to turn the government leaders into minions, by the leading demon in this battle."

"Why is he weak?"

Her eyes narrowed. "Why do you keep asking me things?"

"Curiosity. Besides…" He nodded to Hugo and Erik. "You tend to answer more than they do."

She smiled. "Then maybe I should be like them and shut my mouth."

Collin decided not to ask any more questions for the time being. Gwen's sarcastic replies were starting to get on his nerves and her grinning frightened him a little, as if everything she said had some kind of hidden meaning. She was different, she wasn't herself, or at least what he knew of her. He knew her personally, five years ago. Now, she was a completely different person. She must have been acting in front of Hugo and Erik. She just had to be.

They arrived at Tower Hill station. It was located across the Thames from where they needed to go, but the tube unloaded them right next to the bridge. All they needed to do now was cross, and they were where Gwen recommended they go tonight. Bridge-crossing was faster than changing lines to get to Southwark.

As they crossed, Gwen started to softly whisper a song.

"London bridge is falling down, falling down, falling down. London bridge is falling down, my fair lady."

Her eerie tone convinced Collin that there was something more behind the song. He looked up at Erik and Hugo, but they didn't turn around as she repeated the lyrics over and over again. They knew she was looking for a reaction.

She sang the same song, over and over again, the entire way across the bridge.

They soon reached the other end, and Collin was certainly thankful when she finally stopped singing. He had heard stories of the song's origins, some more morbid than others. He really didn't want to know what part she had played in that incident from history.

"Now." Gwen clapped her hands together. "Where could those rascals be hiding?"

"You're awfully cheerful about catching these minions," Hugo commented. "Especially since they are your creations."

"Hugo, what do you think I've been feeding on for several decades, since turning 'good'?"

Collin's eyes widened. "You've been feeding on minions?"

"Of course. Otherwise I would be a withering mess." She made a motion at her throat. "No energy whatsoever."

"I saw you bite James," Collin added. "Does he give you energy too?"

Collin saw Erik give Gwen a curious look after he said that. He must have not known she had done that. Collin wondered why it would be important.

"You're asking questions again," Gwen said in a little singsong voice. She pointed toward a church. "There's a good place to start."

"By the church?" A thought crossed Collin's mind. "Can your kind even go into churches?"

"We can, it just isn't wise. Everything in there can hurt us, one way or another. So it's not often that any of us will ever follow a person in. Holy water once spilt on me. Burnt like hell."

"Literally," Hugo interjected.

Gwen nodded. "Literally."

Hugo smacked his head. "Now that's what I forgot! Holy water!"

"Why do you need that against minions? There aren't many yet." Gwen kept walking down the street ahead of the rest of them.

"I wouldn't use it against them, I would use it against you."

Gwen stopped and shoved Hugo. "You have the knife. Bring it Gargoyle."

"Gargoyle?" Collin whispered to himself.

Hugo shoved Gwen back. "You would like that, wouldn't you? Summon your minions and then have them attack us!"

She shook her head. "I don't have any minions left to command, you idiot."

"How do I know you aren't lying to us? How do I know your other demon friends aren't waiting for us?"

Collin turned to Erik. "What's their problem?"

Erik watched the two of them keep up their bickering. "They've had many encounters throughout the past. Never been good ones."

"And you?"

"And I what?"

"Encountered Gwen in the past?"

Erik didn't answer, but turned back to Hugo and Gwen. "Knock it off, you two!"

Gwen pointed. "He started it." Hugo glared at her. She started to laugh, but stopped abruptly.

"What is it?" Collin asked.

She put out her hand to stop. "Shh."

Gwen stepped slowly ahead, breathing in the air. Collin found that strange. He didn't know demons could sniff out things or people around them.

"Minions! Come on out!" She started running down

the street.

They followed her. The bit about her being faster was definitely true as Collin could barely keep up with her. He watched as she disappeared around a corner.

Turning around the block, they found Gwen with a minion. The minion didn't try to attack, but instead stood against the wall, staring at her.

"Where on Earth have you been hiding?" She approached him slowly.

The minion stayed in human form, which Collin found to be very strange. Usually, they would have changed and attacked them by now.

"Gwen?" Erik didn't seem to understand either.

"I have hunted down countless minions involved in the second war. I seem to have missed one." She approached the man and grabbed his jaw. "Just look at his blonde hair, blue eyes, chiseled jaw. He was one of my soldiers."

"She can't mean…" Collin began.

"She can," Erik answered, knowing exactly what he was about to ask. An Aryan soldier from World War II, still looking as young as the day he served.

"I'm impressed. I suppose you were the one who told of my whereabouts years ago? You are the only minion left who could have recognized my scent."

The minion didn't answer her. He looked afraid, knowing he couldn't do anything to Gwen now. She had control over him. She was his master.

Gwen chuckled at the minion. "You are correct to fear me but you should answer my questions. Where are the others? Jürgen is here, he has to be gathering you lot. Where is he?" No answer. "Where is he!" she clenched her hands down around his chin.

"Like I would tell you."

Gwen's eyes flashed yellow. "I am your master, minion! Tell me where he is!"

"I can't. I've been ordered not to."

"By whom?"

He smirked, even though Gwen's grip on his chin looked like it could easily kill him. "The one who is coming for you."

Gwen's eyes widened in fear for a moment, then flashed to pure hatred. She clenched her hands down a little more on his jaw, and Collin heard the snap of the minion's jaw and cranium. Gwen let go, and he collapsed to the ground.

"Damn him," she whispered and turned to find them staring at her, awestruck by what they just witnessed. She dashed behind them. Collin turned to see another minion pinned to the wall. Not as calm as the one she had just dealt with. This one scratched at her, tearing at her clothes and skin. Gwen bit into the minion's neck, eyes glowing yellow.

He had seen blood countless times when working with Hugo, but to see the woman he loved digging her teeth into flesh made Collin sick to his stomach. It was a wake-up call, reminding him that she wasn't like him. She was a demon. It didn't make him fear her, just made him remember she wasn't like him. He was human, after all.

Gwen had blood dripping off of her lip. She wiped it

on her sleeve as she looked at them.

"Why you all just standing there? Kill minions, chop chop!" She clapped her hands, then pointed to a space behind them. "Seriously, there's two behind you."

Collin grabbed his own knife and turned. Two minions were coming straight toward them.

CHAPTER 12

Erik pulled out his own knife from his boot. Hugo had the triduanum knife already within reach—he had gotten it ready when Gwen ran off after the minion. Erik could tell Hugo still wasn't too sure about her and, to be honest, neither was he. They had to just play along with whatever she was doing until she turned Collin. Then they could kill her, or at least try.

Erik took note of the situation at hand. Two minions were nothing, he had gone up against more over the years. Many, many more. He figured Gwen could even take the two by herself if she wanted to. She was weak and their blood would help her enough to get over the cravings she had been expressly showing for the past hours he's been with her.

As the two minions attacked them, Erik grabbed one by the throat. He debated whether or not he wanted to kill it or if he should let Gwen feed off of it. In case more minions were on their way, they'd need her strength, so he chose the latter. "Gwen!"

She rushed over and bit into its neck. He never knew of a demon to feed off of a minion, though he had seen enough demons kill them out of pure frustration.

The minion struggled, but it was no match for him or the demon feeding on him. Minions were essentially demonic spirits trapped in human form. They may be stronger than humans, but by themselves they had no chance against anything else in the demon or gargoyle world. In groups, on the other hand, they could do a lot more damage.

Gwen finished taking the blood she needed, so Erik threw the remains to the side. Erik found that Hugo and Collin had already dealt with the other minion.

"So there *were* minions here," Hugo commented as he searched the body of the one he killed.

"What, did you think I lied?" Gwen replied as she rubbed the rest of the blood off of her face with the sleeve of her white button-up shirt.

"I thought maybe you sent us on a wild goose chase."

"Well that wouldn't be any fun now, would it?" Gwen bent down next to Hugo and looked over the body. "This one is recent."

"So Jürgen appears to have followed us." Erik looked around, making sure he didn't see any movement in the shadows. You could never be too careful.

Gwen nodded. "Of course he did. You even said it yourself, this is the next battlefront. The war is always ongoing, whether the humans see it or not. We will always be fighting, you and I."

"What do we do now?" Collin asked.

Gwen stood up and peered around. "We should head back. I think it may have been a bad idea for us to search for minions tonight."

Erik watched her. Her face was serious and concerned. She knew more than she said. "Why?"

Her eyes didn't turn away from the street. "Because Jürgen isn't in the happiest of moods right now and has just sent half a dozen minions our way."

Erik hoped Hugo wasn't correct about her setting them up. "Do you know where he is?"

"He's not going to attack us himself, if that's what you are wondering. He's just hoping the minions give us a good pounding, that's all. A taste of what's to come over the next few days."

Erik wondered if she knew this from experience or if there was something she was hiding. "What about you?"

"What about me?" Gwen questioned.

"If he attacks us, are you with us or with him?"

Gwen smiled. "If he attacks, just throw me at him. I think he would have more fun killing me than killing any of you. Then you could make a break for it, not that I could really hold him off that long. I would just have to wait for morning to come."

"Morning? Why?" Erik asked. She always talked like that and it annoyed him. Again, she was definitely withholding some information from him, which made him trust her intentions even less. He began to understand why Jürgen shot her back in Paris.

Before she could answer him, six minions started to break from the shadows, surrounding them. It was exactly what she had described would happen, only minutes ago.

"Gwen?" Hugo began.

"Yes Hugo?" she answered.

"I hate it when you're right."

She laughed. "Me too."

The first minion attacked. Erik always wondered why they would group together, but other times they attacked their opponents one at a time. It was a stupid move. Gwen took on the one that attacked. To see her in action, fighting against something that wasn't him or another one of his kind was quite a strange sight.

Taking on two of the other minions, Erik jammed his knife into one of their hearts, pulling up and ripping it straight up through the ribs and into the clavicle. He could hear the crunching of the bone as the blood began to pour out of the creature's wound and down his hand, the warmth of it feeling strangely refreshing in the cold English night. Sometimes, they took a little more effort to kill, so he always sliced up and through to make sure it really did die. Red liquid flowed out of its mouth, as it fell to the ground. The other minion didn't even falter.

Stabbing the other in the throat, it didn't have a chance. It collapsed right next to its buddy, its own blood spewing out of the wound, adding to the spilled blood from the other minions that have been defeated.

Erik took a look around. Gwen had taken down a total of two of them, Hugo still was struggling with fighting his minion, and Collin had taken down his one. Six were no problem, but Erik had a feeling there had to be more, especially if Gwen was right about Jürgen wanting to show them what was awaiting them.

"Well that was easy." Collin wiped the sweat off his brow.

Erik knew those were words never to say in a fight, especially when he saw movement in the shadows behind Collin.

"Collin!" Erik yelled as the minion grabbed him and pulled him back, digging its claws into him. Before Erik could do anything, Gwen pulled the minion away from Collin, but not before the minion slammed Collin against the wall, knocking him out. Gwen bit into the minion's neck. It tried to slash her, but it didn't make a difference. Gwen seemed to be used to this kind of struggle.

After finishing off the minion, Gwen rushed to Collin's side, right along with Erik. Hugo was dealing with the remaining minions. Blood poured out of Collin's wounds.

Erik let Gwen feel for Collin's pulse. She kept nodding. "He will be fine. He will heal from something as slight as this." Erik had never seen a demon express concern before for a human being. Her arms shook as she touched him and checked his body for any more wounds. She was truly afraid of losing him, making Erik feel that his doubts about her honesty might be unfounded. A part of him, though, still wondered how much of what she was telling them was true, or what percentage of it was lies.

Erik watched anxiously, as Gwen stared at her fingers to find them covered with Collin's blood. Her eyes turned yellow, entranced with the residue of Collin's blood. Erik could see her struggle, but he didn't try to stop her. She could finish what he needed her to do then and there. Then, they would have the upper hand.

Shaking her head, she wiped the blood off of her hands. "I can't... I can't do that to him. I can't make him like me. I can't make him a demon with a soul."

"Why?" Erik questioned.

"Because he doesn't deserve it."

Fed up with her excuses, Hugo grabbed her by the collar and shoved her against the wall. "You already started this Gwen, now finish it!"

Erik didn't understand why she wouldn't do it. She said she wanted to help them, but she wouldn't do something as simple as this. But that didn't give Hugo the right to get mad at her like this, yet for some reason Erik couldn't stop him.

"I can't."

"Why not?" Hugo lashed out.

Gwen didn't struggle. "Because if I turn him, he will be out of control. You will not be able to control him like you think you will. Believe me, I know. I have done it once before, and that ended horribly, which is why it is forbidden for the Twelve to do so without consequence."

Erik watched her for a moment. Demons never cared

about humans before, he didn't understand how this was different. They thrived on chaos, they liked it when things went completely out of control. Finally deciding to let her go, Hugo dropped Gwen. She turned back to Collin.

"We've got to get him out of here," Gwen started to pick him up. "Jürgen will just keep sending minions at us otherwise. The pub will be perfect, since Jürgen would have to be invited in. Collin would be safe there."

"It will take two hours for us to get back," Erik walked up next to her.

She shook her head. "No, I can get him there in five minutes."

Erik couldn't believe that she thought they would let her go alone. "You can't go by yourself."

"Why?"

"How do I know you won't take him to Jürgen?"

She shook her head. "I won't. He would kill him."

"Then won't Jürgen try to stop you from getting back to the pub?" Erik questioned.

"Yes."

"How will you outrun him?"

Gwen looked at him, her eyes red as if she was about to cry out of frustration and fear. Those eyes scared Erik the most. "Please help me. I won't hurt Collin. I'll stay in the pub until you get there. It's the only way to guarantee his safety. If we walk back, Jürgen will send minions after us until one of them gets lucky and finishes him off completely... Please, I beg you."

Erik knew she was right, it would take too long for

them to walk back, and someone might spot Collin covered in blood, enough blood that he should be dead by human standards. Only the blood of Gwen that still ran through his veins kept him alive. Gwen could get there fast without being noticed by either Jürgen or his minions. The worry in her eyes told him that she was telling the truth.

"Fine." He rolled up his sleeve. "But if you betray me, I will kill you myself."

"Deal." She bit into his wrist. Second time in one day, Erik never thought that would happen. He debated looking over at Hugo to see if he noticed what was going on, but decided not to. He didn't need Hugo's disapproving stare at this critical moment. She took as much as she needed and then backed off.

Gwen grabbed Collin and carried him on her back. "See you later then." And with that, she was gone.

Erik looked at the empty space of where she just was and sighed. For all he knew, that could have been the last time he would see either of them. Glancing around, he realized something odd. Why did she need his energy when she just fed off a handful of minions? That was enough for a demon to get enough strength for several hours. There was something more going on inside her than just not feeding on humans for such a long time.

Hugo had finished off the one remaining minion and witnessed the last moments before Gwen disappeared. "What did you just do? Where did Gwen go? Did I just see her take Collin?"

Erik didn't want to start another argument. There

already had been enough of those throughout the day. "Yes."

"Why did you let her?!"

"Because she can get him back quickly and will protect him with her life." Erik turned to him. "Besides, she'll use all of her strength getting him home. He's covered in blood, Hugo, and there will be no one to stop her from turning him fully into a demon."

"All of this is just to get her to turn him, isn't it?"

"Yes."

Hugo ran his blood-covered fingers through his hair, leaving wet strands. "You really think turning him will lead us to victory?"

"I think it is our last chance."

CHAPTER 13

Gwen ran. She ran as fast as she could with what strength she had, but she knew she couldn't outrun Jürgen. He would be on her like a hawk once he saw she had separated from the Gargoyles. She had to get to Collin's bar as fast as she could.

With Collin on her back, Gwen sped past the buildings of Parliament and the Big Ben. She could sense Jürgen now, coming in closer from behind. Thankfully, Erik had given her the energy she needed beforehand, even though it still wouldn't fully restore her strength. No, she was far from that point, and had been since switching sides.

Street after street, corner after corner, everything flew by quickly, but still Gwen knew it wouldn't be enough.

She had four more minutes to get Collin to his pub, where Jürgen wouldn't be able to hurt him, at least for a while. If she got detained by Jürgen, she would inevitably have to deal with James, which would bring more problems into her world. James would want to deal with Collin personally, and she would have to sweet talk him out of killing him. She wondered how well that would go. If they got to the pub in time, though, she wouldn't have to think of that hypothetical scenario for a little while; it could be delayed. And, maybe, Collin would be safe by then.

The energy drained quickly from her. It took a lot of strength to keep up the speed she had been going for the last couple of minutes. Gwen didn't even know how much longer she could hold out at this pace, but the thought of slowing down and letting Jürgen catch up to her made her keep going. She took another turn. She was so close now.

"Guinevere…" Jürgen's gravelly voice echoed through the quiet night. It sent shivers down her spine. She really didn't want to hear his voice nor his threats. None of them were ever empty. "Do you really think you can outrun me?"

"Oh, I can try!" she replied. Inside she might let him get to her, but she would never show it. She would never give him that satisfaction.

Gwen pushed herself harder. She wouldn't let him catch up to her. Once James was in London, she wouldn't have to worry about Jürgen. James would keep her safe from them, even if he was mad at her. He wouldn't let anyone else take the pleasure of dealing with her. James would want to have her all to himself. Always so selfish.

Only a few hundred meters left.

"You aren't going to make it," Jürgen called out. "And you know exactly what I will do to him if I catch you."

"He's not turned!" she replied sharply.

"I don't care. It's payback. You deserve it."

Gwen wondered what he was really referring to. She had pissed him off so many times over the years that it was hard to keep track. But she had a feeling it was something in particular. "I won't let you. Not today."

"Then you better speed up."

The pub was within sight now. Gwen put all her effort into the last few meters of the sprint. Then, she realized she didn't have a key to the door.

"Shit, this is going to hurt," she whimpered.

Gwen winced as she slammed into the door, the wood coming right off the hinges. Sliding along the floor, she dropped Collin. His unconscious body tumbled across the ground and into the wall. Gwen took a moment to catch her breath.

Glancing over at him, she saw he was fine, just a few more bruises, less than what Jürgen would have done. At that precise moment, Jürgen was standing at the door frame, slamming his hand against the invisible barrier. She chuckled.

"Thought you could come in, didn't you? He lives upstairs. Some rules apply even if it's a pub." Gwen straightened up and approached the door, trying to appear stronger than she felt at that moment. It surprised her that she could even stand up.

"Just wait until James is here. He will do far worse to him than I would have ever done."

"We will see about that." It was her greatest fear, but she wouldn't let Jürgen see that. "A little late to the party, isn't he?"

Jürgen grinned. "He will be here soon enough." He turned toward the street. "Better not get too comfortable with these Gargoyles, Gwen. He will rip away anything you had with those wretched beings." He looked back over his shoulder. "But you already know that, don't you?"

Jürgen disappeared into the night. Gwen watched the street for a few more moments, before checking on Collin. He still lay there in the corner, unconscious. Gwen sighed as she collapsed next to him, her body finally giving out on her. She had done it. She had kept him safe. For now.

Rolling over to face him, Gwen examined his injuries. Nothing too serious, at least not for him. His clothes were soaked with his blood, blood which she craved.

Gwen inched closer. If she drank his blood, he would fully turn into a demon, or at least like one. He wouldn't be truly damned, in a sense, and would still have his soul. But the power and bloodlust would be there, he would crave it and he would be strong and fast just like her. She didn't want that, but she was so weak. His blood would revive her, it would be exactly what she needed, and vice versa.

Her eyes turned yellow. She craved it so much at this

moment. He had her blood in him, keeping him alive. He wouldn't be a minion, as the blood was already coursing through his veins. Minions were humans killed without the blood of a demon. Once Collin was turned, they could run off together, they could be together forever, living on each other's blood.

Gwen's hand flinched back. No, she wouldn't let herself do it. She cared for him far too much to place that kind of burden on him. It would cost her too much guilt and heartache to ever bring him that much pain.

Gathering her strength, she stood up. She needed to get him to his room where he could heal. She took a deep breath, as she lifted him up and carried him up the stairs to his room.

His room, as she remembered, was plain. Nothing on the walls, except some lines. She knew these lines had to represent tallies, which recorded all the minions he killed over the years. It was something she used to do as well until she ran out of room on the wall of her own old flat. She was impressed by how many they had found. She wouldn't have thought he had it in him.

Gwen set him gently down on his bed, which she found to be already covered in blood, the blood she smelled earlier. More still seeped out of his wounds, adding more blood residue to the stained sheets.

Her heart pounded with thirst. With hunger. Just one little drop. Gwen bent in closer to him. The smell of his blood filled her lungs. The temptation almost brought her lips down to his wounds. Almost. She kissed him softly on the lips. She wouldn't let the urge inside of her take hold. She wouldn't.

Backing away, Gwen took one last look at Collin. She wondered, out of the thousands and thousands of humans she killed over the years, why he was different. Why did she care enough now about the beings she once sought to torture? Why, when she felt alone and rejected, did he bring her comfort and, more importantly, acceptance? That had to be it. It had to be the fact he accepted her, no matter what. The first human to ever do such a thing. That was why she couldn't turn him fully. That was why she couldn't cast this type of curse on him.

Her fingers still had his blood on them. She wiped them on the wall, adding a couple of lines to his tallies. It looked a little odd, as his were all in marker. Probably would give people the creeps if they ever came up here.

Gwen shut the door and went back down to the bar. She needed a drink. Searching through the cabinets, Gwen found some Scotch. It was a bottle of Laphroaig, one of her favorites. Grabbing the bottle, Gwen collapsed at a booth.

She couldn't believe the mess she had found herself in. Fallen to Earth, regretting her decision, running away from her destiny, and falling for a human. Gwen took a swig. And humans thought their lives weren't fair. At least redemption was within their grasp. She, on the other hand, was doomed to fall and never get up again.

Checking the clock, Gwen knew the Gargoyles wouldn't be back for another hour or so. So she was stuck here, by herself, with a human they wanted her to turn who happened to be bleeding and she happened to be hungry. Very, very hungry. Now, she understood why Erik let her take Collin back. Because she might give in and change him. That bastard.

Taking another swig, tears started to form in her eyes with memories of the night she left Collin. She had never been so mad at James, she had never felt so much pain as in that one moment. Although he had every right to do what he did, she still ended up using the triduanum knife on him. It took a lot of debating in her mind, to decide whether she should leave some blood for him to heal himself, which she finally did. No matter how pissed she was, she wouldn't let him suffer that greatly, yet she wouldn't let him become what she is either.

Gwen finished her drink and rubbed her face with her hands. James would be in the city soon. Jürgen was right, he would rip her away and wipe out any thought she had about helping the Gargoyles, one way or another. Then, once Jürgen told him about Collin...

Shaking her head, Gwen dismissed any thoughts of what James would do to Collin. She shouldn't worry about that right now. It would only make things worse.

She looked up the stairwell toward Collin's room, debating whether she should go back up there to see if he was alright. Gwen wanted to stare at him, make sure he was fine, but she knew that would only tempt her more. Deciding to stay downstairs, she waited until the Gargoyles arrived.

Gwen took a look at the door she had trampled on the way in. All she broke was the lock and hinges, which was exactly what she hoped for. Easily fixable. She would have to leave a note saying sorry for that, and also not to go outside until they came back later that night. Just as a precaution. He was safe as long as he stayed inside the pub.

Lying down on the booth seat, Gwen closed her eyes. She would let herself rest while she waited, let her mind slip in and out of consciousness. Flashes of memories of cities drenched in blood filled her head. They never went away, no matter how many years it had been. She didn't want to see those faces ever again.

***

Gwen jumped up from the pub booth, as she heard someone approaching her from behind. Hugo and Erik pushed the door out of their way and walked in. Hugo took a closer look at the door. "Didn't think about it being locked, did you?"

"No, I was more worried about being torn into pieces by Jürgen."

"So he did follow you," Erik commented.

Gwen decided to bite her tongue. It wasn't his fault she felt miserable. Well, only a little bit.

She laid back down on the booth. "Followed, threatened, all that jazz."

"And Collin?" He sounded hopeful, which made her want to lash out even more.

Gwen pointed. "Upstairs resting. He didn't wake up for any of it, luckily."

Erik looked up the stairwell. Gwen figured he was disappointed she didn't turn him. She still wasn't sure why he was so keen on it.

He turned back to her. "We should wait until he wakes up and explain what happened. I don't think he would appreciate us leaving in such a hurry."

"He needs to learn to deal with it if he wants to help you," she said.

"You can stop this act, Gwen, I know you care about it him."

She glared at him.

Erik went on. "Sad thing is that no matter what you do, he will suffer in the end. And you know that."

Gwen looked down at her blood crusted hands and closed them tightly. "More than you would ever understand."

CHAPTER 14

James stepped off the plane and took in a deep breath. He could smell it—sweet jasmine with a hint of mint and rose. It was the smell of her demonic blood. It was a smell he missed waking up to. Yes, she was here, his darling Gwen. James smiled. She wouldn't get away from him now. He was ready for her. She wouldn't surprise him this time.

"Where are you off to first? Maybe we could get some breakfast before our vacation begins?"

James turned to face his new friend Katy. He had gotten to know her on the long plane trip, perhaps a little too well. She wouldn't stop talking, but he didn't mind. She had come over by herself and no one was expecting her. She was the perfect person for him.

"Sounds like a splendid idea." He watched as her eyes lit up.

"Great!" She grabbed his arm and started pulling him down the street. "I know of a place just a few stops from here."

James' eyes flashed yellow as he watched her. It was all too easy. He would treat her to a meal before draining her of her blood. He needed a good pick-me-up, before meeting with Jürgen.

As the sliding doors began to close, James and his new friend jumped on the train. The train began to move and Katy almost lost her footing, while getting on.

James wrapped his arm around her. "Don't worry, I got you."

Katy blushed. "Thank you." Those were the only words she could get out. Gwen always commented on how he could make a lady lost for words, except for her of course. He wished he could get her to be as speechless as he could with any human. Then he wouldn't be stuck in this current predicament.

He leaned in a little closer. "No problem."

"So." She fiddled with the end of her sleeve. "So what kind of archaeology are you researching here?"

He had forgotten about that lie. She talked mostly about herself on the plane. "Arthurian legend. I'm actually looking for any evidence of Guinevere."

Her face filled with curiosity. "Really? You think that legend is true?"

"Oh, I know it is," he smirked. "Whether or not the exact tales are true is a different story. But Arthur and

Guinevere were real people. I just don't think they were the heroes everyone makes them out to be. Funny how stories get twisted after time."

"Like Robin Hood?" she inquired.

The name pinched a nerve. They lost a member of the Twelve demons because of him. Now they called him Hugo. "Sure, like Robin Hood. He wasn't the hero everyone makes him out to be either. At least, not from my viewpoint."

"Interesting, I could talk about myths all day. I always found my anthropology classes in college to be enjoyable."

The car shook as they reached another station. It apparently wasn't theirs, since Katy didn't say anything about getting off here. James watched as passengers got off and on. "Oh, what type of archaeology did you study?"

"Just a few classes. Archaeology of Europe, food culture, ancient cities, stuff like that."

"Which did you find the most interesting?"

"I found the Industrial Revolution of Victorian England the most interesting, not that I ever took a class on it. I just did some research on my own."

James remembered that era all too well, especially when the First World War erupted. "It was a very interesting time. Without industrialization, the wars wouldn't have been as fun."

She looked at him puzzled. "Fun?"

He needed to watch his words more carefully. "To study I mean."

"I suppose not." She took a look at the station they had just stopped at. "Oh, this is our stop. South Ealing."

James held out his hand. "Lead the way."

She grabbed his hand and pulled him off the car. He laughed at her eagerness.

As Katy led him down the streets, James debated if he should just end it here and now, or if he should take her out to breakfast, and give it a little more time. Jürgen was waiting for him, but he was a gentleman and should treat a lady to her last meal, even though she didn't know it to be her last. And it had been a while since he'd had a good English scone.

South Ealing was a quiet area beyond the busy streets of London, far less populated than either Kensington or Soho. All the better for what he had in mind.

"Here it is." She pointed at a little family owned café on the corner.

"Looks great," he commented as they entered. It was cozy, to say the least. The tables were close, and it was quite crowded as people had begun to come in for a late breakfast or snack. The walls needed a fresh paint job, but the warm red color was inviting, or maybe that was just him.

They got a little table right near the window, giving them a view of the alleyway full of primroses. The waitress wore, what James noted, a *very* nice uniform. He tried not to admire it, but the outfit was quite short, leaving not so much to the imagination of the onlooker, particularly a demon onlooker. Humans didn't like it when you browsed. Gwen never cared, since she knew he was really only interested in her blood out of anyone's blood.

"Would you like to start with a pot of tea?" the waitress asked.

"Yes, please." Katy smiled. The waitress nodded and left toward the door that led to the kitchen. "It's been a long time since I've had a good cup."

"Agreed." He already knew what he wanted. Scones. Placing the menu back on the table, James leaned forward. "So, tell me, what transportation lines did you work on in Boston?" She had said she was a transportation planner in Boston, but never went into much detail about it on the place. She talked more about the different cities she had been to, and then about her cats. She had a lot of pictures on her phone to show, adorable cat pictures, which he wouldn't admit out loud. Seth would detest to any cat being cute, as he had the worst luck with them in Egypt. Gwen always loved them though, but probably because Seth hated them.

"Oh, I work on subway systems. Make sure they are efficient and that sort of thing," she explained. "I like organizing things."

"That must be a fun job." He didn't really think so, but he didn't dare say it. He was truly bored with this and wanted to get on with his day, but he was a gentleman.

"It's all right, nothing like archaeology though." She sat her chin on her crossed hands in front of her. "You must have some fascinating stories, though."

"I do have some pretty interesting stories, I have to admit." But he couldn't go into detail, not if he didn't want her running and screaming in horror.

The waitress came back with the pot of tea. "Would you two like anything to eat?"

"Yes, an order of two scones." Katy handed her the menu.

James smiled. "The same."

The waitress wrote down the order and left.

"So tell me, what is your favorite finding?"

James thought for a moment. "I guess that would have to be the triduanum."

"The what?"

"The triduanum, also known as the three-day knife, made out of the spear end that pierced Christ's side. Supposedly, if you stab a demon with the knife, they will die in three days' time, unless they get the blood of another demon. It had been used throughout history by the bravest of heroes, such as William the Conqueror, King Richard, President Washington, President Lincoln, and so on. All wars against good and evil," he explained. Gwen had it now, he would have to be careful about her using it on him again.

"Very interesting, I've never heard of it. Where is it now?"

He didn't want to think about the last time he saw the knife. He had been stupid to not pay more attention to it, when he was around Gwen that time five years ago. "A colleague stole it from me."

"Oh, that's unfortunate."

"I'll get it back soon." He took a sip of his tea. "Tell me more about your friend. Why did she bail on you?"

"Oh, she's an aerospace engineer working for NASA. She got a project she had to finish, so she wasn't able to take off. We usually meet in DC and fly to wherever we go."

Space. The final frontier. A place where he could never go. "That's very interesting."

"Yeah, still sad she couldn't come with though. But then again." She grinned. "I got to run into you."

"I will have to thank her," James said as the waitress brought them their scones.

"So." Katy ripped open hers. "What other myths and legends have you studied?"

"Oh, mostly ones that have to do with northern Europe."

"Ever do any study on vampires?"

James almost choked on his scone. "Vampires?"

She shrugged. "You know, Dracula, Vlad, all that stuff. I've always had a fascination with them. Immortal creatures of the night. Sexy and scary at the same time."

"I've done a little studying about them, but not too much detail," he lied. He could have said he studied them a lot, or even admitted they were real, but he didn't want to stretch the truth more, especially if she somehow figured out the truth. Gwen was definitely better at stretching the truth, never lying completely, but wording things in a clever way to hide the full truth. One of the many qualities he missed most about Gwen. He loved her games.

"Too bad."

James just smiled. He could have told the truth, but so

many people think they like vampires until they actually meet one. There was no turning, no falling in love, nothing in the recent movies were true.

"Sorry to disappoint."

They finished their breakfast, talking about other matters in the world, both ones of the past and of the present. She believed in humanity, she had a heart for every person. She really did care and wanted to help society. Apparently someone high up didn't want her to make a difference or they wouldn't have let her fall into his lap.

James paid for the breakfast and they headed out into the quiet street.

"Thank you for breakfast, you didn't have to pay." Katy smiled as they stepped out of the cafe.

"Don't worry about it, it was nothing." He placed his hand on her cheek. Leaning in he kissed her.

In a second, he took her off the street into an alley, where no one would hear her scream.

CHAPTER 15

Headache. Massive headache. Collin's eyes flickered open as he rubbed his head. The pain radiated through his body. He tried to recall the night before, but the thoughts weren't coming quickly. Looking around, he saw blood everywhere. Blood. Minions. Then he remembered. Gwen.

A minion had gotten a hold of him, but before it could hurt him, Gwen attacked it. Then he fell and passed out. He felt like a weakling now. Collin sighed. He got knocked out by a stupid minion because he couldn't keep his guard up. He kept letting himself get distracted by her.

"You idiot," he mumbled to himself as he stretched. Taking a look at his body, he found his clothes ripped and his skin torn. He would be fine, just flesh wounds. His pride, on the other hand, would take a little while to heal.

Collin stood up and heard voices coming from downstairs He didn't think they would have stayed. He staggered over to the stairwell.

"What happened?" He looked down at them.

They stopped talking and peered up at him. Gwen turned and rushed up the stairs in an instant. He almost fell back in surprise. He forgot she could do that, but more importantly, her former white shirt was now speckled with blood. Her arms were covered, and nothing about that and the blood on her shirt fazed her whatsoever. She'd had time to clean up, but she hadn't even tried. Was it because she was spending the time worrying about his welfare? Or was it simply that she didn't care?

"Are you all right?" She tried to help him up, but he waved her away.

"I'm fine." He grabbed onto the railing. "Just explain to me what exactly happened."

She looked concerned, which scared him. Something must have gone wrong. "A minion got you."

He rubbed his temples. "I know that, I mean after. How did I get back here and—more importantly—why are you all still here? I would expect you all to leave unless you had something really important to tell me."

"We stayed to warn you," Erik started. "Come down and have a seat."

With Gwen's help—which he didn't need, but she

insisted on—Collin went down the stairs and sat at the table. He took a look around, finding blood in all sorts of weird places—behind the counter, over all the chairs, over the wine bottles and glasses. Okay, maybe not that weird. He would need to clean it all up before Hywel arrived later.

Collin turned his attention back to Erik. "So, again, what happened?"

"After you got knocked out, Gwen brought you back here as fast as she could," Erik explained.

He looked at Gwen. "As in utilizing her super-speed?"

Erik nodded. "Yes. She had to get you back before the other demon caught you. We stayed to tell you not to leave this pub today. Like Gwen, he can't come in without being invited."

"But why would he be so interested in me? I'm just a puny human." He cracked a smile, but none of them laughed at his comment. Erik glanced at Gwen, and he was sure something else was going on.

"You've killed a lot of minions. You're a nuisance and they want to get rid of you." Gwen smiled. She always smiled like that when she was trying to trick someone. "Believe me, I've gotten rid of many puny humans over the years. Have to admit, though, you are one of the most troublesome."

"Right, you would know. There couldn't be any other reason why they want to come after me? No secrets you three want to share and let out in the open?" Collin looked back and forth between the three of them.

"You know all you need to know, Collin. The rest you

would regret knowing. Just trust us, please." Gwen placed her hand gently on his. Her warm flesh touched his own. Whatever she had hidden was a lot bigger than he thought. "Please."

"Fine, no more questions." He watched Gwen's fear diminish. He did want to know, but the look she gave him made him know that she would never tell him the truth. He would find out one way or another though, in the end. It wasn't fair for him to be left out of the loop just because he was human. Collin checked the clock. "I better clean up before Hywel gets here. I don't need to try to explain why I'm covered in blood. Again."

Erik stood up. "We made a salt ring around the pub. No demon can come in through it, nor can they touch the place. You will be completely safe. Just don't disturb the ring okay? We'll be back tonight. Just stay inside."

"Then how is Gwen in here?"

"We are going to add the last few grains when we leave."

Collin nodded. Having seen how fast Gwen could move, he knew he wouldn't stand a chance against the other demon that was seeking to kill him, in retaliation for the number of minions he has managed to defeat. Hugo and Gwen followed Erik as he headed out the door. As they left, Collin noticed the broken lock. Seeing his worried face, Gwen turned back to him as she left.

"Sorry about the door. Oh, and you are out of salt."

The door shut behind her and Collin let out a sigh. Now he couldn't go outside without supervision. He felt like a kid. A nuisance. He didn't understand why they let him help, he seemed to only cause them worry and problems. Collin knew there had to be another reason, but he hadn't the faintest clue what. Letting that thought sink to the back of his mind, he headed up the stairs to clean off before his shift.

Another set of ruined clothes. There was a reason he bought plain shirts in bulk. Pulling open his drawer, he found only a single one left. He needed to go get some more, but he didn't know when he would have time to do so, especially since he wasn't allowed to go outside. Grabbing it, he cleaned himself off in the shower.

Although there were many nights he and Hugo didn't find anything in the area they searched, Collin was getting sick of all the bloodshed. He wasn't used to seeing so much destruction, and Hugo never had an emotional response to any of it. It frightened him deep down, especially after seeing how much Gwen loved it. The way she looked when she bit into the minion's throat made him shudder. Her glowing eyes, her fangs, her sly smile. Any other human would have likely run away from her, but he knew he couldn't do that. She needed him to be there for her. She needed the human compassion, since no one else in her small world of demons and Gargoyles would be able to give that to her.

She had even given him compassion; they had gone out for a couple of years before she ran away. They even shared an apartment, though that could have been because she had nowhere else to go at the time. That was before he moved into the upstairs room of his pub. His old apartment reminded him too much of her. Then,

James came and ruined everything.

That was years ago, she could have changed—though for her it was probably only a blink of an eye. Five years. Five long years of him wondering where she was, and if she really missed him. Now, he knew. She was fine. She could have come back anytime, but she never did. Collin wondered if he actually meant something to her once, or if he was just something to pass the time with. The more he thought about it, the more this type of brooding hurt him. It made everything that there was between them— those fond memories of some kind of short-lived love affair—seem like a worthless illusion.

Collin decided that he had better clean up the bathroom and bed, in case Hywel decided to take a shower here again.

A new mark on the wall caught his eye. A tally in red. Gwen must have done it. He really wished she hadn't because now it made him feel like some monster, tallying his killings. But that's what it was really, a reminder.

None of them gave him a definite explanation of what had happened at all tonight, but the fact the door was broken and Gwen looked as if she had seen a ghost, or whatever the equivalent for a demon was, made him understand that it wasn't good at all. Also, her admonitions about staying indoors fueled the idea that he wasn't even safe anywhere but cooped up in this pub for the day.

Collin touched his lips. He vaguely remembered Gwen kissing him too. A moment in and out of consciousness, leaving everything as a hazy memory. But even as a hazy memory, it was worth remembering. It was the only moment all night that made him actually believe she still cared, even slightly, about him.

Heading down the stairs, Collin decided to work on the door lock first, hoping to repair it before Hywel came. After examining it for about a second, he knew he would need to call a repairman in to do the job. She must have slammed into it at super high speed. He dismissed the idea of saving the job for Hywel, knowing he wouldn't have the faintest idea of how to fix it. Besides, he would just use the opportunity to yell various Welsh expletives while attempting to fix the door.

Collin grabbed a cloth, and he started to wipe off the smeared blood that covered the booth and some of his favorite dark wood chairs in the pub. Finding an empty bottle of whiskey, Collin made a mental note to make a comment to Gwen when he saw her later. Drinking a few glasses of wine was one thing, but a whole bottle of whiskey was another, especially in combination with the wine. To be fair, he had seen a few humans try just that, just not with wine as well.

After scrubbing everything as hard as he could, and deciding to call the cleaning complete, Collin heard the door creak open.

"Whoa, what happened here?" Hywel examined the door. "Seems to be broken. What did you do to it, lad?"

"Oh." Collin didn't think of the excuse he would give him. "Some kids tried to break in. I scared them off when they realized I was here."

"Bloody hell, stupid kids," Hywel moved around,

taking a better look at the door. "Should we call the police?"

Collin shook his head. "No, it's fine. Just need to call someone to repair it, unless you can fix it."

"Don't think so, the lock is pretty messed up. Better to have someone else who knows doors and such deal with it." Hywel headed toward the telephone. "Always a good start for a day, isn't it?"

"Yeah." Collin glanced around at all the things he cleaned off. "Always."

CHAPTER 16

As they stepped out of Collin's pub and placed the last few grains of salt to close the circle around the building, Erik saw Gwen mentally check her surroundings. She peered around as if paranoid something was watching them, or something would attack. She hadn't done that at all the day before. Someone else must have arrived, another demon perhaps. He wondered if it was her old partner James. After seeing the way she'd dealt with him five years ago, it was no wonder why she was so concerned if he came—James would want revenge for what occurred five years ago. Once she noticed him watching her closely, she stopped and looked straight ahead to their destination.

Although he knew demons were able to sense each

other, he also knew there was a range. By the looks of it, he appeared to be pretty far away. If he was close, she would have warned them, at least Erik hoped. There had to be more to it than them just being former partners. Erik recalled them working with each other more than once throughout the years. They were a deadly team to go up against in those earlier days.

Now that he thought about it, Gwen was still shaking from weakness. He had given her blood after she brought Collin back to the pub. She drank from him and several minions, she should have been much stronger than she was currently. Either she had been putting on an act to look weak or her relationship with James was closer than he ever imagined.

After being sent to Earth, he remembered learning about different rituals demons could perform here. Most of them had to do with summoning, but one in particular crossed his mind. A blood bond.

The blood bond would make two consensual demons closer and stronger. The only downside to it was that if one demon left the other, they would both be weakened in effect, which Erik believed to be exactly the type of process he was seeing firsthand. Gwen even admitted to him that James was weak too. The blood bond had to be it.

So, Erik calculated, seventy to eighty years without sharing blood. That would be a long time. He couldn't imagine the withdrawal they were going through. Nothing could bring them back to that level of energy, and they would always feel weak. Gwen must have a great amount of determination to be able to stay away from him that long.

He looked back at Gwen, who was now humming 'London Bridge is Falling Down' again to herself. Erik realized she could really mean it when she said she wanted to help. But he still couldn't trust her, not after all he'd seen her do. He also couldn't believe that she just wanted to feel better about herself. No other demon regretted what they did, why would she be different? He also didn't think she deserved to feel better about all that she had done. She deserved to suffer for her wrongs.

Gwen noticed him staring at her. "Sorry, that song is stuck in my head now."

Erik shook his head. "That's not why I was looking at you."

"Oh." She raised an eyebrow. "Then why the sudden intrigue?"

"Do you and James have a blood bond?" Erik watched as her face whitened.

Hugo overheard his question and turned around. "No, no demon in their right mind would do that. It's taboo even for them, Erik," Hugo paused, thinking about the possibility. "But that would explain everything. You and James have always worked together. I've never seen you apart other than now."

Gwen didn't answer, but looked at Erik angrily. He didn't know if it was because he figured it out or because she didn't want Hugo to know her weakness. Either way, she didn't want to talk about it. She turned away and kept walking toward the flat.

Erik grabbed her by the wrist and pulled her back. "Answer my question, Gwen. Do you two have a blood bond?"

She looked back and forth between the two of them, as if debating how she would answer their question. "What do you think?"

Hugo put his hands to his face. "You have to be kidding me?! He's going to stop at nothing to find you!"

Gwen yanked her arm away from Erik's grasp. "You think I don't know that? You think I don't know how much he craves me? There's a reason I have been so careful over the years, practically invisible. Until now."

Hugo slid his hands through his hair as he paced around, irritated beyond measure, as was Erik. If he had known, he would have never agreed to bring her here with him.

Hugo stopped pacing. "Then why do you think you can help us? Why in the world are you here?"

"I can get you information. I just want to help..." Before Gwen could finish her sentence, Hugo grasped her throat and shoved her against the brick wall. She looked afraid, knowing that this could be the end for her, but she still didn't try to resist.

Hugo pressed her harder into the wall. "You set us up!"

"This isn't fake," Gwen choked out. If she were human, her hyoid would have snapped by now.

"Why would I believe what you say? Why, Gwen?" He pulled out the triduanum and held it against her throat. "Why would I believe that?"

Gwen's eyes widened with fear. Hugo could easily slice her throat right then and there. Then they wouldn't have to deal with her. Erik was tempted, but he knew it wouldn't be the right thing to do. She was with them to help, even though he didn't agree with her reasoning.

"Hugo, that's enough," Erik said.

Hugo shook his head, pressing the knife harder against Gwen's skin. Erik was afraid what would happen if he pierced it. "We should just kill her now, Erik, then we will have a better chance. James would be weak too. It would work."

"It wouldn't be right, it would be like attacking an unarmed person."

"It would be a lot easier!" he yelled back. Erik had never seen Gwen so afraid. She knew she had no way of getting out of the situation other than trusting him to talk Hugo down.

"It would be, but that's no way to win a war," Erik calmly replied.

"Oh, and what they do to us is so fair. They torture us, let us bleed out until the moment where we should be destroyed, they let us heal and start all over again. How many times have we endured that Erik? How many has it been? Seven? Eight? No! I am not going through that again!"

Erik placed his hand on Hugo's shoulder. "Do you want to stoop to their level?"

Hugo clutched Gwen's throat a little tighter then finally let her go. "No, I don't."

Gwen collapsed, gasping for air. She looked as if she

was going to puke or make a run for it. He wouldn't blame her for running, especially after the threats Hugo made toward her.

As she knelt there, Erik thought about helping her up, but instead he slammed his foot straight into her stomach. He was still pissed that she never said anything to him about the blood bond. Neither Hugo nor Erik had said anything to Collin, knowing they couldn't explain it as fully as Gwen could. She grabbed her stomach, grimacing. Erik was sure he broke a couple of ribs.

"That's for not telling me," he whispered.

Gwen nodded but didn't say anything. She knew there was nothing he wanted to hear from her.

"Get up, we should get back to the flat and figure this out. I don't like waiting in the street to see what may happen." Erik started back for the flat. She pulled herself up, stumbling once, catching herself on the wall, and followed them.

Gwen didn't say a word as she walked behind them. Hugo clenched his fists beside him, but he didn't look back. He kept his fury-filled eyes ahead. Erik looked back every once in a while, to make sure she was still following. At this point he really didn't care. While he didn't want to lose her before changing Collin, he didn't want to find out what James had in store to get her back.

After about twenty minutes, they arrived at the apartment. They went in, Hugo slamming the door behind him. Erik motioned Gwen to go into the living room. She sat down at the couch like a kid caught doing something wrong. This was different. This was worse.

She looked down at her hands, not wanting to make eye contact with either of them.

Erik sat across from her. "Why didn't you tell us?"

She fiddled with her nails. "I guess I didn't think it through."

Hugo looked as if he was about to strangle her again.

Erik rubbed his temple. "Gwen..."

Her head shot straight up. "Because you wouldn't have let me help you if I told you! You know he can sense me anywhere in the city and will stop at nothing to have me. You would have killed me."

"I say we still should." Hugo's eyes stayed on Gwen.

Erik shot him a look. "Is that why Jürgen can't do anything to you?"

She grinned. "Can't completely you mean? He did shoot me a few times and threatened me a lot." Gwen fiddled with her hands again. "What are you going to do with me now?"

Erik sighed. That was a good question, what he wanted to do with her at this point. "I don't know."

"I know what we should do," Hugo stood up. "We should hand her over. Act like none of this ever happened."

Gwen's eyes widened. "No, please don't. I'm not ready to face him."

Erik thought of what to do next. He needed help and the only person who could help him wasn't on earth. He had to talk to him and the only way to do so was to get Gwen out of his hair for a few hours.

"I need you two to go see if you can find any trace of

the demons' headquarters."

Hugo shook his head, as if he didn't believe what he just heard. "Are you kidding me? We can't trust her."

"But we need to find something. Anything. She said she will help us get information. This will be easy for her. It's not like I'm telling you to attack them, just see if you can find out anything about where they are."

"But I would be outnumbered."

Erik turned to Gwen. "How many other demons are in London?"

"Two. Jürgen and James."

"See, nothing to worry about. Besides, you can just throw Gwen at them and they will probably ignore you."

Gwen nodded. "That is true."

Hugo pointed at Erik. "Why can't you come with us?"

"Because I need to go talk to someone," Erik hinted.

Hugo understood. "What if she tries to kill me?"

"You have the knife." Gwen motioned to the door. "Let's get this over with."

CHAPTER 17

Gwen followed Hugo as they headed for the eastside. He walked at a fast pace, reluctant and angry to take her with him. She wasn't a big fan of the idea either, but Erik was right, they needed to search for the hideout. Erik had said he was going to keep an eye on Collin and that he had other things to do. She could only guess what those things were.

Later that night they would ultimately decide on what to do with her. She figured it would be either her getting dumped on James, who would end up finding her anyway, or she would be made to turn Collin into a monster. Not sure which she preferred, Gwen kept on following Hugo, trying in vain to make the fear racing through her mind dissipate.

The moment Gwen had stepped out of the flat, she could smell him. James. To try to describe the sense was like trying to describe the smell of your favorite pillow or blanket. It smelled familiar, lovely, more than words could describe. Most importantly, it smelled like home. Not that she had a home, but being around James always made her happy and by what all the advertisements said, home is where the heart is. And her heart belonged to James.

It wasn't that she didn't love Collin, it just wasn't the same love she felt for James. Where Collin had kindness, James had, well, everything but kindness. Which was exactly why she didn't want him to find her. She didn't want to know what he would do to her for running away from him. Though after seventy-plus years, the curiosity had been killing her, and the run-in with him five years before, she knew, was just the tip of the iceberg.

What she felt from Collin wasn't love in the sense that most people knew it, but love in the sense of acceptance. She never had anyone accept her for who she was before and it felt good. Working with him made her feel like she belonged, if only for a short while. Before James came and ruined it all. For how much James flirted with other women, he was surprisingly jealous. Or maybe it was just selfishness. Either one, Gwen figured, caused him to react the same way. She wondered what he would do once he found out Collin was alive. It had been James, after all, that killed him.

She hoped to be able to use James' jealousy to her advantage though, and maybe she could go back to him in exchange for his promise not to harm Collin. Gwen knew she would have to be careful with her wording, making sure there wasn't a loophole. The two of them were always good with loopholes.

Hugo led her into the underground to take the Tube over to the eastside. She held the pole next to him. Hugo just leaned against it, arms folded, glaring at her. Gwen sighed as the door closed. She really hoped he wouldn't freak out and strangle her again. If he did, there would be no one to stop him.

He didn't say a word as they traveled and she didn't really want to start up a conversation, especially since anything she could say would piss him off even more. Gwen watched as passengers got off and on. Since it was late morning, the car wasn't completely filled. Most looked as if they were just visiting the city while others were just enjoying their day off. Unlike the usual British weather of somber overcast, the sun was shining brightly today. Although this did make the tube a little on the humid side, she didn't mind. Gwen was used to the heat.

They arrived at their destination—Tower Hill station. This time they wouldn't have to walk across the bridge. They would just have to head east toward Whitechapel. That place brought back good memories. She couldn't believe that Jack the Ripper was still talked about even today. No one realized that a demon could have been behind it.

Stepping outside, Gwen stretched in the sunlight. "It's good to be back!"

Hugo didn't even look back at her. "What do you

mean?"

"The eastside. It's so marvelous, don't you think? So much history, so much fun."

He shook his head. "I knew all that stuff was because of you."

"It is, but that doesn't mean I can't enjoy the memories, especially over there." Gwen pointed at the London Tower. "Admit it, you found our run-ins quite entertaining."

Hugo stopped and looked at her. "You really believe that I would think being tortured more than once fun?"

"Maybe not *fun*, but doesn't it make you feel alive? Having bodies that can be destroyed? I mean we just revert to our original form, but we will no longer be on Earth and just be rotting in Hell. It's all that risk and such." She jumped up on a post next to him. "Don't you find it exhilarating?"

He kept the same expression of annoyance on his face. "No, I don't."

He turned and started back up the street. Gwen hurried to his side, letting her senses be open to any threat that could be lurking in the nearby area. She didn't sense anything.

Gwen placed her hands behind her head and looked up at the sky. How she longed to go up. "I guess it's just me. Then again, you lot can suffer here, but not in the other world. While here we can rule with little pain but if we are destroyed, then it will be nothing but eternal torture."

"Precisely why I don't trust you. You have nothing to

gain."

"I can look back and know I did the right thing. I won't have to live with the memories of more bloodshed. Less torture."

"Why don't you think you'll win?"

"Because we thought we won last time. We didn't. Your kind always seems to prevail. No matter the odds."

"Well I hope that's true."

Gwen smiled as she kept her eyes up at the sky. Birds flew around with no care, gliding every which way.

Hugo saw her gaze. "Miss the sky?"

"Like you wouldn't believe."

"I could take you up there," he smirked.

She raised an eyebrow. "So my ankle can burn? No thanks. I've felt that enough through the years, especially since all of you like to throw us up there as high as you can."

"It's fun to watch you scream."

"Right back at ya." She winked. Hugo didn't appreciate the comment, but he had set himself up. She had to say it.

Hugo peered around. "Do you sense anything around here?"

She shook her head. "No, I don't but we haven't gone that far yet. They could also be somewhere else in London, but the eastside is usually the most practical. There are fewer tourists and fewer nosy humans."

"I thought you liked dealing with nosy humans."

"No, I like dealing with lonely humans. There's a difference. One has less consequences, especially when you're trying to hide."

"Words like that make me believe you are still one of them."

"I'm just telling you what I know, Hugo." Gwen looked at him to find him studying her. "What?"

"Then why won't you turn him?" he questioned.

Everyone kept asking her. She was getting sick of it. "What do you mean?"

"Collin. You keep saying you want to help us, yet you won't do that one little task. Why not?"

Gwen sighed. "You two aren't going to leave me alone about this are you?"

Hugo shook his head. "Nope."

She took a deep breath and let it out slowly. "Why do you even want him? You know what happened to the last human we turned?"

"He went insane and tried to burn Rome to the ground two thousand years ago," Hugo answered without hesitation. He knew the story, or at least that part of the story.

"Correct!" she said in the most enthusiastic voice she could make. "Now, do you know *why* he went insane?"

"Because he couldn't handle the power?" Hugo shot a guess.

She made a buzzer sound. "Wrong! If that were the case, why do you think Collin can?"

He was beginning to look annoyed by her remarks. "Because we will be in charge of him, we can keep him under control. He won't actually be a demon, condemned to hell. He will still have a soul."

"You won't be able to because it wasn't the power that drove him insane," she said.

"Then what was it?"

Gwen pointed at herself. "It was me."

Hugo looked at her confused. "What?"

"I got bored one day and changed a human into a hybrid then I manipulated the poor bastard to the point of insanity. It's what I am best at after all." She shook her head. "He had no chance."

"How did you do it?"

Gwen shrugged. "Easy, really. I made him kill people he loved, tempted him, and caused him to forget about any humanity he had left. Proved to be more destructive than anything, hence why we never did it again. They aren't like minions—their souls are still intact. Everything they do, they do it consciously." That wasn't completely true, but that was another long story.

"So if it was you that caused the last one to go crazy, why do you think Collin will do the same thing?"

"Because if I turn Collin, it will be my breaking point. The power will be too great. It's been a struggle to be away from James this long and turning Collin will make it worse." Gwen thought about the feeling for a moment, causing her eyes to turn yellow. "Just the thought of it makes me hungry."

"But he will be with us, we won't let you near him."

Gwen shook her head. "There will be nothing you can do to stop me because no matter what you tell him, no matter how much you think you can watch him, he will come to me. He won't be able to resist his creator. Then I will cause him so much pain, and I will torture him mentally until he breaks. He will be mine."

Hugo stared at her. "So you were telling the truth then, you don't want to hurt him."

She smiled as her eyes went back to normal. "I really don't."

"But then why do the others want to destroy him?"

"Because theoretically you can use him against us, if you were lucky. And we sort of made a pact never to do that to a human again. Caused quite a problem, actually. No creating hybrids, no matter the circumstances. And James gets jealous easily." She knew the last one would be the main reason James would hurt Collin, not because of the pact.

"You just like causing trouble for everyone, no matter the side, don't you?" Hugo jeered.

"It seems that way, yes."

Hugo smiled, which Gwen found weird since she had rarely seen him smile. "Well then, shall we keep searching?"

CHAPTER 18

James approached the meeting spot Jürgen had arranged an hour later than he had scheduled it for, smiling with the satisfaction of his meal, both the food and the girl's blood combined. Mostly just the girl. She was so easy to deceive that it wasn't even funny. Well, maybe just a little.

Jürgen had told him to meet him just outside Borough station, which was really a hassle to get to from Heathrow. He didn't understand why they couldn't just meet at the London Bridge station, it would have been much easier. So James didn't feel bad about showing up late. Not that he would have anyway in the first place.

"Where have you been? I've been waiting an hour!" Jürgen exclaimed as he approached.

James shrugged. "Sorry, I needed some energy. She was a loner and asked me to breakfast." His eyes flashed yellow. "I couldn't resist."

Jürgen grabbed his collar. "Are you trying to get us spotted as fast as you can?"

"It's more fun that way." James grinned. Jürgen let go.

"So why did you take an hour?" His eyes shot James a look, as if he figured the answer. "You bought her breakfast before you killed her, didn't you?"

James gave him the most innocent look he could make. "Of course, I'm a gentleman after all."

Jürgen pointed at the corner of his mouth. "You missed a spot."

James wiped the rest of the blood on his mouth with his sleeve. "Thanks." He had tried to be clean, but there always seemed to be a blood splatter here or there after a meal. It came with the territory.

Jürgen rolled his eyes as they headed down the street. James glanced around. Nothing seemed to have changed since the last time he was here, still busy and chaotic as ever—as creating minions always was. Just the way he liked it.

He could smell Gwen from a distance away, she was walking down the streets somewhere on the other side of the Thames. He would wait her out. He needed to get her away from the Gargoyles. He would figure it out a way to succeed in doing that though, he always did. Then she would be his once more, and they could bring down the last of the Gargoyles.

Peering over at Jürgen, James found him grinning

more than normal, or at least what he considered being a grin. It was always hard to tell with Jürgen.

"What are you smiling about?" James asked, a part of him not wanting to know the answer.

"I found something out that is... let me say, interesting, for lack of a better word." Jürgen's smirk caused James to become even more worried.

"What did you do to Gwen?"

"Always accusing me, aren't you? I didn't touch her. Not yet anyway." He took a pause before ending his thought. "But speaking of Gwen, what exactly happened here five years ago?"

James hated replaying that episode in his mind. He felt like such a fool for letting his guard down for a brief second. If she hadn't gotten him jealous about her being romantically attached to that stupid human, Collin, they would be back together by now. He would have been able to talk her back into coming with him.

"I told you already, I came here, and I found her. She was with that stupid human, so I slit his throat in front of her. Then she got mad and stole my energy and fled England." James narrowed his eyes. "Why do you ask?"

Jürgen stopped and turned to him. "Are you sure you killed that human?"

"Yeah, I slit his throat..." he hesitated, realizing what Jürgen was getting at. He shook his head. "No, don't tell me..." Jürgen smiled. James slammed his fist against the brick wall next to him. Dust spilled off of it. "Damn her!"

Jürgen watched as his face reddened with anger. "He's not fully turned yet."

"What?" That didn't make sense, why would she bring him back but not turn him. "Then how do you know?"

"Smelled him. Can't you?"

To be truthful, James didn't. He was too occupied trying to get the scent of Gwen. He'd ignored everything else.

"I followed the scent and found Gwen outside where he was. I asked her what she did, and she told me to tell you that he didn't deserve to die. Answered my question completely."

"That bitch brought him back." James swung his fist against the wall again. More dust. Passers-by stared at him. He glared back, making them hurry to their destination.

Jürgen watched him, enjoying every minute of misery. "Yup."

Jürgen had hated Gwen even before she betrayed him and he hated how James loved her even after she betrayed them. He took pleasure whenever James was mad at her, which was more often than not. Gwen, after all, liked doing her own thing.

James turned to him. "And she doesn't think she's going to pay for what she did?"

He grinned. "Oh, I think she knows the circumstances, I think she just doesn't care."

Typical, he thought. James rubbed his forehead. He didn't expect this to happen. He never thought Gwen would stoop so low for a human.

Jürgen watched as James became more furious by the

second. "She went back on our deal. We promised not to give a human our blood ever again."

"I know that," he shot back.

"She must have really liked that human to go against you," Jürgen added. James glowered at him.

"Don't start with me Jürgen, I am not in the mood."

He shrugged. "Just wanted to make sure you understand what she did to you, that's all. You know, left you to suffer the consequences of an unrequited blood bond for all those years, attacked you with the knife, and even brought a human back from the dead. All to help those Gargoyles."

"I said shut up!" James tried to punch Jürgen but Jürgen caught it in midair with ease.

"So weak." Jürgen threw James' fist aside. "Look what she has done to you. And I bet you will forgive all of it the moment you see her. Just like you always do."

"Not this time. She isn't getting away with what she has done. She has betrayed my trust for the last time."

Jürgen raised his eyebrow. "Really? For some reason I don't believe that."

James paced back and forth. "We just have to figure out how to get her away from the Gargoyles first."

He rubbed his goatee. "We could use the human."

James looked at Jürgen suspiciously. "What?"

"The Gargoyles know he's been resurrected, but haven't done anything about it," Jürgen explained. "I have a feeling that they want Gwen to finish turning him."

"Why would they want that? Did they not see what

the last one did?" James questioned. The other caused chaos for both the Gargoyles and the demons. It would be suicide for the Gargoyles to try to handle him in that kind of uncontrollable state.

"Yes, but they probably think they could do better than us, those sanctimonious Gargoyles."

"Then they really don't know Guinevere, do they?" And apparently neither did he. He never thought she would bring back a human from the dead. Not after what happened last time.

"Not like we do, no. But we could go talk to them, tell them that if they give Gwen to us, then we will get her to turn him."

"Are you crazy? We would be giving them an advantage."

"James, do you really think they could handle him once he turns?" Jürgen stepped closer. "He will become a bloodthirsty animal. He will come to us and then we will outnumber them by three."

James thought about it. Although they could probably get the human-hybrid to help them, he still wasn't too keen on letting Gwen get what she wanted, nor did he like sharing. "And if Gwen turns him, she'll return to our side."

"That is true. She will go back to her taunting and manipulating ways, although I don't think that aspect of her has ever completely left her," he commented.

James smiled. That was true. She could make any side of a battle pissed, and he loved her for that. "But we still don't know if that human will do what the other one did."

Jürgen shrugged. "Either way, I don't think they would be able to handle him."

"But neither will we be able to."

"Yes, but Gwen might. He loves her, the other hybrid had no feelings for her. It could go either way, really. Besides, maybe in the process, he will kill a Gargoyle."

James laughed. "He won't love her after he finds out what she did to him. He could become an even worse monster than we could ever imagine. Gwen could tear him apart."

"You never know. I say it's worth it, at least you will get Gwen back."

James thought about it for a moment. It was an easier way to get Gwen back than tracking her every movement and hoping for a lucky break. "You think they'll meet with us?"

"Worth a shot."

Jürgen was right. This could be the easiest way to get Gwen back to him, but it also meant theoretically giving the Gargoyles a weapon. Then again, it could work in their favor. He would also have to get Gwen to turn him, since she was the one who started the transformation. Whatever their choices were, they would have to act fast.

"What time is it?" James asked.

Jürgen checked his watch. "Almost eleven."

"Do you know where he is?"

"Yeah, he owns a pub in Chelsea," Jürgen said. "But I'm pretty sure they surrounded the place with salt. I can't sense him as I could earlier. We won't be able to threaten him if we can't touch him."

James thought for a moment. "We could get someone to destroy the salt barrier, then we could cross it."

"Like who?"

"You said he was at a pub, then there will be other workers there."

He nodded. "I presume so."

James started toward Chelsea. "Then all we do is wait for one of them to come out and boom, we have a hostage. Humans are very easy when it comes to threats. He will have no choice, but to let us in."

"Are we gonna kill the hostage even if he complies?" Jürgen followed behind.

"Haven't decided yet, let's see where all this goes first."

CHAPTER 19

Collin cleaned the last of the dirty cups from the night before. Others may hate simple tasks such as that, but it's what made everything more bearable. The simple things. He had sent Hywel to take out the trash. He couldn't really go outside, so Hywel had to deal with anything that involved leaving the building. He wondered if Hywel even noticed.

The door had been fixed, as the repairman came right after they called him. It didn't take much effort on his part, he only needed to replace the lock. Thankfully, the door itself wasn't broken.

Hywel came back inside with a handful of something. "Why is there salt all over? Have we had a bunch of slugs or something?"

Collin saw the clear white substance in his hand. The salt. He had broken the seal. "Put that back right now!"

"What? What's the big deal? It's just some salt."

Collin moved toward the door. "You have to put it back. Now!" Collin opened the door to find two men standing in the doorway. One, of course, was James. He looked the same as the day he and Gwen had gotten into that fight in the alleyway. Messed up dark hair, proud, wore a suit as if it made him look even more proper. His cocky smile was still on his lips just as it had been on that day five years ago. The other man he didn't recognize, but he could tell he was a demon. He had the same hungry look James had.

"Bloody hell," Collin said.

"Long time no see, eh?" James let the moment linger before gesturing to the entrance. "Seems you broke your salt barrier. Shame, really. Now it's going to be a whole lot easier to get in."

He tried to barge in, but it was as if he hit a glass barrier. Confused, James slammed his hand against it. They hadn't realized he lived where he worked. The other demon with him must have known because he let out a sharp laugh. The Gargoyles told him about the little trick. Demons had to be invited into living spaces, so he made his bar his home to keep them out. Minions, on the other hand, could go where they pleased, but they weren't as powerful as demons, so Collin didn't have to worry too much about them.

Hywel looked at James and the other demon curiously. "What's going on Collin?"

"Nothing, just some old friends. Go finish cleaning," Collin ordered. Hywel shrugged and went back to work.

"What do you want?" Collin questioned, watching James closely.

James leaned against the doorway. "I need you to invite us in."

"No," he answered without hesitation.

"We just want to talk." The other man with him smiled. He was taller than James, and scarier too. Goatee, strong build, dark eyes. Collin really wished Hugo was here. "We aren't going to hurt you. Not this time anyway."

Collin shook his head. "There's no way. I'm not inviting you in here."

"Fine, then come out here," James gestured.

"Hell no," Collin responded.

The other demon laughed. "No, if you don't come out here or let us in, we will show you the meaning of Hell."

"I don't care, I'm not letting you in."

"Fine. If you don't let us in," James nodded to Jürgen. In an instant, Jürgen left and came back holding Hywel. "He's a dead man."

Collin just stood there, stunned. He glanced back behind his shoulders to an empty pub. "Hywel?"

"I wanted a smoke. You never said not to go out front. What's going on Collin? Who are these people? How did he move so fast?" Hywel's voice sped up as he began to freak out.

"We aren't people." James' eyes flashed yellow. Hywel began to hyperventilate. The two demons just laughed.

"Now…" James grabbed Hywel from the other demon. "Let us in or say goodbye." He started to bring Hywel's neck to his teeth.

"No, wait!" Collin called out.

James raised his eyebrow. "Yes?"

"You will let him live, as a human." Collin knew to add the last part, otherwise they could turn him into a minion. "If I let you in?"

He grinned. "You have my word."

"That's what I was afraid of," Collin sighed.

He knew it was the only way to save Hywel. They didn't care what they did as long as they got what they wanted. He debated if he should let them in or go out there. Either way, he was outnumbered. He still had his knife stuffed in a sheath behind his back, but he debated what help that would be. He decided what he would do.

"Fine. *You* can come in." Collin stepped out of the way and motioned for James to enter.

"Thank you." James let Hywel go, but before he could run, he smacked him on the side of the head, knocking him out cold. "Don't need him going and telling the Bobbies."

He started to step into the pub, when Collin pulled the knife out from behind his back and tried to stab him in the heart. James grabbed his wrist before the blade entered his chest. Collin knew it was a stupid idea, but he had really hoped it would work.

"You didn't think this through, did you?" James laughed.

"Apparently not."

"What were you going to do about him?" James nodded to the other demon as he started to try to step through the doorway. He hit the invisible barrier.

"I never invited him in. Just you," Collin said.

"Clever boy. I didn't even catch that." Collin heard a hint of astonishment in his voice. "Still doesn't answer what you're going to do now."

Collin hesitated. "I'm still thinking."

"Well, while you are thinking." James nodded to the door. "Let him in."

Collin glanced over. "What?"

"Let him in or I will break your wrist," James grabbed Collin's wrist before he knew it and started to squeeze. "And the longer you wait, the more likely Jürgen over there will beat you into a pulp."

So that was the other's name. Jürgen. James kept squeezing his wrist tighter and twisting it.

"Okay, fine!" Collin gave in. There was no point in resisting, if they wanted him dead there was no way to stop that with his inferior strength. "He can come in too."

Jürgen entered the bar, a little pissed off that he had hit the barrier the first time. James let go of his wrist and let Collin bury the knifepoint into his chest. Collin watched, surprised by James's lack of retaliation to his action.

"See?" James pulled the knife out, dark liquid dripping off of it. "Wouldn't have even worked if you had succeeded."

"How..." Collin began as he backed away, not sure what he could even do next. He was outnumbered, and they were both demons. He didn't stand a chance at this rate.

"Stakes and knives don't work on us, only on minions." Jürgen grinned as he stepped closer to Collin. "It was a myth that started in the middle ages, to keep humans from knowing the true way to kill us."

"Which is?" Collin gulped.

Jürgen laughed. "Like we would tell you."

"Too bad." Collin kept his eyes on both of them.

James kept stepping closer, peering around. "Love what you have done with the place. I wonder what your inspiration could have been, or 'who' I should say."

Collin kept stepping back until he ran into the bar. He had nowhere to go. He took a deep breath, trying to calm himself down, but it didn't work. He felt his heart race as James moved to stand even closer in front of him. He seemed to be enjoying his cresting fear.

James turned and sat down at the bar. "You can calm down, we aren't here to hurt you."

Collin watched closely, making sure it wasn't some kind of trick. He didn't want to let his guard down for even a fleeting second. "You aren't?"

"Nah, we are here to ask you to help us." Jürgen pointed at the stout. "Give me one of those."

Collin slowly went behind the bar and poured him a pint of the stout, eyes flickering back and forth between the two seated casually at the bar. "Why would I help you two? You are demons."

"So is Gwen," James countered.

He shook his head. "But she isn't like you two."

James and Jürgen looked at each other and laughed.

"You're right, she's worse. We wouldn't even do half the things she does," Jürgen said as he took a chug of the stout.

"Like what?" Collin asked.

"She likes playing games, especially ones that lead to insanity. She's manipulative, vile, and downright gruesome," James listed.

"Then why do you want her so badly?"

James laughed. "Because, those are my favorite qualities."

"Even though she manipulates you as well?" Collin knew he shouldn't have said that, but he wanted to see James' reaction.

James shrugged. "What can I say, she's irresistible."

"And you two have that disgusting blood bond," Jürgen commented over his stout.

Collin had never heard of that term. "A what?"

"A blood bond. It's a ritual we can perform to make two demons connected by blood. It marks us as each other's forever." James sounded happy, as if it gave him pleasure to explain that she was his, in a symbolic sense, for the whole of eternity.

Collin couldn't believe it. Gwen has always said she was James', now he knew precisely what she meant by that.

Collin shook his head. "I still don't understand why you're even here and telling me all this."

"We know you are helping the Gargoyles. We want a meeting with one of them, preferably their leader. You get to set it up," James explained.

"A meeting? They would never meet with you."

"Hence why we're talking to you first. They will know since we came to you and didn't kill you that we are serious about our planned negotiation."

"A negotiation? For Gwen?"

"Of course," Jürgen interjected. "What else would we want from a Gargoyle?"

"Gargoyle?" He had forgotten about that word. "Gwen used that same term. What does it mean?"

"It's a nickname since those beings don't have a real name," James explained. "They are the ones who have acted behind the scenes throughout history. Shadows really. So we call them Gargoyles, since they protect the church like those gruesome statues themselves in the front of many aged European cathedrals."

"Aren't Gargoyles supposed to be evil spirits?"

"Yeah, they hate being called that, it's what makes it fun." James pulled out a piece of paper. "Now, I need you to give this to Erik. Have him give me a ring."

Collin picked it up. "Why do you think they'll even give you the time of day?"

"Because we have something to offer as well," James explained.

"Which is?"

"It's really not the business of some pesky human."

"Are you going to hurt her?" Collin asked. Gwen always seemed to fear James, she said she was afraid of what he might do to her, once he managed to catch up with her.

James shrugged. "Depends on how much of a fight she puts up."

Collin shook his head. "I can't let you hurt her."

Before he could blink, James jumped up on top of the bar and grabbed him by the throat, holding him off of the ground. His eyes turned a glowing yellow that brought back a speck of a memory of the time they had met before. A memory that he didn't know he had until being threatened by this deranged ex-lover of Gwen's. All he remembered from that night was seeing Gwen, for a second, speaking tensely with the man that held his throat now, and then he passed out. Now he knew there was something else that happened to him that night, causing him to require the aid of Gwen later.

James held his gaze. "You really think you could go up against us? Your girl is not here to save you. This time you would stay dead."

He let go of Collin and jumped down from the bar. Collin collapsed onto the bar and started coughing.

"The sooner, the better, would be best. Be sure to give them that card." He nodded to Jürgen who downed the rest of his stout.

"Wait," Collin called out after he caught his breath. "What did you mean by 'this time'?"

James simply grinned as he and Jürgen left him lying on the bar, sputtering for oxygen. No one ever told him anything. Sighing, he rolled over and noticed Hywel still passed out in the back doorway.

"Right." Collin stood up and examined Hywel. He didn't seem to have any injuries other than the bump on the back of his head. He would be fine, except he might freak out when he woke up. Another thing to deal with.

He pulled Hywel onto a booth. Collin hoped Erik would come by before he woke up so he could erase Hywel's memories. Again…

CHAPTER 20

Kensington Gardens had definitely changed over the years, even though Erik knew others saw that kind of change differently depending on their life spans. Everything always changed though, inevitably through the course of time. Once a peaceful planet, the Earth was now tainted with darkness, he would never forget what it used to be like before the fall of man. It used to be paradise.

As he strolled through the gardens, Erik wondered what trouble Hugo and Gwen were getting themselves into right about now. He trusted Hugo not to do anything rash. Although Hugo wanted to kill her, Erik knew he wouldn't hurt her. Not badly anyway. Any blood spilt would attract more demons, and he would have to fend them off by himself. No, he wasn't that stupid.

Finding out about the blood bond complicated matters exponentially. It could, theoretically, work to their advantage. He could make a treaty with the demons, giving Gwen back in exchange for turning Collin, but he didn't know how to get in contact with one. They were outnumbered by the demons, and demons could go back on the treaty. They were never trustworthy.

Desperate for guidance, Erik headed toward a quaint little church he had been particularly fond of over the years, a common English church with tall spires and ivy-covered arches. Roses surrounding the church were already in full bloom, their sweet scent masking any exhaust fumes that filled the city streets. It was the perfect place to brood on everything that had transpired-a place where no one would notice him.

As he had hoped, the vicar he worked with in the past was in that day. He had a few questions for him, but that wasn't why had come to this church. He needed a quiet room he could perform a prayer in. Erik approached Vicar Evans.

The vicar pressed his glasses closer to his face. "Haven't seen you for a while, Erik, I was beginning to worry about you." His friendly smile greeted Erik. The man's darkened skin seemed to have acquired even more wrinkles since they had last met.

Erik grabbed his hand and shook it. "Sorry to worry you Vicar, but I've been busy."

He rose one eyebrow. "Chasing that demon?"

Erik nodded. "Yes, but before I bring you up to speed, I need to borrow a room. Have any available?"

"For you, I can pull a few strings. Just wait here a moment." He left Erik in the antechamber. Erik took a look around. The beautiful stained-glass windows brought light into the entryway of the church.

Being the middle of the week, the church wasn't particularly busy. A person would come in every once in a while, either a tourist looking at the old church or a resident looking for some spiritual advice for a particular problem in their lives.

After a few minutes, Evans came back to where he waited. "I have a room that will suit your needs. Right this way."

Erik followed him up to the second floor on a creaking stairway. When they came to the end of a long hallway, Evans gestured to a room. "I hope this one will be to your liking."

Erik took a look around. It was mostly bare with a small altar of candles. "Perfect, thank you."

"Take as long as you need. You shouldn't be bothered. Once you're done, come get me. I need to talk to you about something," Evans said.

"All right, I will."

The vicar nodded and left him alone. That was why Erik liked him so well. He didn't ask questions. He just let it be. It was a rare quality to find in a human.

Closing the door behind him, Erik took a better look at the room. The walls needed a new paint job, white flakes missing here and there. It didn't look like it was used for anything but prayer. Taking out a match, he lit the candles.

Erik called out. "Michael, I need to speak with you."

The surrounding room disappeared in a dark haze, for this world couldn't see the other. The only light that was left was that of the candles. The flames flickered as a breeze swept from out of nowhere.

"Erik, what is it? I am busy," a soft voice answered.

"I need to know what's happening on the other side," Erik said.

"What do you think is going on? War, Erik, war. The demons are getting restless seeing that only three of you are left. They are ready to be released at a moment's notice," Michael explained.

Erik knew all that, but he was trying to ease into the question that was really bothering him. "Do you have any information on the girl?"

"The girl?" Michael inquired.

He knew what Erik meant. He was just making him clarify. "Guinevere. Do you know what the outcome will be?"

"I do not."

"Can you find out?" Erik begged. "Can you find out if she is telling the truth?"

"Erik, you know that I cannot. This has to play out fairly. If I asked for this information, it would upset the balance."

That was the answer he was suspecting, but he still hoped for more.

"I know, but her being where she is now is already

taking the balance out of things," he argued.

"I agree."

"I don't know what to do," Erik admitted. "How much do you know about her?"

"I've heard whispers of her name. She has raised some enemies among the demons but the rest of us, we still don't trust her. She's alone in whatever she is doing."

"So you think I shouldn't trust her?" Erik said.

"I never said that," Michael responded. "But you do know where she stands. She is a demon after all, she did turn her back on our Lord."

"She claims to have changed. What if she is the only one who can actually see her wrongdoings?"

"None of them ever have."

"But what if this one is different?"

"It is up to you, you are the one in charge on this battlefront."

Erik sighed. "She has a blood bond with another demon."

Michael was silent.

"You knew about this didn't you? Why did none of you warn us that two demons shared a blood bond?" Erik knew he shouldn't raise his voice, but he was frustrated. He could have been warned.

"Because we aren't supposed to interfere."

He rubbed his temples. "Can you at least tell me what we should do with the human? Could he help us if we turned him?"

"It would be immoral to use a human like that."

Erik slammed his fist on the table that the altar rested

on. "But it is the only way to win! If we don't win this, the earth will be flooded with demons from the underworld. We can't let that happen!"

"You think I don't already know that Erik? You think I don't know the stakes? I'm just saying think before you do anything rash," he paused, as if something caught his attention. "Now, I must leave, I am needed elsewhere. Be careful, Erik, a lot is riding on this."

"I will."

The light in the room reignited. Erik sighed. He had hoped Michael knew something and was willing to share more information. He figured it was a lot to ask, but they were losing this drawn-out war against good and evil, for the reign of Earth. Everything was literally at stake. This couldn't end without him at least asking for some assistance.

Erik went to find the vicar. Perhaps he'd have more practical advice about what to do with Gwen and Collin.

Erik found him in an office almost as plain as the prayer room. Only a cross hung on the wall behind his desk. Paper littered the desk—notes for sermons and notes about who and what to pray for. The tasks of a vicar were never easy.

Evans stood as he entered. "Done already?"

"Yeah, it was a short conversation, unfortunately." Erik took a seat across from him.

"What did you need to ask him about?" Evans sat back down.

"The demon that half-turned Collin is trying to help us now." Erik knew he could trust the vicar, he had helped him with Collin for the past five years, keeping an eye on his condition between turning from human into part-demon.

"I see. He didn't agree with asking help from that demon?"

"Not necessarily. He just didn't know if it was a wise decision. There's a lot at stake and she is a wild card to play with."

"Is she going to finish Collin's transition?"

Erik sighed. "She doesn't want to. She says she doesn't want to hurt him."

"Then she shouldn't have gotten him involved."

Erik chuckled. "That's what I said."

Evans leaned back. "He doesn't have much longer. The treatments I have been giving him are becoming less and less effective. He has to turn or he will die soon."

"What?"

"He's dying, Erik. You knew this would happen. We have postponed it as long as we could but if she doesn't turn him soon, he won't be of any help to anyone."

Erik rubbed his temples, something he found himself doing a lot lately. Things were just getting better and better. "So this needs to be resolved soon?"

"Unfortunately, yes."

Erik couldn't believe the streak of bad luck he was having. First the blood bond, now this. He could either let Collin die or he could let him become a monster. "I don't know what to do."

"You think he is strong enough?" Evans asked.

Erik nodded slowly. "Potentially, yes. I just don't know

what will happen in the end."

"But it wasn't you who did this to him. It was that *demon*."

"I am the one who is forcing her to make the decision now."

"A decision that could save billions of lives."

Erik stood up and paced around. "That's the problem. One life for a billion. And it's not guaranteed. It could play in the demons' favor."

"So you think it is the end?"

He stopped. "I really don't know."

"Should I begin preparing my people for the worst then?"

Erik shook his head. "No. We never know how anything will turn out. You all should live your lives as usual, not worrying about such a thing."

"I will try my best."

Erik gathered himself. "Now, I must go. I have to attend to my duties, as do you. Remember, don't tell anyone."

"As usual." The vicar stood up and shook Erik's hand. "Thank you."

"For what?" Erik questioned.

"Giving me faith."

CHAPTER 21

Gwen felt it, there was a sudden change in James' location. She turned to face southwest. He was in Chelsea now—where Collin was. Gwen took a deep breath. Collin was fine, she told herself, James and Jürgen couldn't hurt him—not with the salt circle in place.

She turned her attention back to searching for the whereabouts of their hideout. Gwen knew that it probably wasn't in Whitechapel, or even north of the Thames. Before she noticed the sudden change, Gwen realized she had sensed James in Borough. They had established the headquarters down there.

Gwen debated telling Hugo that they were searching in the wrong area. She wanted to help, but the more she thought about telling him where it was, the more she realized that the information could cost James his life. He was the weakest of the demons, at least at the moment, and they could easily destroy him. It had never crossed her mind before that helping the Gargoyles could bring him his death. She couldn't watch him die. If something happened to him, her life on earth would be over and she would have to suffer with the realization it was all her fault.

"Are you sure it's around here Gwen?" Hugo interrupted her thoughts.

"Hm? I can't really feel anything right now," she lied. She couldn't tell him, not yet anyway.

He eyed her suspiciously. "I thought you could sense James."

"Usually, but I'm pretty weak as you know. I can sense he's around, I just can't pinpoint his exact location."

"For some reason I don't believe that."

"Are you accusing me of lying, then?" she shot back.

"It's what you are best at, yes," he said.

Gwen shook her head. "No, actually, there's a lot of things I'm better at, but it's up there."

"So why are you here again?"

"Because I want to help." She smiled as sincerely as she could.

"Right." He rolled his eyes.

They turned down another street and Gwen let out a soft laugh. Buck's Row, now called Durward Street, was still a quiet street, but the blood spilled from the Ripper's first victim from so long ago in history didn't seem to linger in the air any more.

"Mary Ann Nichols," Gwen whispered.

Hugo stopped and turned around. "What did you just say?"

"That was her name. Mary Ann Nichols. The *Ripper's* first victim," Gwen examined the surroundings. Yes, this was the place, it had changed dramatically, buildings were destroyed and new ones added but it was definitely the place. It took her and James months to solve the mystery of who was behind the killings.

Hugo started shaking his head. "Don't tell me that was you."

"It wasn't me directly, but it may have been one of my minions." Which she confessed had surprised even her. Usually minions didn't have such good tactics. It didn't last though.

"Your minions? I thought they only obeyed orders."

"Yes, usually. It was odd, I didn't know he was doing it until a few deaths later. Sometimes minions become more bloodthirsty than they should over time. I stopped him though, threw him in the Thames on New Year's Eve." She licked her lips. "After mutilating him of course."

Hugo looked puzzled. "But weren't there a couple deaths after the New Year?"

"Yeah. Those were me and James. The paranoia it caused was too hard to resist. We had to get in on the fun." Gwen smiled. "They never suspected another killer."

He took a deep breath, so he wouldn't do anything he

would regret. "I loathe you."

"I know."

"Good." Hugo started back down the street. "Just making sure."

They searched further into Whitechapel, but Gwen knew it would be a waste of time. She wanted to go somewhere else, all the streets made her miss James more and more. Gwen usually tried to stay away from the area, so she wouldn't ponder on the memories attached to her feelings for him, but now here she stood, doing exactly what she didn't want to be doing in the first place. Double guessing everything. Again.

"You know," she started as they looked through an old abandoned building. The smell of mold and must filled Gwen's senses, so she couldn't even smell Hugo standing right next to her any longer. The stench was revolting. "I think we should start heading back west and check everything along the way to Soho."

Hugo kicked down a wall. Once the dust settled, he only found another empty room. "Why didn't you say so in the first place?"

"I really thought they would be located somewhere more toward the east, but I don't even sense a minion out here. I think we should head west now." She took another look around the hidden room. This place would have been perfect for a headquarters, if Hugo hadn't all but destroyed all the hidden walls and made a mess of everything.

"How do I know you aren't lying?" he questioned as he wiped off some of the dust that covered his jeans.

She gave him a look as if she didn't understand the accusation. "Me? A liar? What do you mean?"

"You could be trying to hide something that's east from us by making me think it is west."

"Well, I guess you will never know then since you don't have sensing powers," she said. "Just trust me for once. They aren't over here." That really wasn't a lie, they weren't east, but nor were they west. She was just getting sick of the quiet streets and wanted to see Soho.

He examined her for a few more moments, then gave in. "Fine, let's go."

Leaving the building they had just searched, Gwen became a little giddy in getting to go to one of her favorite spots. The streets were overfilled with humans, buildings, lights, history; it was all music to her ears. It was the perfect place to shop...or really shoplift. She didn't really have money, and it was useless for them to shop in the civilized way. So she always grabbed what she needed and ran with all the preternatural speed she had. It was what she was good at, wasn't it?

She wouldn't get to do such things with Hugo scrutinizing her every move, but she would get to make a mental note of where to come back to later. If she got the chance, that is. It really depended how long it took James to cool down.

Gwen let her senses be open to any minion activity as they walked the long streets that led them toward Greater London. Still nothing. She was surprised, since she figured there would be at least some minions out and about. Jürgen was smart to hide them, knowing she had the potential to figure out where they hid based on scent. Usually he wasn't so careful.

The sunshine, to Gwen's surprise, had kept up throughout the day. It felt good to feel the warmth upon her skin. The sun made people stay in better moods, compared to the usual depressing, murky weather England was known for.

They came upon Saint Paul's Cathedral, an architectural masterpiece that has endured through history. She herself hadn't ever stepped inside, but she heard from others that it was magnificent. Not anymore, though, with all of the tourists walking through it day-in and day-out. She missed the old times when a church was a church and a museum was a museum.

"Looks pretty good, especially after the whole bombing," Gwen commented as they approached.

Hugo nodded. "It does. I'm glad it didn't get hurt too badly through all of that. It would have been a shame if the whole place was destroyed."

"Worried about a church? Such a Gargoyle thing to do," she taunted.

He shot her a look. "Stop calling me that."

"Then give me something else to call you by," she countered playfully. He wasn't amused in the slightest by her friendly jesting.

"Just call me an angel, please, like the rest of the world does."

She shook her head. "But you aren't an angel. *I'm* an angel, or at least I was. You're a class above us. Then cherubs, which neither of us are. I wouldn't want to cross one of those in a dark alley." Gwen paused, letting the thought linger in her mind. "Anyway, you are definitely not an angel."

"I'm no Gargoyle either."

"No, I guess not." She thought for a moment, trying to find a good comeback. Grinning, she thought of one. "You are just an innominate!"

"Precisely."

"Innominate," Gwen repeated. "That's hard to say, I'm just going to stick with Gargoyle. Besides, you aren't that hip."

He rubbed his forehead in reaction to her last comment. "Did I already tell you that I hate you?"

She nodded. "Yes, many times."

"Good, just checking."

The streets became more crowded the closer they moved to central London. Shopping bags freckled the sidewalk along with cameras and maps. Gwen watched as a young lad pick-pocketed a couple who were taking a photograph. She laughed under her breath as the boy ran off with the wallet. They should have been more careful.

"What do you think Erik is doing right about now?" Gwen asked.

"It's really none of your business."

Gwen wondered what he could be doing in a time like this. She hoped he wasn't planning on a way to get rid of her, or hand her over to James. No, in order to do that, he would have to meet with the other demons. The Gargoyles had learned their lesson the first time not to try to make treaties with them. Demons were good at wording things in a way where only they got what they wanted. It was a skill that we perfected over the years.

It may have something to do with Collin, and how they are keeping him alive. She had left a vial of blood for Erik, knowing that they could come up with something. Usually if humans died and were brought back to life, they would last a year, maybe two. The Gargoyles were smart beings, they must have figured out a way to keep the process going.

"What made you perform a blood bond?" Hugo interrupted her train of thought.

She looked at him, puzzled by what he asked. She never expected him to ask her such a question. "Excuse me?"

"With James. Why did you do it?"

Gwen shrugged. "Why not?"

"Don't give me that, Gwen. I know that a blood bond is looked down upon even for demons."

"You wouldn't understand, you don't know what it's like."

"Try me. We have a while before we need to find Erik."

She sighed. "I guess we just wanted to be closer."

"Closer than what?"

"Partners. Lovers. Whatever you want to call us."

"How about now?" he asked.

"What do you mean?"

"Do you still want to be together now? You want to help us but what does James mean to you?"

Gwen looked up at the sky. "We will always be connected. We fell together, we suffered together, and we have been through everything together. Nothing will change that, I will always love him."

"Then why are you here then?"

"Because I may love him, but I don't love what I have become for him. I was never in it for the power, I was in all this just to be with him."

"If given the choice, would you do it again?"

Gwen didn't hesitate. "Yes."

Hugo shook his head. "You condemned yourself then."

"I did."

As they made it to the center of Soho, Hugo stopped. "Do you sense anything here?"

She took in deep breath. No, he had gone back to Borough. "Not much, doesn't mean they aren't here."

"Well then, let's start searching for any trace."

CHAPTER 22

"Damn I wanted to kill him," James commented as they started back towards Borough. Seeing the man Gwen had betrayed him with brought his blood to a boil. That human was useless compared to him, yet Gwen still felt something—something strong enough to go behind James' back and bring him back from the dead.

Jürgen didn't hesitate in a response. "Don't blame you, he's the man your girl left you for."

James frowned at him. "She didn't leave me for *him*, she left because she wanted to help the Gargoyles by sabotaging our set-up to kill the last of them and open the gates of Hell. It had nothing to do with that pathetic human."

"And that's better?" he asked.

Honestly, that explanation felt better to him but in reality, it wasn't. She had betrayed everything she swore to fight for, and that was worse than any fling she had with that dull human. "No, it's not, but don't act like she really loves that human, she's just confused."

"Really?" he smirked. "How do you figure?"

"Because she is so low on energy. It makes you do strange things," James explained. It was true, he's woken up in some strange places, due to the absence of years without her blood. Never could remember how he got there, but the taste of blood always lingered on his lips afterword. Weird tasting blood.

"Strange things like forgiving someone who abandoned you to stand on the other side of a war?"

James eyed him. "That's not what I meant."

"I think it is."

James figured he should change the subject before they really started fighting. "Do you think the Gargoyles will agree to the meeting?"

"I think it is the easiest way to get Gwen back, unless she does something stupid before then and they dispose of her. But that might just end in her death rather than back into your arms, like you so dearly want," Jürgen sneered.

"Well then, they can say goodbye to that human of theirs. Not only that, I will make him suffer beyond anything they have ever seen." He smiled at all the things he could do to him. "That will teach them."

"I'm surprised he's lasted this long on her blood. I didn't think he would," Jürgen commented. Now that he mentioned it, James didn't even know humans could last that long.

"That's a good point. It has been five years since he allegedly was killed by me."

"We really have never tested how long they can stay alive on our blood."

"Yeah, but still…" James wondered if Gwen knew. "You think the Gargoyles did something to make him last this long? I know they have acquired a few tricks over the years with their salt and incense."

Jürgen shrugged. "I don't know. I wouldn't put it past them. If they thought he could help their odds of defeating us, they're capable of anything."

"That's for sure. Especially letting Gwen get so close to them. They must be really desperate."

"Anybody would be desperate to want her near them."

There he went again. "Are you calling me desperate?"

"Nah, you aren't desperate, you are just plain stupid," Jürgen remarked.

James stopped in the middle of the sidewalk. "Don't you dare call me stupid after all the wars Gwen and I have won, after the many Gargoyles we have tortured and destroyed. Don't. You. Dare."

"She has caused you more pain than anything, or really anyone, yet you still stand up for her James. Why? You'd be better off without her… if it weren't for that ridiculous blood bond." He started to turn back to go up the street, but James grabbed his arm roughly and pulled him back.

"What is your problem?" James exclaimed.

Jürgen stared at where James was holding his arm, as if he couldn't believe he had grabbed him with such force. "Excuse me?"

"This isn't just about her leaving, what did she do to you to make you so pissed off?"

He shook off James' grip. "It's none of your business."

James studied him carefully, looking for an answer. "So there *is* something."

Jürgen's voice darkened. "I said it's none of your business!"

His tone surprised James. Jürgen rarely got this angry, truly angry. Though they played pranks on each other every once in a while, James never recalled Gwen pissing him off this bad. "Interesting that I don't know what it is. Gwen never used to keep anything from me."

"Other than that human she brought back from the dead."

"She never kept secrets before she ran away," James corrected. It wasn't that she had kept Collin a secret either, he hadn't seen her since it happened.

Jürgen raised an eyebrow. "You sure about that?"

"What do you mean?"

Jürgen stepped closer, bringing his voice to a whisper. "How long has she felt like she was doing something wrong? How long has she wanted to run away from you?"

"She didn't run away from me, she ran away from what she was doing," he said with a slight tinge of annoyance in his voice.

"You sure it wasn't *you* that drove her away?" Jürgen pressed further.

"Why are you saying this?"

Jürgen circled him. "Because you are clearly blind to the fact she betrayed us those many years ago. She betrayed you, James. Why can't you see that?"

"I see that every day since she left—I have lived with the fact she left me! But you know what? I don't care. I love her more than anything. She needed time to herself, and I am fine with that. But I will stop at nothing to get her back, you hear me? Nothing."

He stopped in front of him. "Even if it meant losing this battle?"

James didn't answer, but kept his gaze on Jürgen.

Jürgen shook his head. "If she causes us to lose this battle, I will kill her myself. You won't be able to stop me because if you even try, I will kill you too. You understand?" He let the threat linger.

James nodded, knowing that his hatred for Gwen stemmed from before she betrayed their kind. He still didn't know why he hated her so much, but knew that it was no empty threat. Jürgen turned and stepped down into the underground. James figured they would have to take the District line east until they needed to change trains to get to Borough. The station was still out of the way no matter what direction they were coming from. It would drive James crazy until they left London.

Jürgen didn't say another word to him after the threat. James was sick of the threats from both him and Seth. They didn't understand what love was, they just wanted power. That wasn't why he was there, that wasn't why he fell. He did it for Gwen. The power promised was just an added bonus.

They still hadn't gotten the power they had been promised centuries and centuries before—the power to control the Earth. They lost that battle against Heaven and all its angels, but this would restore it. This battle would determine the ultimate fate of this world. They could either gain full control or they could lose it forever. This would be a fight to the finish.

It was true, in many ways, that this war could have been over if Gwen didn't sabotage the set-up they had for the planned destruction of the last five Gargoyles during the mortal WWII. The moment came back to James. It was 1945, and they had the perfect plan to destroy the last of the Gargoyles. Germany was losing control, it looked like the Allies would win and if all went according to plan, but it wouldn't have occurred that way. The Gargoyles were supposed to overrun where Hitler was hiding to kill him, but instead Gwen shot him, making the Gargoyles realize it was an ambush and retreat from the area.

A couple of demons did take down two Gargoyles though, but three managed to get away in the end. The same three they were still dealing with today. The strongest three. He had run into all of them a few times in the past. All had proven to be a pretty excellent challenge. James was curious how the battle on London's front would play out. Someone would lose a life, he just hoped it wouldn't be Gwen's life that would be lost. He would do everything in his power to make sure that it wasn't her that was in the line of fire.

Gwen could take care of herself in any situation, but the problem was that she, and himself included, were weakened by their physical separation from one another. If he could get to her before anything too terrible happens, she would be fine. They both would be fine.

After changing lines, they finally made it to Borough Station. James was relieved because if he stayed on that train any longer, he may have killed the lone passenger that was in the car with them. Jürgen wanted to stay off of the news before things got serious, just to be on the safe side. They didn't need to arouse too much suspicion of their doings, although it did make things more fun for the pair of them. Maybe in the next city.

He and Gwen always loved starting chaos wherever they went. It was their style. Bring fear to the population and then strike down the government in the end. It had always worked in the past, but then governments grew larger, making it become harder and harder for their method to work. Now they just infiltrated the government through minions and calculated threats. It was working pretty well so far, but they still had to be as careful as they could when doing it, to minimize the risk of unintended exposure of their world.

Jürgen led him to their new headquarters in London. How many headquarters they had around the world, James began to lose count. It had to be every major city, with minions keeping everything in control.

"Quite a lot of minions you have here," James

remarked. He sensed at least fifty of them in the building. Apparently Jürgen had already established a stronghold in the area. Jürgen hadn't been in London that long, he was impressed by Jürgen's masterwork.

"It's amazing how productive you can be when you aren't occupied with other matters," Jürgen replied as they entered a meeting room with a huge conference table facing an LCD screen covering the wall.

"I do my share, you know that."

"Mmm." Jürgen sat down at the table. "Seth laid out plans for us to bring the head of Parliament to our side. I say start tomorrow, since today I presume you want to focus on Gwen. I would think the Gargoyles will contact us as soon as they find out."

"If all goes according to plan, I will have her by next sunrise."

"Right," he coughed. "Anyway, we have a list of names of people we need to make into minions," Jürgen pulled out a folder.

"I presume King William is on there," James flipped through the pages.

"The family has already been taken care of. What we should be focusing on right now is a backup plan in case Gwen tries to play double agent, which I have a feeling she will."

"I concur. What do you have so far?"

"Well, for starters, I don't think she should know how many humans we plan on turning in and around Parliament. We could just let her know about main ones, catch her off guard in case she bails on us, something we should have done before."

"But back then we didn't know she would do such a thing," James said.

"True, but the point still holds. We give her wrong information about times and other such logistics, surrounding our plans, so if she does tell the Gargoyles anything, we will be ready."

James nodded, knowing this was a safe way to play her game. "We just have to make sure we agree on what she will be told and not told."

"Now…" Jürgen flipped open a file. "Let me bring you up to speed."

Chapter 23

Collin checked the time. It was half-past nine. The rest of the workers would arrive in approximately half an hour and Hywel was still passed out on the booth. Collin rubbed his eyes. He was tired, and it wasn't just from his second near-death experience. He felt more and more exhausted all the time, as if his body was about ready to give out on him. He wouldn't let it happen though, he would just have to push through whatever this feeling was that lingered over him.

He let the entire scene play over in his head once more. James came with another demon in hopes to get Gwen back. Collin feared that he wanted to hurt her, but if that were so, he wouldn't have been so careful to get her back. If James wanted to hurt her, he would have just gone straight for her, not negotiate for her, which brought even more questions to Collin's mind. What could they have to negotiate? The question preoccupied him so he didn't notice Hywel start to come to.

"What? Where am I?" Hywel's head shot up on the booth as he glanced around cautiously.

Collin hurried to his side with a bottle of scotch. A nice bottle of scotch. If he could get him to drink enough, he might forget what had just happened. At least that was what Collin hoped.

"It's all right, you are back in the pub." Collin started to twist open the bottle.

"What the hell happened? Who were those men? What, what, what..." Hywel started shaking. "What was wrong with their eyes?"

Collin placed his hand on his shoulder. "Calm down Hywel. They're gone."

"But who were they? What did they want with you? What was wrong with their eyes?" His eyes didn't stop moving back and forth. Collin had never seen someone move their eyes so fast.

Collin handed him the bottle of scotch. He took a big gulp. Collin realized it would take a few nice swigs before he would have any reaction. Hywel really knew how to hold his liquor.

"I mean, I've never seen anything like that!" He swallowed what alcohol he still had in his mouth as he spoke. "They looked possessed!" He took another swig.

Collin watched for any reaction to the alcohol. Still nothing. He would know the difference between sober and not, he dealt with seeing the effects every day amongst many different types of individuals. "Just take a deep breath okay?"

"They threatened me, Collin!" Hywel threw his hands up in the air. "Why? What was I to them?"

They just used him to get inside, but he couldn't explain that to him. "Nothing, you were nothing to them." In the end, he really wasn't. He just was another human to use to their advantage. Just like he was.

Hywel shook his head. "And how did they even grab me? I was in the front and suddenly I was in the back! How the bloody hell did that happen?"

"I really don't know, but please pull yourself together, we have to get ready for the day." Collin checked the time again. Fifteen until ten.

"Get ready? What are you talking about? We need to call the Bobbies on them! There are lunatics out there that need to be stopped!" He was yelling now. The alcohol he kept chugging was starting to affect him almost immediately.

Collin held out his hand, trying to quiet him down. He didn't need more people curious about what was going on inside. "I already took care of it, I had them put away. Bobbies took them and off they went."

Hywel took another swig, studying him. "Really?"

He nodded. He knew it was the only thing to get him to stop. "Yes. They are gone for good."

Another swig. "All by your lonesome?"

Collin kept nodding slowly. "Yes, all by my lonesome."

Hywel looked at him suspiciously, as if thinking about what could have happened. "I find that a little hard to believe."

A blow to his pride. If he only knew about his other job of getting rid of minions. But yes, compared to the two demons, there really wasn't anything he could do to them. He didn't know that for sure, for all he knew they were just odd-looking human beings. "Gee, thanks."

Hywel tapped the bottle on the table. "And why couldn't they come in?"

"What do you mean?" Collin questioned. So he did notice.

"I heard them say you had to invite them in or something." He brought the bottle to his mouth. A third of it was empty. Collin couldn't believe he was still conscious. "And what about the salt? What was so important about that damned salt?"

"Nothing, it doesn't matter anymore." Collin wished he told him about the salt earlier. Then they wouldn't have had this problem.

"None of it makes sense." Another swig. "I mean, first the door, then those weird men. And salt everywhere."

"I know, I know." The alcohol was starting to make him calm down, and over-analyze everything. He started gazing far off into the distance.

"Salt. Salt makes bad things stay away, that's a given." He started gesturing with his hands for everything he said. "Then two strange men show up. Can't come in unless you invited them in. Very strange. Could move fast and used me to threaten you with. Eyes turned all yellow and gross. Weird and cat-like." Hywel slammed his hand against the table for emphasis. "Then he tried kissing my neck. What the hell? Why would a man kiss another man's neck? Especially one he didn't know? Very peculiar."

Hywel took another swig and thought about it all as if putting all the pieces together. Collin just stared at him, wondering what he would put together.

"Salt. Scary eyes. Can't come in. Kissing necks." He kept repeating those words over and over again.

Hywel jumped up. "Wait! I got it! Vampires! They were vampires!"

Collin wasn't sure how to respond. He was beyond drunk at this point, the truth wouldn't hurt him, especially since he probably wouldn't remember later on, once sobriety returned to him.

"Yes, you're right, they were vampires."

"I knew it!" With that his eyes crossed and he fainted from the half a bottle of scotch he drank. The sudden movement probably didn't help either. Collin sighed. It looked like he would have to open the pub all on his own.

Grabbing Hywel by the arms, Collin dragged him across the room toward the stairs. He didn't want Hywel passed out on the booth when customers came in. It wouldn't look very good, especially since it wasn't even lunch time just yet. He also didn't need him screaming vampire either when he woke up, further alarming any guests to the pub at lunch. No one wants their first taste of London to include a drunken Welsh lunatic, screaming gibberish about "vampires."

As he started to pull him up the stairs, the back entrance door creaked open. Collin jumped, causing him to drop Hywel. He hit the ground with a loud thump. Collin turned around to find the head cook Peter standing behind him.

"What's going on here?" Peter examined Hywel curiously.

"Lady trouble. I gave him a little too much to drink to drown his sorrows in and, well…" He glanced at Hywel's unconscious body. "He passed out," Collin lied.

Peter set his things down on the bar. "Lady trouble? I didn't know Hywel had a girlfriend."

"Hence the lady trouble." Collin gestured to Hywel. "Help me get him to my room?"

"Sure thing." Peter helped him lift Hywel up. Luckily, Peter was a well-built man, he could probably carry Hywel by himself, especially since Hywel was a twig of a man. "You had to have given him a lot to drink, Hywel is pretty good at holding his liquor. Did you give him a whole bottle or something?"

"Something like that, yeah. I didn't think he would drink that much from it, but I was wrong."

"Apparently."

They carried him up and placed him on Collin's bed. Peter didn't say anything about the tally marks, and the one red mark on his walls. He knew he saw it because his eyes averted quickly away from the curious sight on Collin's wall.

Heading back down, another one of his workers came

through the door just then. Collin jumped, in fright, every time he heard the door open. He was afraid James would come back and decide he would rather kill him than meet with the Gargoyles.

It was going to be a long day.

As he started his bar up, opening the front door to let in a nice breeze that the sunny day provided, Collin wished Erik or Hugo would show up as soon as possible.

CHAPTER 24

Erik made his way back to Collin's pub. He didn't get the information he had wanted from Michael. But, then again, he never procured the information he wanted from the angelic hosts. It was out of line for him to ask for such a thing, but he had to see whether it might be possible, considering the necessity for such a thing to help reverse the tide of the war in their favor.

The information about Collin he had learned from Evans, on the other hand, was actually quite interesting. Collin was slowly dying and had been since Gwen gave him her blood and effectively brought him back from death. They had definitely prolonged the effect when he found a vial of her blood left for James to use. Two, actually. So he took them both and never looked back, using it to keep on healing Collin slowly these entire five years. He didn't leave one for James, because he really didn't care. He could have killed James right then and there, but it didn't seem right, not when it was Gwen who weakened him. Hugo hated Erik for not taking that chance, but to Erik it just didn't seem fair.

Vicar Evans used the blood in a concoction to be used on Collin, but now it was all coming to an end for poor Collin. It meant that he would have to act fast in getting Gwen to turn him. Whatever it took would help spare the life of Collin, who was someone that Erik was slightly partial to now.

He would have to discuss it further with Hugo. He would be all for forcing Gwen to do it, the problem was more what to do with her after the transformation ritual was done. He didn't think it would be right to kill her, not when she wanted to help, but Hugo was right. She would just make matters worse. After all the things she had done over the years, why should they be any nicer?

The moment he saw the pub, Erik knew something was wrong. The salt seal had been broken. He hurried inside to find Collin busy at the bar. Erik took a deep breath. He was fine, but something had happened. He could tell by the tense atmosphere of the pub.

Collin waved him to the bar. There weren't many customers at this time, being a Monday and all. He took a seat away from the couple that occupied the bar.

"What is it?" Erik examined Collin. He looked worried, glancing back at the door every few seconds.

"James came. He told me to give you this." Collin

pulled a card out of his back pocket and handed it to him. All it had was a telephone number.

Erik looked over the card, then at Collin. "What did he say?"

"He wants to make some kind of deal tonight. He wants Gwen in exchange for something you want," Collin explained.

Well, that was a freebie. He had already been planning the same kind of plan to see if he could somehow get a hold of them to make the same kind of negotiation, now he didn't have to do all that work. "Did they say what?"

"No, just said that you would know," Collin said.

Erik did know exactly what Collin was referring to, but why they were willing to give it to them was questionable. They were willing to finish the transformation of Collin into a demon with a soul in exchange for Gwen. James must have really wanted her back. The blood bond had come in handy after all.

"And that's not all." Collin leaned in closer. "They threatened Hywel and knocked him out. He remembers everything that happened. The yellow eyes, the weird monsters trying to bite his neck. Everything. He knows they are vampires."

Erik sighed. That was all he needed, another mind to erase. "Where is he?"

"In my room. I got him pretty drunk and locked him up in my room. He should come to pretty soon."

"Fine, I will erase his mind then," he said. He was more occupied with wondering what to say to James and how the meeting would go down, than how to handle some human who knew too much.

Collin's voice interrupted his thoughts. "What are you going to do? They want the exchange to occur tonight."

Erik laughed. "Good question."

"Would you really hand over Gwen?"

"If they have what I want, perhaps."

Erik took in the concern on Collin's face. He doubted if he really understood just what she was. "There's a lot at stake here. We really don't know if she will break and go back to being her true self. We just don't know."

Collin shook his head. "I trust her."

"You haven't been in this war as long as we have. She may seem innocent, but it's just a facade, you have no idea all the destruction she has caused throughout the centuries." Saying this made Erik feel older than he cared to admit, but Collin really didn't understand the scope of their wars, not yet anyway. But after the transformation, he hoped Collin would forgive him, knowing that they had to do it in order to keep peace on Earth, and keep the demons in Hell where they belonged.

"What if she had a change of heart?" Collin asked.

Erik shook his head. "It's not the same. We don't experience that like you humans do."

Collin thought for a moment. "So she can't ever be forgiven for what she did?"

"No, she has no reason to help us." Which is what scared Erik the most. It was why he didn't trust her. She had nothing to gain and everything to lose.

"Why can't she be forgiven?"

"Because our rules are different than yours, that's all.

Don't feel bad, she knew the consequences of her actions from the beginning. She knew she could never go back after she was knocked down from the stars," he explained.

"I guess there is a lot I don't understand about your kind then."

"Yes, there is." Erik held up the card. "I'm going to go make this call. Do you have a phone I can borrow?"

"Yeah, you can use the one upstairs where Hywel is."

"Alright, if he wakes up, I will erase his mind. I will be right back." Erik headed upstairs to make his phone call.

This could be their chance to get something they needed. For once, things might work out for them. Erik sat down on the bed next to the pathetic, passed-out Hywel. He picked up the phone and dialed. It didn't even ring once.

"Well, hello there, *Gargoyle*." An exultant voice greeted him. It was unmistakably the voice of a very happy James, expecting their negotiations to take place.

"Ah, James. How I miss seeing you around."

"Miss how marvelous I am, I suppose?"

"More the opposite, but if you would like to think otherwise, I won't stop you," Erik replied.

"I know what you want." Erik could hear the cockiness in his voice. Demons loved being able to use something against them.

Erik looked down at the paper. "Hence the note."

"I was thinking of a truce, let's say in an hour?"

"Fine."

Erik hung up the phone. An hour. Hopefully Hugo

would be back by then. He didn't want to face James alone. Erik rubbed his eyes. He would have to get rid of Gwen, he couldn't have her trying to run away once she found out James was meeting with him. She would be pissed when she found out the truth. But he didn't care, then he wouldn't have to be watching her every bloody second. And Collin would finally be powerful enough to fully enter the fight and, in the end, help them finish this war.

Hywel started to stir. His eyes flickered open. "What happened?"

"Good morning sleepyhead." Erik made eye contact. "I need you to listen to me very carefully."

After making Hywel forget everything, if the alcohol hadn't done so already, Erik went back down to the bar. He found Collin waiting for him at the bottom of the stairs.

"What did he say?" he asked.

"He said he will be here in an hour, but I need you to do me a favor," Erik started.

"What is it?"

"When Hugo and Gwen get back," Erik whispered. "I need you to take Gwen back to Hugo's flat. You know where that is?"

He nodded. "Yes, but why?"

"Because I can't make a deal with James when she is here."

"Because she will resist?"

"Or James will snatch her and I won't get what I want." Erik pulled out a pouch from his pocket. "This is sandalwood ash. Sprinkle it on yourself and neither demon will be able to sense you. I will also give you a knife."

"But I have a knife."

Erik shook his head. "No, this knife can hurt demons, kill them if they don't get blood in time. Trust me, your normal minion-slaying knife won't be as successful."

"That's for damn sure," Collin muttered.

"What?"

"Never mind." He stuffed the bag in his pocket. "So what do you want me to do with her?"

"Just keep her inside the flat until we come, okay?"

"Why can't Hugo take her?"

"Because I need him here with me. I am not facing two demons on my own. It isn't safe."

"And Gwen and me going outside is?"

"The dust will hide you. It should be enough."

Collin let out a sigh. "Okay, fine, I trust you. Will they be back in time?"

Erik didn't want to think about what would happen if they didn't. "I really hope so."

"That's reassuring."

Collin went back to work as Erik took a seat at the bar, thinking hard about how all of this would play out. It could go two ways. Everything could go smoothly and the trade would be made, or everything could go wrong and there would be a fight. Erik knew the latter one had the highest probability but he had a feeling it should play out fine. They had what he wanted, and he had what they wanted. It was simple, yet he still had a bad feeling in his stomach about all of this. There were only a few times throughout history where both the Gargoyles and the demons had met together and only half of such encounters ended quietly. This was different though. This involved a blood bond.

Twenty minutes went by and Erik watched the door carefully, hoping Hugo would walk in at some point. Collin worked at the bar. Knowing what he knew now from Vicar Evans, Erik noticed he did look weak and drained of energy. Erik just hoped that everything would go according to plan and they would have him changed very soon.

After what seemed like an eternity, the door opened and Hugo and Gwen walked in. Erik glanced at Collin and nodded. Collin motioned to Hywel to cover for him and he got ready to take Gwen out of here with him.

"Did you guys find anything?" Erik asked as he approached them.

"No, nothing," Hugo said.

"Stay out of trouble?" Erik watched as Hugo and Gwen gave each other a quick glance and nodded their heads.

"Yeah, just like always." Gwen smiled.

"I'm not even going to ask." Erik turned to Hugo. "Hugo, I need to talk to you."

"Yeah sure." Hugo followed him to the other side of the bar. Collin took the cue.

"The demons are coming here in about ten minutes," Erik said when they were finally alone.

"Wait, *what*?"

"They want Gwen and in exchange they are willing to turn Collin," Erik explained.

Hugo shook his head. "She'll never do it."

"Why?"

"She doesn't want to turn Collin because she'll drive him insane, whether she wants to or not. That's what she did to the last one," Hugo whispered.

Great, more trouble. "We can keep him away from her, it won't be the same."

He shook his head. "No, he'll go looking for her."

"Hugo, we really need this. For all we know, she could be exaggerating."

"I know, I'm just telling you what she told me."

Erik sighed. So many variables. "If he gets out of control, we can kill him."

Hugo raised an eyebrow. "You really think you can do that?"

"If he acts like the last one, yes I can."

He raised his hands in defense. "Fine, I leave it to your hands. As for Gwen, I really think she wants to help."

Erik looked at him. He wasn't being sarcastic. He meant it. "Why the sudden change?"

"It was something she said, I can't describe it. I just know she is telling the truth when she says she wants to help."

"But she can't help, not when she has that blood bond. James will stop at nothing to get her back."

"I know." Hugo glanced at Gwen. "I know."

"James should be here any minute. Collin is taking

Gwen back to the flat. They should be safe there. I don't need either of them knowing about the deal."

"Deception." Hugo smiled. "That's a new one."

"You know it has to be done."

He shrugged. "If you say so."

CHAPTER 25

"Hey, do you want to get out of here?" Collin smiled as he approached Gwen. She raised her eyebrow at him, suspicious about what he was getting at. He seemed to be hiding something.

"Excuse me?"

"I thought maybe we could take a walk, just the two of us. We haven't really gotten to talk much since you've gotten back."

Gwen just watched him, looking for a hidden meaning. "Talk about what?"

Collin shrugged. "I don't know, we could talk about the weather I suppose."

She laughed. "You want to talk about the weather with me?"

"I want to talk about anything as long as it's with you." Collin held up his hand. "Just wait here for a moment while I tell Hugo and Erik that we are going to take a walk."

"They won't allow it, it's too dangerous for you to be out there."

"It's fine, I have some sandalwood ash."

Gwen wrinkled her nose as he left to go talk to Erik. She hated the smell of sandalwood, hence why the Gargoyles used it to mask themselves. The smell neutralized anything around it. It drove most minions away as well. A little trick the Gargoyles had found useful over the years.

Knowing Collin was up to something, Gwen decided to go along with what Collin had planned. Curiosity always got the better of her in situations like these. It made life all the more exciting.

She saw Erik hand Collin something, causing her to suspect that there was more to Collin's sudden need for a walk than he was letting on. Gwen watched carefully as he came back to her.

"Ready?"

"Sure, so it's just the two of us?"

"Yup, Erik and Hugo said they will stay here. We can just meet them back here in a little while," he held out his arm for her to grab.

Gwen wrapped her arm around his. She would play it out to see what the true meaning was behind it all. "Sounds like a plan."

They stepped out onto the street and started north

towards Kensington. He rubbed the ash on his skin, making Gwen almost gag. Reluctantly, she wiped some on her exposed skin. It didn't sting, but the feeling of it applied to her skin made her uncomfortable. She couldn't sense anything now. No James, no Jürgen, no Gargoyles, and no Collin. It felt as if something ripped out all of her sense, temporarily, and she was left with nothing in the way of special sensory enhancements of any kind. Gwen tried not to show how weak she felt, but smiled as Collin held her hand as they j-walked across the streets.

"So, what did you want to talk about?" Gwen gazed over at Collin. His blue eyes shined lightly as they always did. She missed those innocent eyes.

He shrugged. "I just figured you needed to get away from Hugo and Erik, you looked like you weren't enjoying their company very much."

That was true, but she still felt like he was lying. "Ah, well they don't trust me, not that I can blame them."

"Why? What exactly did you do?"

Gwen smiled. "You don't want to know."

"Maybe I do." His lips cracked a grin, as if the things she did were simple pranks, not the actual torture it really was.

"Look, Collin, you are sweet to think I'm innocent enough, but I'm not. The horror stories I have, you wouldn't be able to sleep at night after hearing them. Just know it wasn't good."

"But you regret it?"

"But I regret it, yes."

"That's all that matters to me." He smiled as his eyes watched hers. Gwen felt herself blush. Not something she did often.

Gwen knew if James saw her with Collin as they were now, he would rip his heart out in a flash. Make sure he was dead this time. The danger enthralled her. He shouldn't be anywhere near right about now, but she couldn't be too sure, the sandalwood ash clouded her senses. He was as blind as she was though, so she didn't need to worry too much.

They kept walking casually up the streets, Gwen leaning on Collin's shoulder. She had to admit she missed him. He made her feel content about herself, as if she had the capacity for good. He was the only person who made her feel like that at all. She loved James with all her heart, but she could love herself when she was with Collin.

Memories of the time they spent together five years before flowed through her mind. Collin worked at the same pub but it had a different name back then. She used to visit and coax free drinks out of men. She caught his eye and he started giving her drinks on the house. They got quite cozy with each other, cozy enough to share a flat. Then James came and caught her on the way back from dinner with him. Then everything changed.

"How do I not scare you?" Gwen questioned as their quiet closeness started to make her feel odd.

He laughed at her question. "Because I know the true you, the one you try to hide from everyone else."

"But you never saw me at my worst. You have no idea

what I am capable of."

"I know, but that isn't who you are now—that isn't the girl I met."

"What if I went back to the old me? What would you do then?"

He placed his hand against her cheek. "Then I would stop at nothing to get you back to how you are now."

Gwen smiled and leaned her head back onto his shoulder. That's when Gwen realized where they had headed to.

"Why are we in front of Hugo's flat?" she questioned.

"We are? Oh, how about that?" Collin laughed.

"Look, Collin, I know you are up to something."

He placed his finger on her lip. "Shh, Gwen, don't say things like that."

"But, Collin, I," Gwen began when Collin leaned in and kissed her gently. Gwen felt chills go down her spine as his smooth lips touched hers.

"I just wanted to get you alone for a little while, that's all." Collin kissed her again, but this time more passionately. Gwen pulled his collar in closer to her. He backed her up into the flat's door. Collin fumbled around in his pocket for the key, not letting his lips leave hers.

Once he got it open, they tumbled inside. Gwen pushed the door closed and shoved Collin against it, intertwining their hands.

"James is gonna kill you, you know that?" She leaned in and bit his lip playfully.

"Oh, it's worth the risk." Collin lifted her up and carried her to the couch.

His body felt warm against hers. He ran his hand through her hair, twirling loose strands as he pressed his lips against hers. Collin moved down to her neck. How she wished he was turned and could drink from her, but it wasn't worth it. It wasn't worth ruining his life for. She would settle for a kiss. Wrapping her arms around his waist, she pulled off his shirt. Gwen traced his smooth skin down to his belt. She stopped cold, pushing him back.

"What's that?"

"Oh." He pulled out a knife. It was the triduanum. Gwen shoved him off of her.

"What the hell are you doing with that?" she exclaimed.

"Erik gave it to me in case we ran into any trouble." Collin set it down on the table.

Gwen's eyes didn't leave the weapon. "Did he send you to kill me?"

"What? No, I would never hurt you." He placed his finger on her chin and pulled her in for a kiss. "Never."

Gwen looked back at the knife. "Then why would he give you that? Why would he even let you take me alone anywhere?"

Collin sat up and sighed. "I just asked and he said it was fine." Collin stopped and grabbed his head. "Ow."

Gwen rushed to his side. "What is it? What's wrong?"

"My head." He clenched his hands. "It's pounding."

Gwen smelled it before she saw it. Blood. His nose was bleeding from the pain. Her eyes flashed yellow, she wanted it so dearly. She shook the feeling away. She couldn't hurt him like that. "Collin, your nose is bleeding."

He touched it and examined his fingers. "Shit, what is wrong with me?"

Gwen just stared. It was happening now; her blood was losing its effect on Collin. She was surprised it had even lasted this long, but she figured Erik and Hugo had done something to keep him alive. Either they stopped doing it so she would see his pain and be forced to change him or he really was dying.

"Why are we really here tonight? Was it your idea or was it Erik's?" She pressed again.

Collin sighed as he wiped his nose. "Erik's."

Gwen slammed her palm into her forehead. He knew she would see Collin's state and hoped she would turn him. It was a set-up, they knew she would make the choice alone with him like this.

"He didn't want you to run, so I had to distract you," Collin added.

"Distract?" Gwen paused, realizing her initial idea wasn't correct. Erik wanted to get her away from the pub, not necessarily with Collin, just away from them. "He's meeting with James, isn't he?"

Collin nodded reluctantly. Before Gwen could decide whether she was going to run after them, a knock sounded at the door. Gwen stared at it, not being able to sense anything. It could be either a Demon or Gargoyle.

She held her hand up. "Don't say anything." Gwen picked up the knife and kept her eye on the entryway.

Whoever it was had a key and was beginning to open the door.

"Erik! Hugo! I'm back!" a woman's voice sang out. Gwen's eyes widened.

"Elizabeth," she whispered. "Shit, shit, shit! I have to get out of here."

Collin grabbed her arm. "Wait, you can't."

Before Gwen could explain to Collin that she wasn't running for good, she was just running from the flat, Elizabeth entered the living room.

She looked the same, brown hair long and wavy, but she was dressed for the times now. Last time Gwen saw her she was in a nice Victorian dress and coat. Now she wore jeans with a simple black t-shirt. A look of surprise spread across her face when she saw Gwen, then it turned into hatred.

"Demon!" Elizabeth was on top of her before Gwen could run. She knocked Gwen to the ground and the triduanum slid out of her hand across the floor. Gwen tried to reach for it but failed. Elizabeth pulled her up by the throat.

"Where are Hugo and Erik? What did you do to them?" Her eyes felt as if they could pierce Gwen's soul, if she had a soul that is. Her angelic presence brought anyone near down to their knees. Gwen hated her, but it was only fair. Elizabeth hated her back.

"I didn't do anything!" Gwen tried to explain but Elizabeth didn't hear her. She threw her out the window with enough force to go through the Berlin Wall. Broken glass sliced her clothes and skin, letting even more energy slip from her grasp. Gwen slammed into the cobblestone outside the flat. She didn't have nearly enough energy to fight a Gargoyle, she had to make a run for it. Gwen tried to get up but it was too late, Elizabeth grabbed the knife and sprinted to her. Shoving Gwen into the brick wall, she drove the knife into her stomach. Gwen gasped.

"End of the line, demon."

CHAPTER 26

James took a deep breath as he entered the pub. Two Gargoyles were waiting for him, not just the one he had anticipated facing. He was glad he had brought Jürgen with him. Gwen, on the other hand, he could find no trace of her in the vicinity of the arranged meeting place. While this worried him, he understood that the Gargoyles would hide her from him until the deal was set. Over time the Gargoyles had learned to take caution when dealing with demons.

Jürgen stood at his side, not too happy about the meeting, but knowing it could work to their advantage. Gwen would be under their careful watch and the Gargoyles would have to deal with a confused human-turned-hybrid. Chaotic really, but that's how they liked it.

The pub wasn't crowded that night, so it made it easy to spot the Gargoyles. Erik and Hugo. These were the two gargoyles who his darling Gwen was trying to help. James found this interesting since Hugo had been one of the Gargoyles Gwen and himself fought against countless times at certain points in history. Gwen and Hugo were like archenemies.

Then there was Erik. He couldn't believe Erik would let her near him after what she had done. Hell, if it had been him, James would have been scared of her for quite some time.

James nudged Jürgen toward where the Gargoyles sat. Both Hugo and Erik kept a steady eye on them as they approached, which made James grin. They had not one ounce of trust for them yet they were desperate enough to agree to the meeting.

Erik stood up. "James, I would say it's a pleasure to see you again but it really isn't."

"Surprised you have the guts to meet with me, especially after what happened the last time we saw each other." James' eyes didn't leave Erik's fierce glare.

"Well, I slipped from your grasp. I figured if the time comes, I can do it again."

Jürgen chuckled. "I believe those were the last words of some of your colleagues."

"And yours as well," Erik replied.

"Touché, Gargoyle, touché," James commented. "Now, shall we get down to business? I am surprised you agreed to meet us here, you must be desperate."

"You have some nerve threatening Collin to get to us," Hugo growled.

James turned to face him, finding his comment ironic. "You are the ones that have been keeping him alive through some questionable means. Surprised, really. How did you manage it?" Not that they would tell him, James knew. But he was curious.

The edge of Hugo's lips curled into a slight grin. "Dealing with your kind for so long, you develop tricks to work to your advantage."

"Speaking of tricks, I can't sense Gwen. Sandalwood ash I presume?" He hated the stuff. He thought it was unfair. He saw Jürgen crinkle his nose next to him.

"Good guess," Erik answered.

James looked back and forth between the two of them. "Where is she?"

"Her location will be given to you after we make our deal." Erik gestured to the chairs. "Now, please sit."

The four of them sat down, never letting their eyes leave the other for a second. As the glares were kept, a waitress came by. "Would you like anything to drink?"

"No, we are fine, thank you." Erik didn't even look up at the young girl. Usually James would have watched her walk away, but he knew he shouldn't let his eyes leave his enemy's for even a fraction of a second.

"Now, on to the treaty," Hugo began.

"Ah, I would think after all these years you would be wary of making treaties with us. I figured seeing your friends' hearts ripped out of their chests would turn you from even the idea." James heard Jürgen laugh at his comment.

Hugo clenched his hand into a tight fist. "No, now I know how to word such treaties with such low-life, vile, deceiving scum such as you."

"We'll see about that." James turned back to Erik. "You know I want Gwen, alive and well, but let me hear what you want. Let me hear those beautiful words."

Erik took a deep breath, not very enthusiastic about James' wording. "We want you to make Gwen fully turn Collin into a hybrid."

James smiled. "You are willing to cause a human such pain in hopes of gaining an ally?"

It was the first time a Gargoyle had ever wanted to do such a terrible thing to a human. He found the whole situation delightfully ironic.

"He's dying either way," Erik began. "Besides, it wasn't me who started his transition. It was your girl."

"But you are still sentencing him to a life of misery. Can you really do such a thing and not regret it?" Jürgen added.

Erik didn't waver. "I can because I will know that whatever pain he will feel is caused by you, not me."

James raised his hands up in defense. "So quick to point fingers, but do remember that it was your kind that threw us out of heaven, not the other way around."

"You rebelled," Hugo retorted.

James shrugged. "It was for a good cause."

"Keep telling yourself that, especially after you lose this war and are stuck in the dark abyss that is Hell for the rest of eternity," Hugo added. They held each other's gaze.

James laughed. "And what makes you think you will win?"

Hugo shrugged, mimicking his style. "Because, we always do."

He raised an eyebrow. "Cocky, that's a new one."

"I guess your attitude has rubbed off on me," Hugo said.

"Or you just have been around Gwen too much recently. She tends to make her mark's ego go up before she destroys them completely."

"Talking from experience? I do believe she left you." Hugo grinned.

Jürgen coughed, causing James to give him a scowl and said, "while I do love this banter, we really should get this deal over and done with, as soon as possible."

"I agree," Jürgen grunted.

"So Gwen for Collin, that's the deal?" James inquired.

Erik nodded. "We give you Gwen but you must get her to turn Collin within four day's time."

James glanced over at Jürgen who seemed to be just as confused as he was. "Why four days?"

"Because, he doesn't have much longer," Erik explained. So that was why they needed him. They didn't think they could make her change him in time.

"Sounds like a deal." James began to stand.

Erik shook his head. "No so fast, you really think I am just going to take your word for it? Don't be ridiculous."

James sat back down in his seat, folding his arms on the table. "Then what do you suppose we do?"

"A blood pact," Erik answered taking his knife and slicing it across his palm.

James' eyes flashed yellow. It took every ounce of determination for him not to give into the urge to tackle Erik for that blood. Taking a deep breath, his eyes turned back to normal, and then his mind registered what Erik had asked him to do. He couldn't believe it. It was rare for such a thing to be done, not as rare as a blood bond, but still he only heard of a handful of such times. Before James could say anything else, a waitress hurried over.

"Um, are you all right?" She looked between the four of them, frightened by what was happening right before her eyes.

Erik turned and smiled. "Don't worry about it, just go back to work. Forget about this table and move on."

She nodded and walked away, affected by his act of compulsion. They could make a human do or forget everything they wished. Such skills would work wonders if the demons had the same ability. But making minions do their dirty work would suffice.

"And the terms?" James asked.

"If you don't change Collin within four days, your dear Gwen will die. You share the blood bond with her, you can make this pact with your blood," Erik explained as he handed James the knife. So he knew about the blood bond. He wondered how long it had taken him to figure out.

"Fine." James cut along his own palm. "But in return, if Gwen is killed by any of your kind between now and twenty-four hours *after* she turns Collin, Erik, you will die."

"Erik, don't," Hugo began.

Erik ignored him and held out his bloody hand. "Deal."

James shook his bloodied hand with Erik's blood-stained hand. The pact was sealed by the fatal combination of their blood, sealed by their symbolic handshake. James licked the excess blood off of his hand. Hugo gave him a revolting look.

"What? You expect me to waste blood like this?" James questioned.

"You disgust me," Hugo responded.

He smiled as he licked the remaining drops. "That's fair, your kind disgust me as well."

Erik started to stand up. "Shall we make the exchange then?"

He nodded. "With pleasure."

Following the two Gargoyles outside, James and Jürgen could sense something amiss. The smell of someone else filled their senses.

"Is there another Gargoyle in the city?" James asked.

Erik turned around, confused. "What?" Then his eyes widened. "Oh no, Elizabeth."

"Elizabeth is here already?" Hugo questioned. "But she would go straight to the flat. Didn't you send Collin and Gwen there?"

"Yes," Erik slammed his hand onto his forehead. "Stupid, stupid."

"What is going on?" James inquired slowly, suspicious of a trap.

"The other Gargoyle doesn't know about Gwen." Erik spun around and started running. "We have to hurry!"

That's when he smelled it. Gwen's blood. Jürgen hesitated, smelling it as well.

James rushed to Erik's side. "She's hurt! Where is she?!"

"The flat is three blocks north!" Erik answered. James was gone in an instant.

CHAPTER 27

Collin rushed to the broken window. It had happened all so fast, he couldn't do anything to stop her. He just hoped Gwen was okay, or at least what passed as okay for a demon. If she was a human, she would have been dead by now.

He had met Elizabeth a couple years earlier. It was a brief introduction, but even then he could see she wasn't one to forgive and forget. If Collin was right, she and Gwen had a run-in with each other in the past, just as Hugo and Erik did.

As Collin jumped through the gaping hole that was once the window to Hugo's apartment. He discovered, to his horror, the sight of Elizabeth preparing to stab Gwen with the triduanum. Gwen gasped as the knife sliced into her stomach.

"Wait! What are you doing?" he called out.

Erik had said that the knife could hurt demons, even kill them. Elizabeth must not have known about the meeting between Erik and Hugo and the demons. She didn't know Gwen was trying to help them.

"I'm purging this heinous creature from the earth once and for all!" Elizabeth replied as she stabbed Gwen again. Gwen didn't yelp in pain, but took it quietly as if she deserved the punishment.

"No! You can't!"

Elizabeth didn't hear him. She pulled out the knife and threw Gwen to the street. Collin tried to rush to her side but Elizabeth blocked him.

"Get away Collin! This beast will kill you for energy," she warned.

He shook his head. "No she won't, you don't understand."

"Oh, but I do. I have run into her before." She turned back to Gwen. "She won't let anything stop her from getting what she wants. She'll use you and when she is done, she'll dispose of you as she has done with countless others. She's a demon and she will forever act like one."

"But she's..." Collin began.

"She's right Collin, just leave me be," Gwen whispered.

Elizabeth pointed at her. "See, she even admits it, or she is trying to get your pity. Which is it?"

Gwen laughed. "Know me too well, Elizabeth. How

long has it been? A hundred twenty years? No, a hundred thirty. How time flies when you are having fun."

"If you consider destroying people's lives having fun."

"You know that I do." She smiled. Collin knew she was trying to distract herself from the pain, though whether that be mental or physical, he didn't know for certain. "So if you are alive, that means Daniel and Hatori were killed in the trap. A shame, really. They were both good sparring buddies. They always put up a good fight against me."

Elizabeth kicked her in the stomach. "Don't worry, I will do to you what was done to them."

"I sure hope so. I'm exhausted." Gwen closed her eyes. "Just get all this over with."

"You would like that wouldn't you? A quick death compared to all the slow tortures you have orchestrated over the years."

Collin couldn't believe how calm Gwen was being.

"I admit," Gwen said. "I do miss them. Although if you have the strength to do such a thing to me without crumbling, go ahead. I won't stop you."

"Masochist," Elizabeth spat.

Gwen's eyes opened as she looked up at Elizabeth. "Nah, I like to think of myself more as a sadist, but you're right, I could go either way."

Elizabeth shook her head. "You disgust me."

She tried to lift herself up, but tumbled back down. "You all always say that. What is it that disgusts you? I say you are all just jealous that we can take pleasure in things that you cannot."

Elizabeth kicked her in the stomach again. "That's it! Get up demon!"

Gwen didn't budge. "The knife is making that a little difficult."

"Oh, I'm sorry," she sarcastically replied. "Does this spear make you feel pain?"

"Actually, that spear is the worst thing I have felt in a long time," Gwen remarked.

"What is so special about that knife? Why can it hurt her?" Collin asked.

"This spear is poison to creatures like her. It speared the side of the pure and they can't handle it. Just as he rose three days later, they will fall three days after being stabbed."

"Wait, she will die in three days from that?!" Collin exclaimed.

"Not if she gets the blood from her kind, to replenish herself. Their blood is healing to all," Elizabeth explained. "Now, demon, get up!"

"I already said I can't," Gwen whispered as she spat out blood.

"Fine, I guess I will just finish you off then." She pulled Gwen up and placed the knife under her throat.

"No!" Collin exclaimed as he ran to Gwen. "Erik needs her!"

Elizabeth eyed him. "What?"

"He is meeting with the demons to trade her in exchange for something he wants," Collin explained.

"Trade?" Gwen whispered. "Damn him." She looked

as if she wanted to run but was too weak at the moment to do that.

Elizabeth shook her head, as if she didn't believe him. "Why would he do that? Why would he risk such a thing?"

Collin shook his head. "I don't know, he wouldn't tell me."

"Where is he?"

He gestured down the street. "At my pub. I was supposed to distract her while he made the treaty."

"He trusted a demon in your hands? Is he crazy?" she questioned.

"No, Gwen has changed. She wants to help us now."

"I don't believe that. I don't believe such a creature would ever be able to change. Especially her."

"Well then you have trust issues."

Elizabeth stared at Gwen. "All for a good reason."

Collin stepped closer to Elizabeth. "Just please, give me the knife and wait for Erik to explain things further. She can't even move, she is weak. I promise everything will be fine."

"She will kill you, Collin!" Elizabeth warned.

"No, she won't," he replied as he knelt down next to Gwen. "Gwen, are you okay?" He saw the wounds from the knife. Black lines, like poison, stretched out from each wound.

"It spreads like a disease." Gwen had seen the way he looked at the wounds.

"What do you need?"

"I need..."

"My blood," a voice said from the shadows. Collin looked to find the figure stepping closer. It was James. "Don't you, love?"

"You can't take her!" Collin yelled. He knew it was an empty threat since he was a mere human, but he had to try to improve things around him anyway. He didn't want her to suffer whatever punishment James had planned for her defection so many years ago, during World War II.

James just laughed. "I can't, eh? I would like to see you stop me." His eyes flashed yellow. "Besides, I think it would be in your best interest to get away from her. You never know when a girl like her will go mad with hunger."

Confused, Collin looked at Gwen. Her eyes glowed yellow, staring at him with the steadiness of a predator. It was like something out of his nightmares, only this time it was real. He remembered seeing her eyes like this five years ago, but they weren't directed at him. Collin knew he should leave her, but he couldn't make himself.

Gwen shoved Collin away from her. "Get away from me!" she yelled at him, now taking deep breaths, trying to calm herself down.

While he didn't want to leave her in James' hands, he knew if Gwen said to get away she meant it. He backed away slowly. Standing next to Elizabeth now, he knew he couldn't do anything, and that sickened him.

"Looks like I came just in the knick of time." James smiled down at Gwen. "Otherwise you would have bitten him, wouldn't you?"

"No thanks to you," she replied at him angrily.

"You started all of this, now I have to clean it up," he replied. Gwen glowered at him.

"What are you going to do now?" Collin questioned, only half wanting to know the answer.

"What I should have done a long time ago—take her away with me."

"Are you going to hurt her?"

"Really depends on her." He nudged Gwen with his foot. She grimaced. "If a good few hours suffering from the effects of the triduanum will knock some sense into her, then I won't have to do a thing."

Collin looked at Gwen uneasily. She looked like an injured animal lying there on the street. Blood pooled beside her. Collin glanced around. So far no pedestrians had come to this part of the alleyway. He was thankful Hugo lived in a quiet part of South Kensington.

James knelt down beside Gwen. "Darling, I've been so worried about you."

She shook her head. "Fuck you, James. Have to make a treaty to get me back? Bunch of games."

"Well, I learned from the best, haven't I?"

Hearing someone running toward them, Collin turned to find Erik and Hugo.

"What's going on?" Elizabeth asked.

"The treaty has been made. James is taking Gwen," Erik explained.

Wondering if Gwen had heard what Erik said, Collin looked back to find her in shock. Her eyes widened, she started shaking her head, appearing as if she was about to cry.

"Erik, no, please help me." Gwen reached out to them. Collin looked back at Erik. He had his back turned and was walking away. "You won't get what you want! You hear me?!" she called out. "You hear me, Erik? Never!"

"Collin, let's go," Erik said.

"Did you hear that, Gwen?" Collin heard James whisper as he followed Erik. "They don't need you, but I know a few demons who do."

Collin looked back to find Gwen still watching him, heartbroken. She reached out once more for help as she collapsed, unconscious. James pulled her up and gave Collin a look of satisfaction. He watched as they disappeared into the dark of the night.

CHAPTER 28

"Now tell me Erik, why was there a demon in this flat?" Elizabeth asked as they all entered back into the flat. Hugo ran toward the broken window.

"My window," he moaned.

Elizabeth patted his back. "Sorry about that. I was in the moment. But Erik, please, tell me what's going on."

"We traded Gwen for something we needed," Erik began.

Elizabeth looked at him as if she couldn't believe what she was hearing. "Which was?"

Erik eyed Collin. He couldn't explain it all with him standing there. He didn't need more people mad at him. "Collin, I think you should head back to your pub."

Collin just stared at him, offended by the request.

"What?"

"You've been gone for a while, Hywel will start to worry. We don't need him to get any more suspicious, especially after what happened this morning."

"But what about Gwen? We left her for that demon."

"It was part of the deal," Erik explained. "She will be fine."

"How can you say that? She looked horrified."

"Collin." Erik tried to make his voice demanding, but not angry. "I need you to go back to the pub."

Collin looked at him for a few moments, debating whether or not he should protest. "Fine." He started for the door, more pissed off than he had ever seen him be for the short time he's known him.

"We will be there tomorrow. Let us say, eight AM?" Erik inquired gently.

"That works. See you then." Collin waved his hand behind him as he left.

Erik sighed, pinching the bridge of his nose. One headache gone, another one to face ahead of him. He turned to find Elizabeth staring at him.

"Well?" she demanded.

Erik went into the details of all that has transpired over the past couple of days. He told her of Paris and of the blood bond between Gwen and James. She already knew of Collin's situation, but he went over that piece once again, as well. She didn't know he was dying and why they had to act quickly. Hugo still stood by the window, listening to the story once more and nodding. The entire time Erik talked, Elizabeth looked more and more furious with him for not being informed about any of this.

"You did all this before asking me if I was okay with it?" she asked.

Erik nodded his head. "We had to act fast and you were already on your way here. We had no way of contacting you."

Elizabeth turned to Hugo. "What about you?"

"What about me?" Hugo stared at his window, still upset that it had been broken during the fight that broke out due to the misunderstanding.

"You went along with this charade?"

Hugo shrugged.

Elizabeth rubbed her temples. "So you made a deal with them?"

He nodded. "Gwen for Collin."

She leaned back. "They have Gwen, how do you know they will keep their word about Collin?"

Hugo turned to them. "He performed a blood pact with him."

Elizabeth stood up. "You did what?!"

Erik gave Hugo a look. Out of all the things he could say, it had to be that. "It had to be done. As you said, they won't keep their word otherwise."

"What were the exact terms of the deal?" she inquired, cautiously.

"If he doesn't have Gwen turn Collin within four days, she is dead. If we kill Gwen between now and a day after she turns Collin, I die," he explained.

Her eyes widened. "So if I..."

He nodded. "Yes, I would have been dead."

She sat back down, rubbing her forehead. "See, this is why we consult each other before making stupid decisions."

"It was the only way to get them to turn him, though," Erik said.

"Why didn't you just keep Gwen until she turned Collin, and then kill her?" Elizabeth questioned.

Hugo sat down on the couch next to Elizabeth. "Because she and James have a blood bond, we couldn't wait any longer."

"So when James got here, you had to get rid of her." Elizabeth took a breath, letting it out slowly. "Why wouldn't she just turn him to begin with? Don't they like toying with humans?"

"Because she actually cares for him. She doesn't want him to get hurt," Hugo explained.

"But he would have been dead by now if you hadn't prolonged the effects."

Hugo shook his head. "She's smart, she knew we would do something."

"Then tell her he's dying," she said.

"It's not that simple," Hugo said.

"Why not?"

Hugo sighed. "She's the one that caused the other hybrid to go crazy. If we do this, she said she would cause Collin to go crazy as well."

Erik admitted this scared him a bit. If she did the same to Collin, he could turn on them and make things worse. He just hoped Collin would be stronger than that. He had faith that he would be.

"Who doesn't go crazy being around her?" Elizabeth started. "What does she care? What is so special about this human?"

Erik shrugged. "We don't know, all we know for sure is that she cares about him, and he also cares about her. He doesn't see her for the demon that she is."

"Well, he will learn. I can't believe she would keep her act up for this long."

"I don't think it is an act, I think she really wants to change," Hugo stated. Erik agreed, after all the things he had seen her do, there was no way this was an act. She looked horrified when James came to take her away. She looked as if she was about to die.

"What makes you say that?" she questioned.

"She told us," Hugo explained. "She said that she doesn't want to stay in eternity in hell, regretting everything she has done."

"So she thinks a quick switch will solve all her problems? Highly unlikely."

"Which is why we decided to deal with James. She will be out of our hair and Collin will be turned," Erik said.

"Then what?"

Erik shrugged. "Then we fight."

Elizabeth looked out the broken window. "What about London?"

"We can still save London. We can still stop them before they take over the city with their minions."

She turned back to him. "Can we? I thought you said

we can't hurt Gwen until a day after she turns Collin. If that's true and she goes back to her old self before then, she can attack us and we can't do anything to stop her."

Erik was silent.

She looked at Hugo. "And where were you in all of this? Why didn't you try to stop him?"

He held his hands up in defense. "I tried."

"Well you failed miserably," she retorted. "Now we have to be really cautious or have to abandon London altogether."

"Not yet," Erik said.

Elizabeth shook her head. "You are so dense."

"Let's just wait it out and see what happens," he started. "We are all on our guard now."

"Yeah, but we need to find a new flat," Hugo commented. "I loved this place too. Right location, right lighting. It was perfect."

"You will get over it, but you are right, we need to move quickly. Gwen has been invited in and we don't know how persuasive James can be. We should pack up and leave as soon as possible," Erik proposed.

"It's late, you really think anyplace will take us in?" Elizabeth inquired.

"We can stay at a hotel for the night then find something else in the morning."

"Fine." Hugo grabbed a bag to fill. "Let's go."

CHAPTER 29

A billion little lights. That was the first thing she saw when she woke. It took a few seconds for her eyes to adjust to her surroundings. Gwen found herself lying on a bed, alone.

This was James' bed. She could smell him.

She moaned as it all came back to her. The Gargoyles had traded her to James in hopes that he could get her to turn Collin. They had used her and didn't care what the demons would do to her. She wanted to help them and this was how she was repaid. Her heart filled with anger. They would get what they deserved in the end, she would see to that.

Gwen stood up, but had forgotten all about her wound. Pain jolted from her stomach, echoing throughout her body. Biting her lip, she placed her hand on it, hoping that would alleviate some of the pain. It didn't. She had forgotten how much pain that damn spear brought to her kind. Being shot was more fun than one little cut.

Though, it wasn't just her stomach that ached in pain. She reached down to her ankle. It felt as if it were burning. The invisible shackle that kept her down to Earth. But that meant she would have to be up high.

"What the hell?" Gwen mumbled as she stepped to look out the window.

She could see the entire city around, twinkling lights that lit up the night. She had to be inside the Shard, the tallest building in all of England. How James had gained access to a place like this was beyond her. They must have hacked into banks or turned important people into minions. It was the only way.

Looking up to the sky, Gwen found it to be a crystal-clear night. Even with all the city lights, she could see stars perfectly. Those damn stars. Another reminder of what she had lost.

Gwen pulled up her shirt to examine the wound more closely. Black lines radiated in every direction from the stab wounds. Poison in her blood. A death so slow. She deserved it, though, after everything she had done.

"Hurts huh?" James said behind her. She spun around to find him leaning in the doorway.

"A bit," she replied, not moving an inch.

He looked the same as he did five years ago, and every day before that. His dark, messed-up hair he always sported, looking as if he had just rolled out bed. His deep green eyes. His cocky smile. Everything she once loved him for, though a part of her still wondered how many of those feelings still persisted.

He took a step toward her. "Imagine my surprise when I woke to find you had used it on me."

Gwen felt her heart race. There was no running away this time. She had to face him. "You deserved it."

He raised his eyebrow. "Did I now?"

Frozen, it took everything for her to make a shrug, but she didn't want to seem afraid of him even though she was terrified of what he might do to her now that she was in his clutches. "You killed him."

"You left me," he replied with a bit of anger tinged in his voice.

"I didn't leave you, I left the life. I left everything that I was doing. You just happened to be a part of that life," Gwen explained. It did make her heart ache, knowing that she had to leave him behind, but it was for her own good. She didn't want to feel that pain anymore, the guilt from all the atrocities they'd both caused throughout so many scores of centuries.

"Doesn't mean it didn't hurt. You were everything to me and still are…." He stepped closer. Gwen backed into one of the windows that filled the apartment. The cold glass echoed through her body. "You don't have to be afraid, I'm not going to hurt you."

She tried to let out a small laugh. "I find that a little hard to believe."

"It's true, I'm only here to help you Guinevere, I just

want you back."

Gwen took a look behind her, gulping. He could easily shove her through the window and down she'd go. "Really? Then what were you doing five years ago? You were ready to stab me with that knife of yours."

"I was mad okay? I found you with that human. You know how jealousy can get the better of me sometimes." He gently brushed a piece of hair out of her face and behind her ear.

It was her turn to cock an eyebrow. "Sometimes?"

He smiled. Oh how she missed that smile. "All right, more often than not. But you are the one who gave that knife to the Gargoyles."

"They wouldn't trust me otherwise," she argued.

"Then they used it on you," he replied.

"That was because one of them didn't know about me."

"And that makes it all better?" James placed his hands on her shoulders. Gwen took a deep breath. His skin felt so warm on hers. "She almost killed you. If I hadn't come when I did, you would have been dead."

"No, if Collin didn't stop her, I would have been dead. Good thing he was alive, huh?" She grinned, knowing it was true.

"If Collin wasn't alive, we wouldn't be in this mess." He mimicked her smile.

"Then you wouldn't have had anything to bargain with," she said.

"Then they wouldn't have let you near them. They wouldn't need you for anything."

"Erik would have come around."

James laughed at her statement. "No, he wouldn't have, you are a demon. They would have never trusted you."

That part was true but Gwen just shook her head. "I can't go back, James."

He gazed at her with confused eyes. "What do you mean you can't go back?"

"I can't do this anymore. I can't... I can't hurt any more of them." Tears began to form in her eyes, tears she thought she would never shed.

James saw and wrapped his arms around her, tightly. "Shh, it's okay. It's okay."

She shook her head. "No, no it's not. I can't come back, no matter what you think. The others hate me, they will rip me to shreds when they get a hold of me."

"I won't let them get a hold of you," he whispered into her ear.

"You can't protect me forever, James," she said, half wanting to believe he could. She felt safe in his arms, but she knew she couldn't hold onto that feeling forever. She had enemies on both sides now. Even if James wanted to, he couldn't protect her from the enemies she had made on both sides of the struggle.

He kept his arms around her. "I can try."

"Why? Why would you risk them hurting you just for me?"

He backed away so he could look into her eyes. "Because I love you Guinevere. No matter what you do, I love you."

"You're just saying that to get me to return to you."

He wiped away her tears. "No, I'm not. I don't care what you did; I just want you to be safe."

She didn't want to believe him, but in her heart she knew she felt the same way. "Then why didn't you leave me be?"

"The one Gargoyle was trying to kill you and the other two used you for their own devices. Did you think you were really safe with them? Why would you want to help them?" he asked.

"Because it was the right thing to do."

"Right thing to do? Are you kidding me?"

She knew he would never understand, no matter how many times she explained. He would never understand what it meant to do the right thing.

"James, just let me go." She grabbed her stomach, wincing. It was spreading.

He tried to help her stand. "Gwen, you need to drink my blood. The longer you wait, the more pain you will feel. A drop will make it all go away." The thought taunted her, but she knew she couldn't.

She shoved him away. "No, I can't. I will lose control. You know how long it took me not to want to come crawling back to you?"

"Oh," he whispered. "I can imagine."

"I didn't want to hurt you, I just couldn't be around all that death anymore. Day in and day out, James. How many lives have we destroyed over the years? And for what? What was it all for?" she pleaded for an answer, something that would solve everything she felt poorly for. An answer that would satisfy the pain that she felt.

"For revenge. For control over this world."

It wasn't the answer she had hoped for.

"You should have just left me alone, James," she whispered.

"You know I would never leave you alone." He stroked the side of her cheek. "We need each other. We need each other's blood."

"I can't drink your blood."

He traced her jawline with his finger. "Then whose are you going to drink? Collin's? His blood would work to heal you now, thanks to your foolish idea of saving his life. I saw the way you looked at him tonight. You were thinking about it."

"Shut up," she said.

"Gwen." He bit his wrist and let the blood drip down onto the floor. Its dark, crimson hue took away the metaphorical purity that the white carpet once possessed. It had been tainted now, never able to go back to the color it once was. Her eyes turned yellow with lust for the few drops that fell onto the ground.

"I know you want to drink my blood, admit it. Just give in. It's natural. It's who we are," he whispered enticingly.

"But I don't want to be who I once was," she argued.

"But you can't go back, we can never go back to what we were..."

She gave him a look. "I know that."

"Do you? Do you really." He grabbed her and spun her around to face the sea of lights outside. "Look out there. See those stars?"

"Yes," she nodded.

"Do you remember the war like I do?" Gwen felt his breath against her ear. It made her body ache. "Do you remember being cast down from those stars with chains grabbing us and pulling us to earth? Binding us here for eternity?"

"You don't have to remind me," she answered.

"All we are trying to do is to get even—get back what we deserve."

"You really think that will ever happen?"

"If we can kill all the Gargoyles, we will be free."

She laughed. "And you believe that?"

"It is what He promised us."

Gwen shook her head. "Those billions of lies He has told us. Those lies are what got us here in the first place."

"Don't say things like that," he replied.

"But it's true."

"It also will get you tortured for eternity."

She laughed. "No, what I did in Germany will."

"Not if you help us end this war. Not if you just take one drop of my blood and remember who you are." He wrapped his arm around her in a suggestive way and placed his wrist in front of her mouth.

Seconds passed as she stared emptily at the blood running slowly off his arm. Gwen took a deep breath, thinking of all the possibilities of just what she could do. She didn't want to go back to him, but there was no place for her back with the Gargoyles. They had used her, they had let James take her away in this manner. They didn't care what happened to her now, they just wanted Collin turned into a demon. They had used her, even though she wanted to help them. The alternative, take a drink of James' blood and let herself slip back into his arms, a place where she knew she belonged, even if it ate her up inside.

Grabbing his arm, she pulled it to her lips. The warm blood met her lips in a welcoming way, reminding Gwen of every feeling she used to enjoy without guilt. The seduction. The feeling of her heart racing against his. Everything she had thrown away only to be rejected and used.

Gwen bit into his wrist, letting his blood flow into her, gifting her with the energy she once had. It felt warm, as if her body had been frozen for a long time and this was the only way to revive it. Slowly everything came back to her. The power, the memories, and the lust she once had for the demon that stood behind her. She could feel the poison retracting slowly back out of the wound, created by that damn Elizabeth. The black lines disappeared and everything went back to normal.

Letting go of Erik's wrist, she spun around to face her love. Pulling him in close, she kissed him. James wrapped his arms around her and returned her kiss with a passion that had been bottled up for nearly seventy agonizing years. She never stopped loving him; she just didn't want to hurt anymore.

Gwen shoved him against the wall, ripping away his collar from his neck. Piercing his skin with her fangs, she let the sweet taste of his blood energize her even more. It was the one thing she didn't want to do after all these years, knowing it would drag her back to his side and his life. Now here she was, and she didn't care whatsoever about the lasting repercussions of this one forbidden choice. All she wanted was his body against hers. And their blood mixed together for eternity.

She kissed him again on the lips as he pushed her down toward the bed. James' soft lips moved to her neck as he collapsed onto her.

"See, isn't this so much better than helping those Gargoyles?" he whispered into her ear as he slowly bit into her neck.

CHAPTER 30

Collin paced back and forth in his pub, checking the clock every minute. Erik had told him he would be back here at eight. It was fifteen past, and he was beginning to worry if he'd ever show up now. They were never late, or at least he didn't think they were. They usually never gave him an exact time for when they would show up, so maybe there wasn't any reason for him to worry. Nonetheless, he still did.

Letting his mind drift back to the night before, Collin stopped pacing and brought his palms to his eyes. Last night, he watched Gwen be taken. He watched as she reached out for help. Damning himself, he knew he should have done something, anything to help her.

It would have pissed Erik and Hugo off if he disrupted

their plans, but he decided he wouldn't have cared. They didn't trust her like he did. They didn't know the real Gwen, the one she trapped inside. He had seen it; he had seen her true self emerge when they were together five years ago. It was the little things, really. A smile to a child. A treat for a puppy. A coin for a homeless person, granted she did steal the coin off of a tourist, but that was beside the point. She did care for this world, she just wouldn't let them know it. Now she was with James and she would go back to the creature they all feared, the being James created her to be. A facade, really, to make him happy. At least, that is what Collin thought.

Collin heard a knock at the door.

"Finally," he whispered to himself as he reached out to the door. Then he hesitated. What if it wasn't them, he thought to himself, what if it was James returning to finally kill him or inform him that Gwen was dead?

Collin pulled the door open to find Erik, Hugo, and Elizabeth all standing in his doorway. He stepped to the side. "Come in, please."

Hugo nodded and the three of them entered his place. Collin shut the door behind them, half expecting them to give a reason for being almost half an hour late, half knowing they wouldn't explain it to him. They never did.

"So, what's next?" Collin questioned, finding the silence both awkward and even a little frightening. It made him feel as if they didn't want to share whatever was on their minds, which made him always ponder the question as to why they even talked to him in the first place. Sure he was handy with a sword, sure he dated a demon, but why did they care. Why did they really want him?

"We need you to pack your bags and leave this place," Erik stated, taking a quick glance around. He felt as if his jaw was going to drop to the floor. It came out of nowhere.

"But this pub is my life," Collin began. It truly was. Ever since he ran away from home, he dreamed of making a place where people felt welcome and safe enough to be themselves. It took him nearly a decade to make this place become a reality. They couldn't be asking for him to just give up on it, to give up on his life.

"They will come for you and destroy this place. You need to stay with us. Or do you not want to be a part of this anymore?" Hugo asked.

Collin knew he shouldn't get so worked up about his pub. It was just a pub after all, even though it meant the world to him. It was selfish of him, really. He should be out there saving the world from demon overlords. But the thought of never seeing the faces he had grown accustomed to seeing, each and every day, ate at him. He would get over it. There was more at stake now.

"I want to be a part of it. I will help," Collin said.

"Good, because I have a feeling we aren't going to win this round and we will have to move out of the country when the time comes. You have a passport, right?" Erik inquired.

Collin nodded. "Of course."

"Good. You will need it. Now, go on and pack your

things. I'm not sure if you will get another chance to," Erik said. "Oh, and while you are at it, change into a suit."

Collin nodded, not really wanting to ask why he needed a suit. He had only one suit for special occasions, which was rare since he didn't talk to his family and the only friend he really had was Hywel, and he was pretty sure that man didn't own a suit.

Quickly, he left them in the bar while he went up to his room. He didn't have much he needed to take, he always tried to keep to the bare minimum. Grabbing a backpack, he stuffed it with the handful of clothes that weren't covered in blood. Everything he had built up in his life was now gone and he would be on the run now, maybe for the rest of his life. Everything fell apart the moment Gwen walked into his life. But he still didn't know if he considered that to be a good thing or a bad thing.

After filling his bag as well as he could, he changed into the only suit he had. He tried his best to be hasty, but suits were not something you could ever change into in a hurry. Maybe James Bond, but not him.

He never cared for suits. They felt too formal. He hated the tie, the uncomfortable shoes, and the tight shirt. Just a waste, really. James had come to him, dressed in a casual suit. It made him hate both him and Jürgen, and the whole lot of the demons, even more.

Collin scratched the blood that Gwen had placed on the wall. He didn't want to seem psychotic to Hywel, if Hywel decided to live here either temporarily, or maybe even permanently. He would give him the deed of course; he trusted that Hywel would be able to take care of the bar when he was gone. Hywel put in just as much effort as he did to keep the place running.

Finally having everything he needed, he headed back down the stairs, saying goodbye to his upstairs flat that he had spent the last few years of his life in.

"Is that everything?" Erik questioned as he took the last step, eyeing his small bag of items.

He shrugged. "Yeah, everything I need."

As if he knew he was needed, Hywel walked into the pub, earlier than he normally entered the pub.

"Sorry I'm late, I..." He saw the four of them standing there, including Collin with a packed bag and a suit on. "What's going on Collin?"

"Hywel, I have to go somewhere for a while. You can take care of the pub, right?" Collin asked.

"Yeah, no problem, it's just." He looked at the three others. "It's really sudden."

"You have my cell, if there are any problems, call me."

"When will you be back?" Hywel asked.

Collin eyed Erik. He shrugged. "I don't know but I will check back in a few days."

"Alright, keep me posted. I just hope everything is fine," Hywel said.

"Don't worry about it." Collin took one last look around. "Just keep her safe."

"Are you ready?" Erik gestured to the door. Collin nodded.

He would be back later in the week to give Hywel the deed and to say goodbye to the other workers. It had been fun working with them. They would ask questions why he was suddenly leaving, but he wouldn't be able to answer them in a satisfactory way. He would just have to say something came up, maybe blame it on the family, although Hywel would know that was all a lie. He didn't talk to his family. Collin would have to think of something else later.

The three Gargoyles led him down the streets toward their new flat. Collin understood that he had to leave his pub behind, but it still hurt him. He put so much of his life into that pub and it was hard to just let it go. He kept telling himself that being a part of this was better, it meant more.

"You think she's okay?" Collin questioned again. He knew they didn't have the answer, but the question had been on his mind all night.

"I'm sure she's fine," Erik answered. "She's a demon after all, it wouldn't be the worst situation she has found herself in."

"Ain't that a fact," Hugo murmured. He had been quiet since he had stepped into Collin's pub. A lot had happened in the last day, Collin figured he must not be the only one overwhelmed with all of it.

"So we are heading to the new flat?" Collin tried to get rid of the awkward silence. He hated that they ignored him when he asked about Gwen, not giving him any straight answers. But something inside of him understood. They were creatures from Heaven fighting demons. Gwen was a demon who had tortured them again and again, whose whole purpose was to destroy

Erik and the rest. He could understand how had they used her to get what they wanted.

"Yes, we have found a nice place not too far from here. Just a few more blocks," Erik explained.

"Still not as nice as my old one," Hugo mumbled.

Elizabeth rolled her eyes. "I already said I am sorry about your stupid window. Besides, we would have had to move since you idiotically invited Gwen into the flat."

"I didn't want to, Erik made me." Hugo glanced at him.

"She passed out, we couldn't just leave her on the street," Erik argued.

"Yes, we could have," Hugo retorted. Collin had no idea what they were talking about, but he just listened. A part of him, though, was quite troubled by the slight note of glibness on the subject of Gwen's safety at the moment. He didn't understand why the plan had to involve her being in her demon ex-lover's clutches.

"Get over it, it's just a flat."

Hugo pointed at his chest. "Yes, but it was my flat. Mine! When you have a place, it's always nice and nothing ever happens to it, but when it comes to my things, boom! It's destroyed one way or another! First my hut, then my nice country home, then my ship! Now my flat! Seriously, it's not fair."

Elizabeth placed her hand on his shoulder. "It's alright, you will get over it."

"I can never have nice things. Never."

Collin had to keep himself from laughing. To see a heavenly being getting so worked up about materialistic things. It seemed contradictory, but he could understand if everything Hugo tried to make nice inevitably got destroyed century after century, it would have ticked him off too.

"Speaking of nice things, why did you want me to change my clothes?" Collin questioned, now realizing he neglected to ask earlier about it. He got used to odd requests with no explanation from the Gargoyle gang.

"Because," Erik smiled. "I'm going to try to get us an audience with the King."

CHAPTER 31

James opened his eyes to find Gwen lying next to him. Her hand was gently resting on him, soft hands he loved to kiss. He smiled. It was something he had missed for far too long, being able to wake up and see her face. Stroking her cheek tenderly, he got up as carefully as he could, not wanting to disturb her. It had been a long night after all.

Stepping into the shower, James thought about what his next actions would be. There was a lot to be done in a short amount of time. They needed a different plan of attack or just an entirely new strategy. He, Gwen, assuming she'd be willing, and Jürgen would need to surprise the Gargoyles. They had been using the same tactics for far too long now and change was needed, all of them agreed. They had to act fast this time and go straight for the top, no matter if people noticed. All they wanted to do was start chaos, not a full-scale war. The war this time needed to be within, not against the countries. That was what was happening in both France and the United States, now they needed to start it here as well.

His thoughts turned back to Gwen. He couldn't believe what she had said. She cared for these humans; she felt remorse, fear, and pain for everything she had done in her past. He couldn't understand it, this sudden moral transformation. When they fell from the heavens, none of them looked back. None of them regretted what they had done, yet, after thousands of years, she just snapped. Why she did it was beyond him. There had to have been something that led up to it.

After listening to her last night, he knew she would try to help the Gargoyles again, one way or another, even though they had used her for their own greedy plans. This brought up another problem. What was he going to do about Collin? He would have to get her to change him or he could lose her for good. James knew if he admitted that he made a blood pact for her life, she would be pissed. No, he would have to play this one out carefully, getting her to complete Collin's hybrid transformation without knowing the price James paid.

Grabbing the towel from the rack, James dried himself off in the shower. He had to get ready before Jürgen stopped by, which would be very soon. He had left him to deal with Gwen last night, knowing he might not be able to control his temper. Jürgen really hated Gwen, and James still wasn't sure about the exact the reason why. He needed to ask Gwen while Jürgen wasn't around, but they would be busy for a while and at this point it wasn't that important. It would have to wait.

Wrapping his towel around his waist, he stepped out of the shower to find Gwen sitting on the counter. All she was wearing was his shirt. Damn, she was beautiful no matter what she wore.

"How long have you been sitting there?" he asked.

She shrugged. "A few minutes now."

He grinned. "Admiring me as I bathe?"

"Just waiting for you to get out," she replied, not letting him get the satisfaction of a yes, even though he knew that he was right.

James lifted her up off the counter and kissed her. "I missed you."

"I missed you too." She smiled as she shoved him against the wall and bit into his neck. He closed his eyes, letting her take what she needed.

The door to the bathroom swung open. James looked past Gwen to find Jürgen standing there, rolling his eyes at what he found. "I smelled blood outside, and I got worried. I should have known you two were just fooling around."

"Then why did you bother?" James questioned as Gwen slowly moved behind him, hiding.

"Worried that she might do something to you." He glared at Gwen.

"Oh, Jürgen, you don't have anything to worry about."

She smiled.

"Really? Then why are you hiding behind him?" he asked.

"Because I know you too well, you didn't like me before I left and sure as hell don't like me now."

"You know I can't hurt you while he's around." Jürgen shot a look at James.

Slowly Gwen stepped forward, worry filling her face. Without hesitation, Jürgen threw a punch at her face. She caught his fist in midair.

"Jürgen!" James yelled.

"I didn't hurt her, I was just seeing how aware she was." His eyes didn't leave Gwen's.

"I passed I presume?" Gwen questioned.

Jürgen grunted. "We need to get going. Seth is waiting for our call."

"Ah, Seth." She let the name linger on her rosy lips. "So that's who's calling the shots these days?"

"No thanks to you," Jürgen murmured.

Gwen shoved Jürgen and James out of the bathroom. "Okay, I'll be out in five. Find me some clothes I can wear. Mine are a bit gory." She winked at James as she shut the door on them.

James glanced at Jürgen. He was staring at him.

"What?" James asked.

"You sicken me," Jürgen replied.

James knew that wasn't what the look was about. "Seriously, what happened between you two?"

"She betrayed our trust."

"That's not what I am talking about," James said.

Jürgen just sat in silence.

After Gwen came out of the bathroom, smiling as if the past seventy years had never happened and everything had been a joke. They left the apartment and headed toward the headquarters in London. He and Jürgen had decided the day before that they would make her feel as if they somewhat trusted her. Then they could watch her closely and make sure she would betray them just as planned. It would be a set up for the Gargoyles and hopefully end up with the loss of one of their lives.

They made their way down toward Borough, where their headquarters resided. Fortunately, it wasn't that far from the Shard, so their journey wouldn't take too long. As they walked, James slipped his hand into Gwen's hand and kissed her cheek. He was glad to see her after all this time, even though she was probably lying to him. Something was better than nothing. Either way, he would get her back completely, it would just take some manipulation on his part. It wasn't like she hadn't played the same game before; he was really just taking after her.

As they approached the building the headquarters was in, Gwen chuckled. "I knew it would be around here."

"Did you say anything to them?" James inquired. He wondered what exactly she figured out for the Gargoyles but hadn't gotten around to asking, not that she would tell the truth.

"No, I didn't say anything, at least not where your headquarters was," she said. He debated if that was a lie or not.

"Why?" he asked.

She shrugged. "Didn't seem like good sportsmanship and anyways, I wasn't totally positive about my assumption on whether it really was here or not."

"You're one to talk about sportsmanship, and loyalty for that matter," Jürgen interjected.

"Aww, who woke up on the wrong side of the bed this morning?" she asked. James rubbed at his eyes. They weren't going to stop arguing. They never stopped arguing.

"I'll show you the wrong side of the bed." Jürgen pulled back his fist. James caught it.

"Jürgen, what did we agree to?" James warned.

"Yeah Jürgen, just pretend it's the old days when we used to have fun. Terrorizing villages, attacking camps, pirating the high sea..." Gwen added.

"You mean when you acted like a demon, not a selfish bitch?"

"Exactly," Gwen replied.

James laughed at her comment as they entered the building. Gwen never let anyone get under her skin, which made her all the more fun since she could get under anyone's skin, including his.

The minions had the video chat all ready for them. Seth was already on screen, waiting for them.

"About time you two showed up, you have any idea how long I've been waiting?" Seth caught a glance of Gwen. "Ah, Gwen, I see you have decided to join us after all this time."

"Indeed I have," she said.

Darrell poked his head behind Seth in the video screen and waved at them. Even though he was the one who told Seth about Jürgen running into Gwen in Paris, he and Gwen were best friends. Gwen waved back smiling, happy to see her buddy again all in one piece. It wasn't anything James worried about, they acted like brother and sister. Darrell picked on Gwen and she always liked to prank him back in return. It was interesting the things they thought up together.

Seth shot a look at Darrell, making him pout and disappear from the screen, then he turned his attention back to them. "For some reason I find that hard to believe, especially after only one night."

"You underestimate how persuasive James can be." Gwen traced her finger on his jaw and smiled.

"Doesn't mean you won't betray us again. I presume you two will keep a close eye on her?" Seth watched as Gwen gave him an innocent look, as if she wouldn't do anything.

"I will never take them off of her." James grinned and put his hand on her thigh.

Jürgen apparently saw the worried look on Seth's face. "Don't worry sir, I won't let anything happen."

"Good. At least there's one person there with whom I can trust to keep a level head about all of this," Seth said. "Now, has Jürgen filled you in?"

James nodded. "On arrival yesterday, yes."

"And Gwen?"

"Haven't had a chance," Jürgen grunted. "James had her all night."

"Well then, I will leave it to you two to catch her up," Seth said.

Jürgen nodded. "Yes, sir."

"And Gwen?" Seth turned his attention back to her.

"Yes, Seth?" she asked.

"I'm watching you. Don't think I will let all of this go. I still want to yank your heart out and make you watch, and if you give me any reason to, I will." With that, he disconnected from the video chat.

"Glad he's in a good mood," Gwen commented in the silence that overtook the room, after Seth's departure from the chat.

"That's what happens when you betray your own kind," Jürgen said.

"So worked up over nothing. The past is the past." Gwen motioned with her hand dismissively. "Get over it."

Jürgen glared. "It was yesterday."

James interrupted their feud. "So what's the plan Jürgen?"

Jürgen pulled five pictures out of his pocket. "These are the men we need to turn. They are all guarding the Prime Minister tomorrow. If we can get to them, we can get to the Prime Minister."

"Wouldn't the Gargoyles see that coming?" Gwen asked.

"Yes, which is why we are doing it so soon. They won't expect us to act so quickly," James commented.

She looked through the pictures. "Are you sure about that?"

"We have this all planned out, unless you are going to do something that will compromise the mission—again." Jürgen glared.

"I'm not."

"Sure you won't. At any rate, we have a list of the pubs they usually go to. Tonight is game night so more than likely they'll be there. We turn them tonight. Tomorrow the Prime Minister himself. We will attack at morning at 9 AM. That way it is after rush hour. Fewer people to witness, not that it will matter," Jürgen explained.

"Tomorrow at nine," Gwen repeated.

"Yes, is that a problem for Your Royal Highness?" Jürgen remarked.

"No, just memorizing the plan for tomorrow," Gwen said. "Before we do anything, James, I need some new clothes. Jürgen ruined my favorite jacket." She shot a look at him then turned back to him. "The rest are a little worn and yours just don't work for trying to persuade men like that into the alleyways where I can turn them."

"Of course, the first thing you want to do is go shopping," Jürgen murmured.

"Want me to be able to turn them or not?" she questioned.

"I will take you, don't worry." James grabbed three of the pictures—men that happened to go the same pub. "We will take these three. Jürgen, you can take the other two."

"Fine." Jürgen looked at Gwen. "Sure you will be able to turn them? Been awhile, hasn't it?"

"Don't worry, Jürgen." She grinned. "I'm back."

CHAPTER 32

Erik took in the surrounding area, letting the details come to him slowly. Everything had to go perfectly or he would be thrown in prison for a long time. Not that he couldn't get out easily. It was just a hassle that he didn't want to deal with. He looked through the bars of the gate toward the handful of guards that were on watch. Their red suits and black caps looked clean and polished, as they always did.

He needed to get inside Buckingham Palace and the only way to do that was to establish eye contact with at least one of the guards. They all looked straight ahead, as ordered. None of them looked at the crowds of tourists or at the cameras these tourists all had. They just looked straight on with a stoic gaze.

Not many people know this, but establishing eye contact with one of the royal guards was like trying to roll a seven with a six-sided die. It couldn't be done. At least not without a little outside help, usually from another die. Erik nodded to Hugo. He needed him to distract the tourists so he could jump over the gate without getting noticed, except by the guards, which was exactly what he wanted. Then he could establish eye contact, since they would be after him.

They had brought Collin along with them. Erik wanted him to become more accustomed to the tasks they did, other than fighting minions and demons. Collin looked anxious about meeting the King. Erik would be too if he was a human, but he wasn't and after meeting many leaders of various countries throughout different times in history, he learned they were only human. But King William was their leader, he represented Collin's country. It surprised Erik that Collin didn't ask to sit this venture out, out of pure fright, but curiosity probably got the better of him in the end.

Collin didn't ask questions, just did what was asked of him. Erik liked the kid's obedience, rare for humans to do what they say without complaint. Then again, he had been dealing with them for only five years now. Collin knew what was at stake and that questions would only slow them down.

He heard a loud crash behind him, accompanied by gasps and shouts. A mad rush of people moved behind him. Erik wanted to look back to see exactly what Hugo had done, but there wasn't any time to waste. He grabbed Collin and jumped over the twenty-foot fence with ease.

It didn't occur to Erik before this, but he wasn't sure if Hugo had ever explained to Collin that gargoyles could fly. They rarely would use their ability since humans freaked out at the sight of them flying overhead and would run away, causing a large scene that they didn't need. Causing chaos was the demons' job, not theirs.

Collin's expression was what triggered this thought about the flying. He looked as if he was going to scream bloody murder, but thankfully he didn't. He must have been used to weird things after being with Hugo for so long.

They got the attention of the guards right away. The guards ran over at them, pointing their rifles straight at them as if they could manage to hurt him. "Oi! Stop!"

Collin, again, looked as if he were about to scream but he resisted the urge. Erik really should have explained the whole plan to him. Lesson learned.

Erik held out his hand, calmly. "It's all right, I just need to talk to the king." He looked at each one of them in the eyes. Slowly, but surely, they lowered their weapons. "Please, can one of you take us in? It is urgent."

One of the men nodded. "Of course, right this way."

They followed the guard into the palace. Collin gaped as they entered. He admitted the scarlet, gold, and pearl decor was truly exquisite. Everything was set out perfectly, nothing out of place. Dozens of chandeliers decorated the halls, bringing an even, resonant golden tone to each and everything the light touched. Rows and rows of paintings hung on the walls, reminding the observer of the power each and every one of these people had.

"It's much more incredible in person," Collin commented as they walked quietly through the halls, following their escort.

Erik nodded.

"By the way." Collin leaned in closer. "I didn't know you could fly. You really should have said something."

"Sorry about that. Not used to explaining it to others," he said.

Nothing seemed to have changed since the last time Erik had walked through these halls. Sure, an added thing here and there, but overall, it looked virtually unchanged. He felt as if no time had passed and indeed, from his immortal vantage of life, it hadn't. Just another battle had gone by, and another was here to take its place.

They came upon the room that the King resided in. The walls were covered in a jade green with curtains to match. A gold and white interlaced rug covered the aged wooden floors. King William sat at his desk, talking to his wife, Princess Kate. Their conversation stopped when they stepped in.

"King William, these men have come to speak to you." The guard nodded to the two of us.

William looked concerned, shuffling through some papers as if checking through them. "I don't recall having an appointment. Who are these men?"

The guard hesitated, realizing he didn't have an answer.

"I am an old friend of your grandmother's. I believe she may have told you about me. My name is Erik." He hoped that she had, otherwise he would have to tell the long and confusing story all over again.

William turned to Kate. "Please excuse us."

She nodded then left with the guard. They were alone.

"Please." He gestured. "Sit."

Erik obeyed, as did Collin. The chairs creaked as they both sat down. Collin looked as if he was afraid to touch anything, keeping his hands folded in his lap.

William looked long and hard at Erik, as if trying to evaluate who he really was. Finally coming to his own conclusion, he shook his head. "You can't be the Erik my grandmother told me about, that was in World War II. You don't look a day over thirty-five."

Erik laughed at his accusation. "I'm not human, age has no meaning to me."

"So she said." He fumbled with a few papers. "What brings you here?"

Erik's voice softened, sad that he was condemned to say the same words at many intervals throughout time. "The same thing that brought me here last time—war."

He looked over the papers at him, as if he didn't hear clearly. "You can't be serious, our country is finally at peace, and you can't let me believe that another world war is brewing."

"It isn't the same kind of battle as the last one, your highness. This is not as blatant. It is an internal battle, one of resistance and rebellion," Erik explained.

Looking between him and Collin, he said, "How do you know this?"

"Because the same thing has happened in Paris and in the United States. It will happen here too."

"Who is behind these attacks?" he asked.

"The same as the last war, demons."

"Demons?" He chuckled at the word, as most humans did these days upon hearing the ludicrous term used in a literal sense. "You can't be serious."

Erik sighed, not wanting to deal with yet another leader who didn't understand the ramifications of what was happening right now. "Did the Queen not tell you about the war?"

"You mean the war between heaven and hell for the control of Earth?" King William's voice became serious, realizing that this wasn't some kind of joke. "I thought those were just stories."

"They aren't stories, the war is real, and it is ending. It is important for you to help us," Erik said.

"How can I help in a war of that magnitude?"

"You can warn your prime minister and set up defenses, double your guards for every important member of Parliament. Make sure none of them gets turned."

The King raised his eyebrow. "Turned?"

Erik wondered now how much the Queen did tell him, and how much she left out, in order not to scare the poor boy. "Demons can kill a human and use their body as a host for other demon spirits. They aren't smart, but they are ruthless. They can deceive anyone into believing they are human."

He didn't seem to react as Erik thought he would, or was capable of holding his composure well. "How can you tell if a person is one of these creatures or just a human?"

"Salt, silver—either of those two can hurt them," he said. Collin nodded in agreement, since he understood all the things demonic creatures couldn't handle.

"Just like in all the stories?" It was more a joke than a question.

"All stories have some truth behind them, one way or another." Erik had seen most of those stories, and their outcomes. It was interesting how many myths had truth at their core.

William rested his elbows on the desk in front of him. "It isn't going to be easy, you know, setting up high security without questions arising. What will I tell them? How can I warn them about something like this? They would think me mad."

"Tell them you were tipped off about an assassination attempt. That's what your grandmother did."

He shook his head. "But the enemies were more known then. Germany had already invaded Poland. There already was someone to blame. Who do I blame now?"

"I'm sure you can think of something, your highness, your family always could," Erik reassured.

The door opened to reveal a worker with a silver platter. "Your tea is ready sir," he brought the plate to the

King. He was hesitant to touch the platter and the utensils.

"Thank you, I was just finishing up here." He turned back to Erik. "I will keep your warning in mind, Erik. I will post guards at Parliament at once."

"Thank you for listening." Erik bowed and turned toward the door. Collin bowed as well and followed him out.

As they left, Erik heard the echo of a spoon hitting the ground.

CHAPTER 33

Gwen rushed through the racks of clothing, tracing her fingers along the soft fabric. Fresh, non-bloody fabric that smelled clean and hadn't been worn yet by anyone. Pulling out a black pleather tube-top that had Victorian designs down the middle, she smiled. It was perfect. She grabbed the beige shorts to match the top.

It had been a while since she had gone through a department store, especially one where she could pay for what she was going to buy. All the clothes she had since she left the demons had been stolen, or what she liked to call, temporarily borrowed. Although, she never did give them back. You would be surprised by just how many pieces of clothing you could go through in seventy years.

She grabbed a few more shirts, a jacket, some shoes,

and a couple nice pairs of jeans. She knew James had the money, especially after finding out where he was staying. He loved to live in luxury. Minions came in handy when you needed money, all you needed to do was turn the right human and presto, you had all their assets.

"Why do you need all these clothes, Gwen? You seem to be going a little overboard," James commented as she handed him a dress.

"You know how long it has been since I could actually shop for what I want? A long time."

"Well whose fault is that?"

She gave James a look. "Either way, I need something nice for tonight. Have to look my best, don't I?"

He took a quick glance, up and down, as if he didn't agree. "You always look your best."

"Of course you would say that. You will say anything to get a taste of my blood." She winked.

"You know that's not true." James gently kissed her lips. "Speaking of which, what did you do for clothing? I presume you had no money."

"I stole clothes and money for apartments. Anything I needed really," she explained as she handed him another pair of boots.

He laughed. "That's ironic, given that you wanted to be good and all."

"Materialism means nothing to our kind and you know that. Besides, I would have paid for them if I could, but I couldn't and now here I am."

"Here you are with me." He kissed her again.

"I can't believe I made such a huge mistake leaving

you."

He stroked her cheek. "Don't push it, Gwen." His voice sent chills down her spine. To someone eavesdropping, it sounded like he was saying something sweet to her, his tone a little cheerful but Gwen knew the real emotion behind it. He meant it as a threat. "I know you aren't keen on being back and since you can't do anything to go back to them you are acting as if nothing had happened. Don't lie to me."

Gwen studied him. He knew her all too well. She wanted to be with him, but not in this way. Not fighting against the Gargoyles. She still wanted to help them, even though they did turn their back on her. Erik had just stood there as James took her away. He had been using her, but she couldn't really blame him. She would have done the same thing in his shoes.

"I won't lie to you James, I'm sorry," she finally said.

"Good." He pulled her a little closer. "Because if you ever run from me again, I will rip your heart out. Do we have an understanding?"

Gwen grinned playfully. "Jamesy, you know exactly what to say for a girl to love you."

His eyes narrowed. "I mean it. Don't you ever do that to me again."

She looked at him. He really meant what he said. He had never been this serious with her at any time during the last few centuries and it frightened her. Gwen didn't realize how much she hurt him when she left. She didn't leave because of him, it had nothing to do with him, which could be the problem. She never thought about how it would affect him, and it hurt him that she never considered his feelings. She broke his heart and his trust. How long would it take her to mend what she had done? She didn't know now, but she knew she wanted to, eventually.

"I won't. Not after how they betrayed me like that," she said. Whether that was a lie, she didn't know. She wanted to help them but she wouldn't run away from him again, that was for sure.

"Good." He let go of her arm. "Now, are you almost done?"

"Just about." She bit her lip, thinking of the last things she needed. "Here, pay for these while I go grab something real quick." Gwen grabbed his wallet and pulled out a wad of notes. "Be back in a jiffy."

James sighed as he grabbed the clothes. Gwen smiled and ran off with the money in the other direction. She needed to grab a certain shade of lipstick that she had been eyeing for months now.

Dark Side, by M.A.C. was what it was called. Gwen didn't need to try the shade on, she knew it would be perfect for her. The dark red matched that of her blood, a sinful crimson would catch every man's eye, even the good ones.

The fancy clothed ladies that were also shopping in the store eyed her thrashed wardrobe. A loose t-shirt, loose jeans, white converse, and a leather jacket of James'. Gwen definitely felt like something out of *Grease*, not that she cared. She could destroy any snob's glance with an even stronger intimidating glance of her own, or even a couple of straight fingers.

Gwen handed the worker the pounds for the lipstick, along with some other essentials, and skipped back to where James waited for her. She was happy to finally get what she wanted. It wasn't something she could steal since they didn't give you the item until it was paid for. She could have stolen the demo version of the lipstick but that was just gross, even by her standards.

James gave her a suspicious look as she approached.

"What was that about?" he inquired as they started down the street. The weather wasn't as nice as the day before, with overcast and a slight chance of rain. It made it feel more like London. Damp.

"Oh, just needed some makeup. Figured you wouldn't mind." She held up the little bag and shook it. The items rattled inside.

He rolled his eyes. "You and your lipstick, I swear."

She smiled. "Oh, believe me James, it makes all the difference in convincing men to come into the shadows with me."

"I would go into the shadows with you with or without lipstick." He gave her a little peck on the cheek, hinting at something more.

"You knew what I meant."

"I did, I was just simply agreeing to it," he commented as they stepped down the steps into the Underground.

People with shopping bags, just like them, rushed to their train. One little girl, like a dog with a big stick, got her bag stuck in the little gates each person had to walk through to get into the station. An Underground worker yelled at her to get going, using his own card to reopen the gate. She hurried along, embarrassed. Silly girl.

As they entered the fork between the Bakerloo line and the Piccadilly line, Gwen pointed down toward a different route than what they had come on. "Can we get on the Piccadilly? I need to pick something up."

"And what's that?" James questioned, sounding suspicious.

"My bike," she grinned widely. "It's at the Gargoyles' flat, which I presume is vacant now that you took me back."

"What if it isn't?" he asked as they stepped onto the car.

"Well, then, wouldn't that be a fun surprise."

The train jerked back and forth as it made its way down the tracks. People held on as the darkness of the tunnel engulfed them. Gwen and James just leaned against the back of the car, watching as passengers went about their business. They didn't have a clue about the war brewing around them.

They got off at South Kensington station. It was a good area with moderate traffic, but not too much in the side streets. It was the perfect place to hide, as the Gargoyles had done in this area often. Unlike James, they actually had the sense to find a small place that didn't stand out like his ostentatious condo did.

They found her bike, which was still parked out in front of the building. Gwen hurried over and hugged her heap of machinery.

"So that's where my bike went," James said as he

approached.

"You mean *my* bike? She was mine and has always been mine. I told you that then and I'm telling you it now, mine," she retorted.

"Alright, it's yours. I don't want that monstrosity anyway," he commented, trying to make her mad. It did. "Where's the sidecar?"

"Long gone. I didn't need it any more. I always rode solo. Besides, I liked using the back seat better than that thing," she explained.

He gave it a look over. "How did you keep it running for so long?"

"Why do you act so surprised? I learned the ins and outs of this thing a long time ago."

"Just surprised you didn't run it off a cliff or something. You do like to go crazy on it."

"Yeah, I have to admit it's pretty sturdy, not like the new stuff, I would break one of those in a week. Did once, actually," she replied.

He stopped in front of it and laughed. "We are going to stand out on that thing, you know that right?"

"Would you rather stand out on a nice ride, or have to backtrack through the Underground because Jürgen picked the stupidest place for the headquarters?"

"Bike it is. Now come, we better go and get ready for tonight."

Gwen climbed on the bike and James behind her, still holding the bag of clothes from earlier.

"Hold on," she said as she revved the bike and raced down the street.

CHAPTER 34

Collin couldn't believe what had just happened. He had sat in front of the king himself in Buckingham Palace. Even though he spent his nights routinely doing things no other human did, this made him feel more special than ever before. He tried not to look as giddy as he felt.

Despite the excitement, something nagged at him. Through the entire conversation, King William had stared at a platter and cutlery that was laid before him, without picking them up by accident. And, Collin noted, it was silver. As they already were aware of, silver was one of both the demons and minions' weakness. The King couldn't touch it, at least not without burning himself.

"The demons got to him first, didn't they? And made

him into a minion?" Collin asked as he and Erik walked through Saint James's Park. Hugo should be meeting up with them shortly.

Erik didn't say anything to his comment, but kept his eyes forward, thinking. It answered his question. They had gotten to him first. The demons were winning this war thus far.

"What are we going to do now?" Collin asked.

Erik looked up at the sky. "I don't know, they're moving faster now. Jürgen got here the same time we did, and he's already turned the king into a minion. This time is different. They took the others slowly, stirring up a rebellion. I didn't see this coming."

"How do you know they didn't start five years ago when James was here? He could have turned the king then. We just didn't know," Collin suggested.

"Maybe, but highly unlikely. It doesn't seem like anything else is on his mind other than Gwen. He puts her first and everything else second."

"Surprising a demon can put anything before power."

"To him, she is power. It's a feeling of rebellion for them to be together. It's against many rules in the Heavens to be together in that way, especially with that blood bond of theirs."

"James mentioned that. What exactly is a blood bond?"

Erik turned to him and sighed. "It connects them through eternity. It's a taboo, even for demons, but they did it anyway. That's why James is so keen to have her. Together they are stronger and it explains why they have won against many of us over the years."

"Oh." Collin became silent, letting what he had just said sink in.

That's what a blood bond was, a connection through eternity. Collin repeated the words over and over again. Eternity. He couldn't believe he had been so stupid not to realize it in the beginning. When she had said her heart belonged to someone else, she really meant it. It wasn't just some nasty breakup, there wasn't even a breakup. There could never be a breakup. His heart raced. What then, he thought, did he mean to her? Was he just a toy for her boredom, or did she actually care?

It made sense now why James had gone to so much trouble to get her. It wasn't just about her being a demon or the possibility of her betraying the demons, it was about her betraying James. She left James to pick up the pieces as she ran off to help the Gargoyles. But where did Collin came into the equation? He still didn't quite understand it all.

"How did it go?" Hugo ran up from behind them, panting.

"Hugo? Are you okay?" Collin had never seen him out of breath, or, well, human-ish. It was strange.

"Oh, had to run away from a mob. This entire time in fact. Demons may run faster than people, but I sure can't." He wiped the sweat off his brow. "I really hate running. Fighting I can do. Running, not so much."

"The demons got to him first," Erik said, not wanting to dilly dally on small talk. Hugo just stared at him with undisguised horror.

"What? That can't be."

"Someone brought in silverware. He couldn't touch it. I heard him drop the spoon as I left. He's been turned."

Hugo ran his hands through his sweaty hair. "Then we have no help from the inside."

"Nope. We can't do anything to him either or the entire nation will go into a panic. They thought this one through," Erik explained. Collin agreed, there was nothing they could do about King William. If they tried anything, there could be great consequences from the human world.

"Indeed," Hugo whispered.

"I think we should get ready to leave after…" Erik paused, not wanting to say the next word. "The contract. Don't you agree?"

Hugo nodded. "But what until then?"

"If we keep trying, we might catch a break."

"Our luck seems to have run out if you haven't noticed…" Hugo held up three fingers. "There's only three of us."

"We are still alive Hugo," Erik said. "And that's all that matters."

"I thought you two got something in exchange though?" Collin was curious if they'd finally tell him what it was. They just stared at him.

Hugo broke the silence. "Right, I guess there's that."

"What *did* you two get in return?" Collin questioned.

Erik winced. Collin looked back and forth between the two of them as he impatiently waited for an answer.

"Seriously, someone say something!" Collin yelled out.

"You," Erik blurted.

Collin blinked in confusion. "What?"

"You," he repeated sadly.

It still didn't make sense to him. "What about me?"

Erik grabbed him by the scruff of his neck and pulled Collin toward him.

"What the..." Collin began.

"Remember that night, five years ago. Remember all of it." Erik stared into his eyes.

It came back to him in a flash. That briskly cool night when he and Gwen were walking back to his flat. She wore that cute little white summer dress he had picked out specially for her. Her eyes glistened in the moonlight and her hair was in tight curls, how she usually had it. Life seemed to be perfect, at least for that moment in time. Then, from the darkness, a man stepped out of the shadows. He didn't know that it was James at that time. Collin remembered the expression on Gwen's face. Horror. She knew him. She stepped back in fear, holding her arm out in front of Collin, as if trying to protect him. He found this odd at the time but now he knew better.

James and Gwen stared at each other, not letting their eyes part for a moment.

"Gwen, do you know this man?" Collin asked.

James chuckled playfully as he stepped forward. "Who is this Gwen?"

"None of your business James," she growled. "Walk away."

"You really think I'm going to walk away? You really think after seventy fucking-long years I am just going to walk away?" he questioned.

Gwen stepped back. "James, I'm warning you."

"If this man is bothering you, we can just leave." Collin tried to get her to pull her away, but she wouldn't budge.

"Is this the guy you left me for?" He took a quick look at him. "Some human?"

"I didn't leave you for him."

"So you won't mind if I dispose of him then?" James smiled.

Gwen's eyes narrowed. "Don't you dare!"

James moved toward him. Collin had never seen anyone move so fast. He wouldn't have gotten out of the way in time if it hadn't been for Gwen intervening in the nick of time. She grabbed James and shoved him against the wall in the alleyway. That's when his life fell apart. The moment she showed him her true self. Gwen's eyes turned a monstrous yellow. He felt his body freeze with fear. He watched her teeth piercing into the neck of the man she held. She was a demon.

"Gwen!" He didn't know if he said her name out of fear or surprise, but it was enough to distract her for a second, which turned out to be a second too long. James got away from her grasp and went straight for Collin. He should have run, when he had the chance, but he knew now it wouldn't have made a difference. The feeling of something sharp stabbed into his neck.

Collin fell to the ground, dead.

No wait, Collin thought, he couldn't be dead. He was standing there, that couldn't have happened. Then more memories came. Opening his eyes, seeing Erik and all the blood. Lots of blood. He remembered panicking and Erik telling him to look into his eyes.

"You erased my memories," Collin said, coming back to the present. "You kept this from me this entire time!"

Erik glanced around. "Shh, don't cause a scene Collin."

He wanted to punch Erik. He had lied to him. James had killed him, yet he was still alive.

"How?" he questioned.

Erik sighed. "Gwen gave you some of her blood before you fully passed away."

"What?" Collin paused, trying to put the pieces together. "What does that make me?"

"A hybrid, but you aren't fully turned. That was our deal. Gwen has to fully turn you."

"And you didn't think to ask me first?"

"You don't really have a choice, Collin. You're dying. Her blood should have only kept you alive for a year, maybe two. We expanded it," Erik said.

"For five years?"

"It took a while to track her down after James spooked her but yes, for the past couple years you should have been dead."

Collin ran his fingers through his hair viciously. He was dead, he should be dead. Those weren't words a man wanted to hear. "What's a hybrid?"

"It's a human demon," Hugo began. "You have the powers of a demon but your soul is still intact. No demon will ever possess you."

The information overwhelmed him. He needed to get away. He needed to walk this one out. He couldn't be around Erik and Hugo, not after finding out they had lied to him all this time.

"I gotta take a walk," Collin spun on his heel and started in the other direction.

"Collin, wait!" Hugo called after.

"I will meet you both back at the flat later. Don't worry about me, nothing will happen. You made a *deal*."

He left them standing there.

CHAPTER 35

James watched as his love fixed her lipstick in the mirror. Gwen pasted the dark crimson on her puckered lips. She was right, it really did make a striking difference. She had crimped her hair for that night and wore the little black dress he had bought for her. The black lace that made up the top portion made her light skin look that much more seductive. He had to admit, even after centuries of being together, she always looked as good as the day they fell.

Gwen closed the cap of the lipstick and came out of the bathroom to where he had been admiring her. She gave him a suspicious look.

"What are you looking at me like that for?" she asked.

"That's an interesting color of lipstick, what is it

called?" he questioned.

"It's called *Dark Side*." She let the words linger on her lips.

"Fitting. I like it." He leaned in and kissed her.

"That's the point," she remarked as she went back and fixed what she had smudged.

"That it's fitting, or that you wanted me to like it?"

"That it is fitting. You liking it has nothing to do with why I picked it." She snapped the cap back on.

James smiled as they headed outside. It was dark now and the street lights began to flicker on.

Their job now was to find the three men that guarded the Prime Minister and convert them into minions. Jürgen should be working on his two while they found their lucky three. From what Jürgen had found, the three men James and Gwen were after hung out at a bar near Tower Bridge on the south side of the river. It was getting late; hopefully they already had a few drinks in them to make the job of turning them effortless.

"Come in a little after me. Don't want to look like a couple," Gwen said to him as they stood outside the entrance.

"Of course." James gave her another kiss and watched as she turned to the pub. He tilted his head as he watched her enter the bar. Her dress came up pretty high. He made a mental note to not get blood on that dress.

After waiting a few minutes, he himself went in. Gwen was standing next to a table near the back, a glass of red wine in her hand. She was talking to a group of men. The three men they needed to turn. James stepped up to the bar.

"I'll take a scotch. Laphroaig. Neat."

The bartender quickly poured it out and handed him the glass. James placed the money on the table and turned, scanning the area for a seat. The only available one was near where Gwen stood, with a group of girls. It must have been his lucky day.

"Evening girls, mind if I join you? Can't seem to find a seat in here." James smiled.

"No problem, you can sit here." The red head bit her lip, pointing to an unfilled seat on their table.

James nodded. "Thank you." He sat down. "My name is James."

"Mine's Jennifer," the red head said. She pointed to her two dark haired friends. "This is Kayla and Melanie."

"Pleased to meet you," James smiled.

"So," Melanie began, stirring the drink in front of her. "What brings you to this pub? I haven't seen you around before."

"Oh, just the game. I'm supposed to be meeting someone here but they haven't showed up yet. Once they come I can get out of your hair," he explained as he took a drink. It was a lie. He didn't even know who was playing.

"Oh, don't worry. You aren't a bother." Kayla winked flirtatiously.

James wished he could give the table full of girls more of his attention, but he had to keep an eye on Gwen. He didn't trust her yet, but he really wanted to see how far the girls at the table would take him. Acting as if he was turning his attention to the game, James listened to Gwen.

"If you don't mind, we're trying to watch the match," one of the three men said to Gwen. James glanced over at them. She looked shocked. It must have been a while since she tried to coax men out of a pub.

She smiled. "Sorry to be a bother." Gwen turned and headed for the bar. James debated following her. He didn't want to seem to be with her, but he also knew she would be upset, otherwise. Sometimes, women can be so damn difficult to read.

Just as he was about to give up and go talk to her, one of the three men got up from the table and approached her. He was the youngest of the bunch, short brown hair and a fresh tattoo on his arm. It was of a number. James tried to deduce what it was for, but couldn't come up with anything. He started pleasantly talking to Gwen.

James decided to move to the bar. The girls at his table looked upset, and he wished he could stay but he needed to make sure Gwen wouldn't say anything stupid to further piss those guys off. A seat had opened on the other side of Gwen so he took it. Setting his now empty drink down, he ordered another.

"Sorry about my friends back there, it was rude what they said to you," the man said to Gwen.

"It's no problem, I'm used to things like that." Gwen gave him her sweet smile, irresistible to most men, if not all including James himself. James was just used to it, or at least he liked to think he was immune to its disarming effect

The man ordered a Guinness. "Now, tell me, what's your name?"

She held out her hand. "Gwen Erebus." James just about choked on the scotch he just sipped.

"Erebus?" the man commented as he shook her hand. "Isn't that something from Greek mythology?"

Yes, James thought, yes it was.

"Yes. It's the primordial deity of darkness." Gwen bit her lip, waiting for the man's reaction.

"Really? How did your family end up with a name like that?"

"It's just a name. I'm not even sure really how it got attached to our family." She had picked the name up in Greece a long time ago. It was what they called her.

"Well that explains why you look like a goddess then," the man commented, edging closer towards her.

Gwen laughed. "I wouldn't go that far."

"Well then, maybe you are just an angel that fell out of the sky," the man flirted.

James had to try to not laugh. If he only knew the truth behind that statement.

"What's your name?" Gwen changed the subject, resisting the temptation to reply to the fallen angel comment.

"John Smith," he answered.

"No, really?"

"That's my name," he smiled. "A lot of people don't believe me."

"Well, it's nice to meet you John Smith." Gwen sipped her wine. "You know, I knew a John Smith once, looked a little like you. Long time ago though."

James rubbed his face. She always liked saying whatever was on her mind.

"Yeah, there's a bunch of us out there," John agreed.

"Through time and space, yes," Gwen added. "So tell me, what do you do?"

"Oh, I'm an accountant."

A lie. A lot of men in his line of work lie, not wanting to compromise their job. It was standard procedure.

"That sounds... interesting," Gwen said.

"It's a job, that's for sure." He leaned his elbow on the bar. "But let's talk about you. What do you do for a living?"

"I'm a travel writer. I go around Europe, writing about different places and adventures I've had."

"That must be a lot of fun."

"Yeah, it gets lonely though, especially when you have no one to travel with."

James shook his head. She caused herself to be lonely with this whole quasi-redemption twist in her life.

"That's too bad, maybe you will find someone," he said.

"Yeah, hopefully I will find someone who likes traveling as much as I." Gwen looked down at her drink, stirring it.

"Well," John began. "I really love traveling so if you don't find someone soon, I might just have to join you for an adventure."

"I would love that." Gwen paused. "You know, I'm supposed to check out a new club just down the street. Want to join me?"

"You know, I would." He stood up. "Let me just tell my friends I'm leaving."

Gwen watched as he left.

James turned his head towards her, whispering. "You know, if you asked me to join you on your travels, I would have gone."

Gwen shook her head. "I knew you were going to say something like that. Now turn away. I don't know you."

James looked back at his drink as John came back to the bar.

"I can't stay too long, I have to get up early tomorrow. Big day at my firm."

"Sure, that's fine," Gwen gestured toward the door. "Ready?"

He nodded and opened the door for her. James counted to five in his head before following them, telling the table of girls he would miss them.

They had already traveled a ways down the street. James watched as the man wrapped his arm around Gwen. She must have said she was cold. James fought off the temptation of ripping his head off right then and there. They rounded a corner, and he ran after them.

As he got to them, Gwen already had the man against the wall, eyes yellow.

"What the hell?" the man yelled.

Gwen bit into his neck. James smiled. To see his girl enjoying the lust for blood once again made him feel content, as if her leaving never happened, even though in the back of his mind he knew it did. In the back of his mind he knew she could pretend to do anything, even look as if she never changed.

She backed off. "Well, now we just have to wait until he wakes up a minion, then we can get the other two."

"What did you say to make the others ask you to leave?" James questioned, curious as to why they had sent her away.

"I just asked if I could take a seat."

"Really?"

"Yeah, the other two are married so I must have been too much of a temptation to let me sit near them." She grinned.

The newly-created minion stirred awake. Gwen pulled him up. "Now, I need you to get the two buddies of yours to meet us out here. You understand?" Gwen licked his wound clean. It had healed already.

He nodded and left.

"Got your lust for blood back," James commented.

She laughed. "Funny thing is that it never went away."

Moments later, John brought the other two outside. "What the hell John," one commented. "What was so urgent for us to come out here for?"

"Us." Gwen's eyes flickered yellow.

They were upon them in a matter of seconds. James had his turned in a flash, biting his neck and letting the venom enter the man's body. It was an easy process, he had to admit. They could just bite the victim, venom entering their body and killing them. Then a spirit from hell came and possessed the body. That was it. There were countless numbers of demon spirits in the underworld; they battled it out to be the next ones to have control within a human body. It was quite fantastic.

Gwen, on the other hand, still held her prey, not turning him. She just stared at him as he screamed.

"Please, I have a family, I have children! Don't kill me!"

James watched as she hesitated. He had thought that maybe she didn't care about the humans, that she left those thoughts behind. Apparently he was wrong.

He ran up next to her. "Gwen, hurry up! You're going to draw attention."

"Right." She bit his neck. Letting the body fall to the ground, she turned to him with a smile. "I forgot what I was doing. Funny."

James just stared at her. She wasn't back, she still felt for these worthless beings. Everything had been a ruse. She had lied to him.

He would have to do something about that.

CHAPTER 36

Erik watched as Collin walked off, retreating into the dark streets beyond. He didn't want Collin to know about the deal quite yet, but he hated lying to him over and over again. He needed to know the truth, Erik knew, but he had always been afraid of his reaction. Collin actually took it a lot better than he thought he would. Erik expected cursing, name calling, yelling, and stomping off, then never being seen again. Collin only got to the stomping off part, but he would be back sooner or later. Collin knew it was important for him to help their mission, now he just knew the reason why.

At least now he could prepare for what was to come.

"What do we do now Erik?" Hugo questioned after Collin had left their sight. "You think he will be back?"

"He will be back, don't worry. It was probably better for him to know now rather than when Gwen turns him," Erik said. "Then he would be pissed and powerful."

"That's true," Hugo sighed. "You think he will let himself be turned?"

Erik looked around at all the humans surrounding them, going about their day cheerfully. "One thing we have learned over the years is that humans fear death, no matter what. If given the choice, they will prolong their life, no matter the consequences."

Hugo nodded. "Even so, we still should be careful."

Erik examined the expression on his face. Hugo looked concerned, whether it was for Collin or for their future, he wasn't sure. "You want to follow him?"

"It would make me feel better, yes."

"Then go ahead. I trust him enough to go on his own, but if you want to check on him, you can. I'm not worried about any demons hurting him, given the deal." Erik gestured toward where Collin had gone.

Hugo kept his eyes focused on where Collin had disappeared. "Alright, meet back at the flat?"

"Yeah, sounds good."

With that, Hugo hurried after Collin. Hugo had better be careful about not being seen by Collin, or else Collin may get even angrier with them. Hugo was good at following people though, even demons, given the right equipment.

He knew he should go straight back to the flat and let Elizabeth know what they had found, but Erik also needed to take a walk. He needed to calm his head after everything that happened that afternoon. It was almost dinner time now, and the streets were beginning to get increasingly crowded with hungry Londoners.

Just north of him was Hyde Park, a place he hadn't ventured into for quite some time. Deciding to meditate on everything there, he headed in that direction.

It was busy this time of year with people from all over the world walking, cycling, and sitting in the park. The nice summer days brought everyone out to enjoy the sunshine, if not just for the warmer weather. It was like a little taste of paradise. Children, adults, the elderly, they were all of different generations but here for one thing, to enjoy this rare beautiful day.

Erik watched as bikes rode past him. How he wished he could relax for one moment to enjoy such a day as this. He hadn't been able to relax for the past two thousand years, since the beginning of this war, and even before then. He didn't know the real meaning of the word. After this war maybe, but not today. Never today.

Erik took a seat at a bench and watched the passersby. They went on with their daily lives, not knowing what was going on around them. Destruction, corruption, deception, lies, all of it crafted by angels who used to stand for something right, something glorious. Then they fell and now here they were, playing in the filth they got blinded by.

He needed to figure out what to do with Collin. Now that he knew everything, he felt even worse than ever. It was only a matter of time before James made Gwen finish what she started. He just hoped everything would run smoothly. It never did but he still hoped.

As he sat with these thoughts, a little boy sat right down next to him. Erik looked over at him. Probably only about five or six years old, his golden blonde hair would have shined if it wasn't so cloudy that day. His bright green eyes stared up at him with curiosity.

"Can I help you?" Erik asked cheerfully. He found children to be some of the funniest creatures there was.

The boy didn't falter. "What are you doing?"

The statement puzzled Erik. "What do you mean?"

"Why are you just sitting here staring at the park when you should be out doing other things?" the boy questioned.

"Like what?" he inquired, curious where the boy was going with this conversation.

"Like stopping those bad men before they destroy everything," the boy said.

Erik blinked. This was exactly why children were funny. Before Erik could say anything more, the boy's mother came and grabbed her boy by the hand and started to drag him away.

"Come on, Justin, what have I told you about talking to strangers?" she exclaimed.

"But mother, he's not a stranger, he's an angel." Justin tried to pull his mother back to Erik. She didn't budge.

"Don't be absurd, angels don't look like that," she replied sharply.

Erik watched as they walked away. He chuckled. It was strange how children could see the truth a lot clearer than adults. They were more open to the truth than what people tell them is true, he supposed. Although he technically wasn't an angel. An angel was a messenger, and he was far more than just a messenger.

Deciding to head back to the flat, Erik got up and started walking down the paths that filled the park. Magnificent statues littered the park, representing different people throughout history, stories, wars, ideas, and thoughts. Humans took pride in monuments for those who had passed, as if it will cause their spirit to stay with the Earth forever. They thought if people didn't remember that these people once existed, then the memories of these people from the past would be lost forever. He didn't understand how they could care so much about this world and be blind about the one that was to come after it.

As he admired a statue that memorialized the veterans who were lost in the Second World War, he heard some yelling coming from the north section of the park. Having to know what it was, Erik hurried over to get a glimpse.

Shouts and signs engulfed the crowd, then Erik remembered. This was preacher's corner where anyone or any group could stand up for what they believe in. He took a look at the people. Signs were held for almost everything. Signs about love, signs about law, signs about loss. Everything that wanted to be said was said.

As he listened to the different speakers, he heard one of them call out sinners. The person told everyone they were sinners and that none of them knew the true love that God provided. He assumed everyone didn't believe the "truth" the way he saw it and called those "others" liars, adulteresses, cheaters, selfish, name after name. Some people in the audience had made signs of their own, including one that said 'if he's going to heaven, I'd rather go to hell.' Erik felt sorry for them for not understanding the real core of ethical good, but he felt most sorry for the preacher who didn't understand what 'love your brethren as yourself' truly meant.

One sign stood out to him. It soberly declared that "The end is coming!" It was something humans had been exclaiming for generations. They had always feared it no matter the time period. It was something they didn't quite understand yet thought it to be true. Little did they know that maybe this time they were right.

Erik made his way through the crowd. He wondered how many people out there actually cared about what the people were saying or if they just found the whole thing amusing. Lots of people ignored the preachers as they walked by, but Erik enjoyed reading what people had to say in the form of expressive signs and banners. What they considered to be freedom.

It was starting to get late and Erik knew he should be getting back to rest, but there was one thing he wanted to check since he was in the neighborhood. He wanted to check whether Gwen had taken her bike back. He had left it there for her to take, he knew how much it meant to her.

Rounding the corner, he saw that it was gone. She had gone back to their side, otherwise she wouldn't have shown them where they had been staying. Or the bike meant that much more to her. Either way, he knew she would take it. That bike seemed to mean a lot to her and he still didn't understand why.

Sighing, he headed back towards their new flat, where the rest of the group would be waiting, he hoped. He told them they needed to wait until the demon's first move but that doesn't mean they would listen. He himself needed some fresh air to think. Now that he had it, he was ready for whatever lies ahead.

CHAPTER 37

Gwen didn't feel like celebrating with James. It had been a long while since she had drunk human blood and the neutral feeling about it hadn't come back to her just yet. She used to take pleasure in it, now there was something inside of her that made her want to stop, that made her hate what she was doing. Despise it, really. She couldn't explain it to James, it was just a feeling. A feeling she didn't know she had until that day when she sabotaged everything they had planned and let the Gargoyles live another day.

James had noticed her hesitate with the man she was told to turn. She couldn't help it, he had a family. She had never thought about their families before. It had never occurred to her through the years. She tried not to think about it as they walked, not when James walked right next to her. They had been so close that he could read her thoughts by her body language. He would see how she acted and start asking more questions, none of which she had an answer to.

She'd tried to make a joke out of it, but she saw the way he looked at her. He didn't believe her, but he didn't say anything either. He had to be planning something to get her to fall back to his level, but what that was she didn't know. She didn't want to know.

Gwen held James' hand as he led her to the venue. James knew where he was going, which wasn't a big surprise. He knew where the parties lasted all night and people were high off their asses. Easy marks.

They came upon the club. It was just the type of club they needed: dark, loud and busy. There shouldn't be too much suspicion, kids did crazy things in places like this. No one would think twice about it.

Jürgen was already standing outside the venue, eyeing them as they walked up. "Did you get them?" he asked.

"Yes, all three. Exactly as planned," James said.

"So no problems?" Jürgen glanced at Gwen as if she would instantly be a problem no matter what. She took offense to that, even though they almost did have a problem because of her, but he didn't have to suspect her automatically. It was uncalled for.

"None," James lied for her.

Gwen wasn't surprised he would lie to Jürgen like that. He thought he could handle her and didn't want the others breathing down his neck about how she was supposedly acting up in some way. Out of all of them, he probably was the only one who could handle her, but she didn't let him know that. It would increase his ego way too much and he would become cockier than he already was. What fun that would be.

"How about you?" Gwen asked. "Did you get yours?"

"Of course, and a few others in the mix, just to be safe," he grinned.

"Why did you bother coming if you already had fed?" Gwen questioned, putting her arm around James as if she didn't need Jürgen wasting their time. She didn't want to spend any more time with Jürgen than necessary. Not after what she had done.

"Just wanted to make sure your end was taken care of. Don't want to find things unfinished," Jürgen said.

Gwen raised an eyebrow. "Are you suggesting that I would sabotage this mission?"

"Yes," he shot back.

"Hey, stop it. We're here to have fun," James interrupted their pre-fight banter.

"That's right, Jürgen." Gwen winked as she grabbed James' tie and pulled him toward the door. "Let's have some fun."

Gwen was the only one who had to show her ID. She hated how people treated younger-looking folks nowadays. They acted as if they had no rights and couldn't do anything. She was smarter and stronger than all the beings on this planet but she was always treated as a child. What they didn't know was she would get her revenge soon.

They entered to find music blaring. Gwen winced. It had been a while since she had been to any sort of club. Back then the music was quieter. A lot quieter. In fact, she realized that the last time she scouted for humans at a club was in the twenties with all the fun music and the real dancing and mixed drinks. Life definitely was much more fun back then, when she didn't have a care in the world about "redemption," or remorse over the atrocities she'd caused.

"Things have changed," she exclaimed to James.

"Yes they have," he answered. "But I guess you wouldn't know, you let all that time slip by without a care."

She ignored the last part of the comment. "In the twenties the music wasn't this loud. I liked it better then."

"So did I but we can't really do anything about that."

"Well, we could," she jeered. "It just wouldn't be practical."

James smiled. If they had time to waste, they could easily turn enough humans into minions and bring back the twenties, relive their glory days for a short time. It wouldn't be that hard, they could start up a vintage twenties themed club and such, but it still wouldn't be the same. It wouldn't be as fun as it was back then, before what inevitably happened around World War II.

Gwen noticed Jürgen's face. He didn't look too happy about being there. He didn't like scouting humans like this and she was surprised he had even come. He must really not trust her and wanted to see if she really had changed back. She would have to prove herself to him so he would stay off of her back. This was the perfect place to do it.

"Ready when you are," James exclaimed over the noise.

Gwen nodded and turned to the dance floor. Crowded with people, many she didn't even think were old enough to be there, she started dancing, or at least what humans considered dancing these days, and looking for single young men. She had many to choose from. Picking a young dark-haired man out of the crowd, she made her way toward him.

"Hey, crazy here isn't it?" She greeted him with her seductive smile.

The boys checked out her rather, she had to admit, short dress. Not the most revealing dress she had worn, but it was up there. He decided she was hot enough to acknowledge, as if she might not be.

"I've seen it crazier, actually."

Why couldn't he just agree? Was she really going to get another rejection? By the way he was looking at her, she really doubted it. She licked her lips.

"So, you care to dance?" she asked.

The boy gave her another glance through. "Sure."

He grabbed Gwen's hand and brought her in close. By the way he flirted with her, she doubted he had a girlfriend. This would make it easier to coax him toward the back of the club where no one would see them.

He ran his hands along her back, leaving them a little lower on her back than she would like. Gwen wrapped her arms around his neck, letting her eyes gaze into his. He had green eyes, a little like James, but his were a lot brighter and bold. Collin's were blue.

Gwen shook the thought of Collin out of her mind. She didn't want to think about him right then, or ever, for that matter. Not after the last moment she spent with him, when she wanted to take his blood so she wouldn't feel the pain of the triduanum any longer. If James hadn't stepped in, she may have done it.

Back to the boy she danced with. He wore casual clothes, as most boys that era did. No one dressed nicely anymore. It was a pity, really, people used to look nice all the time, professional and maybe even a little fake. She missed that.

Peering around the room, she saw James with a young blonde. She never got jealous as she knew all he saw was food or pawns in a war. She was the only being that ever truly mattered to him.

He, on the other hand, did sometimes get jealous when she was with a human. It was rare, actually, and she didn't know what set it off, but he would sometimes intervene with a target she had acquired and end it before she even started with the human guinea pig. It puzzled her, really, because back then humans didn't mean anything to her. It wasn't until Collin did she ever really feel any sort of true affection for them. It was then that James had a real reason to get jealous.

Three songs passed as they danced intimately with each other, tracing the curves of each other's body. Gwen was ready for James to show up at any second and beat the boy into a pulp, but he never did.

She placed her hand on his shoulder, leaning in. "Hey, want to head toward the back," she whispered. "It's getting a little too crowded for my tastes."

He glanced at her hand but didn't move it. "Oh, I probably shouldn't. I have a girlfriend back home."

Gwen was surprised, he really didn't act like he had a girlfriend, though it wouldn't be the first time. "Back home?"

"Yeah, in America. I am here on vacation with some friends."

"Well." Gwen leaned in closer. "I won't tell anyone if you won't."

"When you put it that way." He grinned.

Gwen smiled as she pulled him toward the back of the club, into the shadows. Once she felt that no one would see, Gwen shoved him against the wall and kissed him firmly. He wrapped his arms around her and pulled her even closer to him. Gwen slowly made her way down to his neck and quickly placed her hand on his mouth so he couldn't scream as she bit his neck.

He passed out in a matter of seconds. Gwen kept him upright, waiting for him to awaken as a minion. She licked the excess blood off of his neck. She didn't want to waste it. Every drop counted. She needed to bring her strength up, just in case James figured out what she was about to do.

She realized she never got the boy's name. Gwen tried to take a guess at it. Jeffery maybe, Tom, Charles, she really didn't know. It didn't matter anymore, he was no longer that person. His soul had left and in its place was a demon spirit.

Gwen felt him jerk back to life. His eyes were glassy and dark, as most minions' were.

"Now, I need you to do me a favor," Gwen whispered into his ear.

CHAPTER 38

Collin kicked a tree stump in anger. He cursed, regretting the action. Now he was pissed off *and* his toe hurt. Great. Shoving his fists into his pockets, he sauntered further through the park.

They had lied to him, suppressed his memories, and used him. He felt like a pawn in their game now, slowly making it to the other side so he may be turned into something more useful. Used beyond repair. How could they, he thought, how could they just think he would be okay with it?

He was just a human, perhaps that's why they didn't bother mentioning it. He wouldn't understand, he would break, and he would be too weak to handle it. They were wrong. He could handle this, and he would show them exactly that.

What they had told him explained a lot. It explained the reason he could sense them before they approached, as if a smell lingered with them. He had sensed Gwen in London before he even knew she was around. It's also why Hugo and Erik had kept him around and wanted him to help with finding minions. More importantly, it explained the horrifying nightmares he'd had since the day Gwen gave him her blood.

Collin stopped abruptly and replayed that thought. Gwen gave him blood. Her blood. She defied James just to save him. She cared enough to save him. He let a smile form on his lips, even though he was still pissed at Erik and Hugo for not telling him.

The question now was, why didn't she finish the job? He would have died if Erik hadn't prolonged the effects. She must have known they would do something and let them do it. She probably hoped she wouldn't have to finish it if they figured something out.

That wasn't the case, though, he was dying. He didn't know how long he had. Gwen was supposed to turn him soon, part of the agreement with James. How long would he be a hybrid? How long would he be some unnatural creature?

Questions kept rolling through Collin's mind as he made his way toward Kensington. He didn't know he was heading toward there; it was just on instinct. West toward Chelsea and to his pub. To his home. But it wasn't his home anymore, he had to give it up. Now he knew why.

He would need to get the deed signed over to Hywel. He would ask questions but Collin knew he wouldn't be able to answer them. Where are you going? Why are you leaving? Are you coming back? He didn't know the answer to any of them so he figured he would just make up some lies. Say a job offer came up in the United States or something believable like that. Not helping to fight a war against good and evil.

Collin knew a place he needed to go before he left. He was already heading that direction, it wouldn't be too far of a walk. He quickened his pace, trying to get to his destination before rush hour really kicked in.

The neighborhood was nice with well-kept gardens, a quaint little church, and not many visitors. It was a good community to retire in. Collin opened the little gate and stepped on the stone steps that led to the home. It had been a while since he visited; he hoped she didn't hold a grudge but he wanted to see her one last time.

"Auntie." Collin opened the door. "It's me."

The home smelt of spices, bread, and fresh-cut roses, as it always did. Trinkets cluttered each and every room. Little dolls sat on shelves, staring at him with their beaded eyes. He always diverted his eyes from them. The shaggy carpet felt soft under his shoes. He thought about taking them off but he knew she didn't care.

"Collin?" her raspy voice came from the nearby room. He stepped into the doorway so she could see him. "It is you, how marvelous!"

He always lied to himself when he said he had no family. He didn't consider his great-aunt Claire to be family since he hated the rest of his family. The word family had negative connotations to him. No, he considered her to be a dear friend, or a mentor of some kind. Not his family.

"I'm sorry I haven't been around lately, I've been very busy at the pub," he explained as he gave her frail body a soft hug. She looked weaker than the last time he saw her, her skin clinging onto her bones as if she had nothing else left.

"Come, come, I know a busy boy when I see one. I understand your time is precious and you must use it wisely."

Her eyes still sparkled as they always did, letting Collin get a glimpse of the beautiful woman she once was. Wrinkles now drooped over her high cheekbones, her once black hair now white as the snow on a peaceful winter's eve. Aged to perfection, she always had said about herself.

"That's what I came to talk to you about, I'm leaving London."

"Pish-posh, you wouldn't leave this lively place." She grabbed for her walker and tried to lift herself up. "Now, let me get us a pot of tea."

Collin jumped up. "Let me get it, Auntie. I know where everything is."

"Such a sweet boy, knows his way around the kitchen. Much more helpful than that pesky father of yours." She scowled at the thought of him. Collin smiled at her comment as he went into the kitchen and readied the tea. "You are definitely a black sheep, you know? You are the only kind person in the whole family, except for myself of course."

"Of course, Auntie, of course." Collin brought the platter into the living room. "One sugar or two?"

"Do you really have to ask?"

Two it was. The clink of the sugar cubes filled the silent room and Collin poured the cream, waiting for the tea to steep.

"That's why I never told them. I never told them where you went." Claire crinkled her nose. "I wouldn't give them the pleasure of tormenting you any longer."

"And I'm very grateful."

"You should be." She was known for her sassy tone. She would tell anyone what she thought and couldn't care less about their reaction to it. Collin poured the tea and handed the cup to her. "Thank you."

"You're welcome."

She took a sip of the tea and placed it on the table next to her. "Now, tell me about this trip."

"It isn't a trip, I'm leaving for good," Collin explained.

She looked at him, as a bit of sadness appeared on her face. "Why all of a sudden? Did they find you?"

Collin smiled. "No, nothing like that. Just some things came up and I need to get out of here."

Her eyes sharpened. "Are you in trouble? Did you get involved with the gangs? I heard they found bodies in the Thames recently."

"No, nothing like that," he answered, even though the bodies were the minions he had killed.

"Then what is it boy?"

"It's a girl," he answered, knowing it would get her off his back, and it technically wasn't a lie.

She clapped her hands in excitement. "A girl! How wonderful! What's her name?"

"Guinevere."

"Is she pretty?"

"She's an angel, auntie, a complete angel." Collin almost choked on his words. He had to say it, just once.

"I wish you could bring her here," Claire hinted.

"It's complicated. She has…" He paused, trying to find the right word. "Relations she is trying to get away from. That is why we have to leave."

"Where is she from?"

Heaven. "Cornwall."

"Marvelous, Collin, I am very happy for you." She reached for her walker. "Help me up, will ya? I have something to give you."

He helped her stand. "Auntie, you really don't have to give me anything."

"Pish-posh." It was her favorite saying, he swore. "You are leaving and I may never see you again and those relatives of ours aren't getting this."

She went over to a drawer and pulled out a ring. It was thick and made of a white gold, with a large garnet set in the middle. "This ring was snatched by our ancestor Grace Gallagher, one of Ann Bonny's pirate crew, from one of the fiercest pirates she ever came across. In some of the stories I was told, the pirate was said to be Satan himself, or herself. It depends who you talk to in our family, really."

She placed it in his hand. He examined it. The sides had carvings of intertwining designs like one would see in a church.

Collin shook his head. "I can't take this."

"I'm not going to take no for an answer Collin, and that's final. I don't want anyone but you to have it, you are the only one who would treasure such a thing, the rest of those dingbats would probably sell it on eBay for some drinking money," she rambled on.

"All right, I will keep it." He placed it on his right ring finger. Perfect fit.

"I wouldn't let you leave without it." She smiled.

Collin checked the time. It was almost five. "Auntie, I have to leave soon, people are waiting for me. I just wanted to say I am thankful for all the things you have done for me over the years."

"I know, you are sweetie." She wrapped her arms around him and kissed his cheek. "I won't tell anyone that you left either, or that you are happy. They might try to put a hex on ya or something."

"Thank you so much." Collin helped her back to her seat. "If I'm ever in London, I'll come by."

"I'm looking forward to it. And Collin," she began.

"Yes?"

"You are a good boy, don't let anyone tell you differently."

He smiled. "I won't."

Collin left the house, feeling heavy-hearted. He didn't want to leave her but it was for the best.

As he headed toward the gate, he ran into a familiar

face. "Vicar Evans?"

Evans jumped, not noticing that Collin had just walked out of the house. "Oh, Collin, what a surprise. I was just coming to check on your great-aunt."

Then it hit him. "You knew, didn't you?"

The vicar looked at him innocently. "What do you mean?"

"About everything. Erik and Hugo, Gwen, me getting turned. You *knew*."

Evans' shoulders sagged. "Collin, I'm sorry."

"You're my aunt's friend. How could you lie to me like this? Why didn't you tell me?"

"Because when two angels come to you and tell you to do something or not do something, you listen to them without question." His voice didn't waver. "Do not judge me for orders I had been given."

Collin shoved past him and left the garden. Evans called after him, but it was for nothing. He couldn't turn back. There wasn't a way to turn back.

CHAPTER 39

All the girls loved James, he found that to be a fact through most of his extended life. No matter when or where, they hung onto him and never seemed to want to let him go. It was just his unnatural charm he supposed. All the girls wanted a piece of him which was ironic because he wanted a piece of all the girls. Except in his case, it was literal.

James took note of Gwen. She was in the back with that dark-haired boy she had been dancing with. She seemed to have a thing for dark-haired men. It made him a little jealous this early in the game, but he wouldn't act on those emotions. He would let it slide for now. He was just a little overprotective of her, and now that instinct had grown in intensity after he found her with that human, Collin. Although he wasn't human anymore, which really made the situation even worse. He promised to get Gwen to turn him completely, but he didn't particularly want to. However, he didn't have a choice anymore. He knew if he could get her to change him, she would be back to her old self, mentally torturing the poor soul. He couldn't wait to watch that spectacle unfold.

James felt his eye twitch. Although it would be fun, he still didn't want that monstrosity to live. Though the Gargoyles would have to deal with him themselves, he still feared it would end the same way as the other one did. With the death of a demon.

He turned his attention back to the girls surrounding him. So many to choose from. He debated whether he would make them all minions or drink them dry. It was really a hard choice.

"This place is a snore, how about we go back to my place?" the blonde asked. He believed her name was Jessica.

James smiled. Those were the exact words he needed to hear to help make his final decision. Drink her dry it was.

"Yes, let's! It will be a lot more fun if we can go somewhere a little more intimate," Vicky said. She had red hair and cute little freckles dusting her cheeks.

They all were going to the same place. Even better, now he didn't have to choose one and make the others jealous, at least until the morning news came on. Then they wouldn't be jealous. They would also be able to ID him, so it really was better that they were all coming along.

"I'll go anywhere you want me to," James said. All the girls giggled.

They started pulling his tie in firm tugs, leading him toward the exit. He motioned for Jürgen to come to him. Jürgen rolled his eyes, knowing how girls acted around him. He said it was ridiculous but James knew he was just jealous.

"Hold on girls, I need to let my friend know I won't need a ride home," he said, pulling his tie away from them. He turned to Jürgen, who didn't have a very pleasant look on his face, not that he ever did.

"What?" Jürgen grunted.

"These lovely ladies are taking me back to their place. I don't know how long we will be." James eyed them as they waited for him at the door. "Do watch over Gwen while I'm gone. Make sure she isn't doing anything she isn't supposed to."

Jürgen looked at him squarely in the eyes, as if weighing his options of what he would do to her if she did. "You trust me to watch her?"

"I trust you know your place. Tell her I will meet her back at the apartment. Then we will meet back up with you tomorrow morning at the designated area," James didn't let his attention leave his girls.

"Fine," Jürgen glanced at the girls. "Don't do anything I wouldn't do."

"Oh, trust me." James eyes flashed yellow. "I will."

He walked out of there with his arms around two of

the girls. There were three of them. That would supply him with enough energy for tomorrow. It was going to be a big day after all. They were taking over the British Parliament and maybe killing one or two Gargoyles as well.

James knew Gwen, he knew she would somehow tell the Gargoyles what they were doing. So he gave her the wrong information of what was happening tomorrow. It was a set-up. If she didn't tell, no harm done. If she did, well, then she would pay for her betrayal with the life of a Gargoyle.

The girls dragged James down the darkened streets and toward their apartment, their high heels clicking on the cobblestone. He could never figure out how they walked in those wretched things. Gwen always wore boots, she wasn't dumb enough to wear heels, not with all the running she did. If a victim got out of her grasp, she would have a hell of a time going after them.

James loved girls like these. He didn't have to seduce them, they invited him into their home without all that sweet talk some girls took. It was all too easy. He debated how far he would let them go before devouring them. He needed to get back to Gwen sooner rather than later. He decided he would just have a little fun with them then for a short time.

Making it to their apartment, the girls grabbed him by his shirt and pulled him inside. He had already been invited in, luckily. It wasn't fun trying to explain the invisible wall that he sometimes was pulled into. Usually that killed any chance he had with getting with any of them, especially after all vampire stories being popular on the telly that warned them of such classic rules. No, he didn't have to worry this time, this time he took the precaution and made sure to be invited beforehand.

The girls began to rip away his shirt, staining it with the dark lipstick each of them had. Gwen was right, lipstick did make a difference. She wasn't going to be happy finding his shirt a mess like this but it wasn't his fault. Actually, it was because he could have killed them all by now, but he wanted to have just a little more fun before that.

They shoved him down on the couch. He hit it with a loud thump. The couch definitely looked softer than it felt. Vicky cranked up the stereo. Some sort of modern music played, James could never keep up with music these days. It all sounded the same to him. However, James wasn't against the music blaring because the louder it was, the less likely someone would hear them scream.

Jessica started to pull his tie to her and kissed him firmly on the lips. She ran her hands through his hair and started to pull off his shirt fully. He decided to let her kiss him a little more before he would end it all. The other girls went to get some beer out of the fridge.

The girl's breath tasted of cigarettes and cheap ale, which disgusted him. He was more of a cigar type of guy. Her lipstick smeared against his mouth, leaving that pasty feeling on his lips. Although he loved seeing it on women's lips, he hated the feeling against his own. He would have to live with it though, especially since Gwen loved her new shade of lipstick.

"What about your friends?" James asked as she kissed his neck.

"They'll be back, don't worry. Think you can handle all three of us?" she whispered playfully, pulling herself closer to him.

"Oh, believe me." His eyes flashed yellow as he moved her hair away from her neck. "I can."

He bit into her neck. That's when the screaming started, drowned out by the music. He let her body fall to the floor, covered in blood. James turned to the other girls. Hysterical, the other girls tried to run for the door, but none of them could beat him. He was a demon, he could travel faster than a mere human like them. He shut the door as they tried to open it.

James eyes flashed yellow. "Where are you going girls? The party has just begun."

CHAPTER 40

Erik laid out the map on the table, its crisp edges slicing his index finger. He jerked back from the sudden prick of pain. Good thing Gwen wasn't still with them, she would make sure none of that blood went to waste, even though only a drop fell to the ground. He rubbed the wound with his thumb and it vanished in an instant, leaving only dried blood that stained the surrounding area. Just like with demons, paper was troublesome. It never gave warning before an attack, just surprises you with a cut.

"So, where to next?" Elizabeth sat down across from him.

They didn't have any furniture other than a couple of bean-bag chairs and a few mattresses. They didn't bother making it cozy, not when they would have to leave again so soon.

"That's what we are going to figure out." Erik glanced at Hugo. He and Collin were back from their journey, not that Collin knew Hugo had followed him, or at least he didn't think so. Collin kept quiet, not arguing. Collin had accepted everything and moved on. Erik was impressed, not many would have done that. "What do you think, Hugo?"

"Well, they have France, the United States, Spain, and part of England. My guess is they will head east." Hugo pointed. "They do love Germany."

Erik nodded. "I'm surprised they didn't start there, though I guess they took the countries that gave them the most trouble the last time."

"That's for sure," Elizabeth commented, tapping her finger on her chin.

"They still would have won though, if it weren't for her," Hugo added, still staring deeply at the map. "Even though their army was collapsing."

"What did she do?" Collin questioned. It was the first words Erik heard him say in thirty minutes.

"She sabotaged everything for them," Erik began. "They had a perfect trap, she set it up of course, and something happened inside that strange little mind of hers and she made a distraction so we could get away."

Collin stared at him, as if he was waiting for something more. "Which was?"

"She shot Hitler," Hugo answered.

He looked at them, shocked. "I thought he committed

suicide."

Erik shook his head. "No, she shot him right in the head. I saw it. Then she ran, distracting the demons, especially James. They went after her instead of us, but she still got away. She has been running ever since."

Stepping up to the map, Collin sat down on one of the bean-bag chairs. A cloud of beans flew out of the back. They should have gotten better chairs. "How many demons are left?"

"Five." Hugo raised his hand. "Five little demons."

Elizabeth shot him a disgusted look. "Don't you dare start that. That's her game."

Hugo raised his hands in defense. "I'm sorry, it slipped out."

"What game?" Collin asked.

Erik didn't want to go into details of the whole hobby Gwen had set up in her head, it would only confuse him. "It's nothing really, just a rhyme."

"A foul rhyme," Elizabeth commented.

"Back to what we were talking about, there are five demons left. Gwen, James, Jürgen, Darrell, and Seth." Erik counted on his hand. "We haven't heard much of Darrell and Seth, I presume one of the two are the masterminds behind this battle of the war."

"What makes you say that?" Collin inquired. There was a lot he still didn't understand.

"Usually the mastermind hides in the darkness until the battle is near its end," he explained. "They don't want to risk getting killed."

"Smart plan."

Erik sighed. "It is, yes, but that makes it all the harder to track him. He could be in control of all of this from anywhere. He will just send different demons to different countries."

"So we will just have to try to predict which countries it will be." Collin took a look at the map studying the different areas they had already marked.

"I'm putting my money on Germany," Hugo said.

Elizabeth nodded. "So am I."

"It's a bit predictable though." Erik rubbed his chin. "Unless they want us to predict their plans, and then set us up."

"That is a big possibility," Hugo agreed.

Erik sighed. He hated war, he hated it so much. Years had passed and the wars never seemed to change, just where they were held. First heaven, now earth. Even if this war ended, another one would rise. That's what happened when there was good and evil, a never-ending fight for the top, even though evil would never prevail where he came from, which was exactly why they targeted earth. Here, they had a chance, here, they could rule if they really tried. Erik couldn't let that happen, he couldn't let such a thing happen to this poor defenseless planet. It had so much more to gain, it had so much more to explore.

"Collin." Erik turned his attention to him.

"Yes?"

"Once you turn, you'll be able to sense them a lot clearer. Not just Gwen. You can help us determine where they are," he explained.

He fidgeted. "When will that be?"

"Soon. Are you ready?" Erik raised an eyebrow.

Collin shot a sarcastic smile. "As ready as a human can be before they turn into some kind of demonic creature."

That answered worked for him. "I'm going to take that as a yes."

"Fair enough."

Erik turned back to the map. "They could go to Russia, that is another possibility."

"Or Italy," Elizabeth pointed out.

"Both good places. Collin will help us decide which. Usually we'd split up but this time I think we need to stick together."

"Because we're low on numbers?" Hugo asked.

"Yes, we shouldn't let them single us out. I have a feeling for the next few battles, they will group together to outnumber us," Erik explained.

"Which is why you need me," Collin interjected.

Erik nodded. "Exactly. We need to increase our numbers. If we can get a demon alone, they can be easily killed, but when there are more of them than us, we start to lose hope."

"Then why didn't you keep Gwen?" Collin questioned.

"Because of that blood bond of theirs, James would stop at nothing to get her back. Besides, she was too weak to help." Erik knew Collin wouldn't accept "because she's a demon" for an answer. He didn't understand how evil she really was inside. She had tortured them countless times, but then again, they never met the Gwen Collin knew. The Gwen that felt love for a human.

"But she can tell you where they are in the city better than I can," he argued.

"Not worth the risk of dealing with James or her going back to her old self all of a sudden. She switched sides once, she could do it again," Erik answered. "Erase any thought of her helping us, Collin, it isn't going to happen."

The sudden sound of someone thumping their fist on their door echoed through the unfurnished flat. All four of them stared apprehensively at the colorless door. They didn't know anyone who would or could, come to this place. They set up the salt barrier, they set up the incense, they were well hidden.

"Who could that be?" Hugo finally questioned. The knocking became louder.

"I don't know." Erik slowly got up and stepped up to the door.

He debated about opening it, it could just be some person with a wrong address or even a child playing a prank. He looked out the peephole to find a young man standing there.

He opened the door to find that the young man was really a minion. Erik just stared at it for a moment, wondering how it found them. The minion didn't attack, not that it could have with the salt barrier in place. Erik could easily kill it but he decided to wait and see what it wanted.

"I have a message from Gwen," the minion finally

said. The poor boy had to be in his early twenties, a college student perhaps. "They're planning an attack on members of parliament tomorrow. The attack is set for nine. Use this information or not, it is up to you."

Without hesitation, the minion turned around and stepped out into the street.

Erik reached out. "No, wait!"

But it was too late. An oncoming bus smacked into the boy. It came to a screeching halt, people screaming at what they had seen. Erik quickly slammed the door closed, shutting his eyes, trying to erase what he had just seen.

"What just happened?" Hugo rushed to his side. Elizabeth and Collin stood up, concerned about what had just transpired.

Erik took a deep breath. "Gwen just sent us her version of a telegram."

CHAPTER 41

Gwen watched as a group of girls at the club pulled James toward the door, yanking his tie like a leash. That was his style, wherever they went. Girls liked to just hang off of him. She didn't blame them, he really was perfect, or at least for her. He wasn't perfect for them but they would come to that conclusion on their own when it was too late.

James motioned Jürgen over and after a brief conversation, Jürgen turned sharply in her direction with a look of annoyance.

"He didn't make him guard me, did he? Selfish bastard," Gwen mumbled under her breath.

After a little more talking, James walked out with the girls in his arms. They would be regretting their choice in men soon, not that it would matter.

Jürgen stomped over to her. "Seems I'm to watch you for the rest of the time here."

"Oh goodie," she remarked as she downed the rest of the drink she had grabbed after converting that boy into a minion.

Jürgen grinned. "That's what I said."

"Did you even feed?" Gwen questioned.

"I fed before I met you two here. This place isn't my sort of style."

"You have style?" she smirked. Gwen glanced around, she didn't care for the place either. "Do you want to get out of here?"

He raised his eyebrow. "Did you feed enough?"

"Yes," Gwen answered.

Jürgen's fist came straight toward her face but she blocked it without hesitation. People around them gave them an incredulous look, but went on with what they considered to be dancing.

"Fine." He backed off. "But you are still a little on the weak side."

"No human blood will fix that. I need Jamesy's." She gave a little pout. "Do you know when he will be done?"

He rolled his eyes at her expression. "Not sure, he just said for you to meet him back at his apartment."

Gwen laughed. "That sounds about right."

"Does that bother you?"

She gulped down the rest of her drink. "No, but I hate that he dumped me on you."

"Don't worry, it's mutual."

"Then let's get out of here." She gestured toward the door.

Jürgen nodded, and they turned for the doors. The streets had become quiet now with only a lone stranger appearing every once in a while. The tubes were all closed for the night. The dark, cool air felt nice against her skin. It made her more alert, which she needed to be with Jürgen walking next to her. He could do anything at any moment.

"So, tell me Gwen, how does it feel to be back on the dark side of things?" Jürgen asked.

She shrugged. "Normal."

"Really? Then why did you leave?"

It was for reasons he would never understand. Gwen shook her head. "I don't have to answer that."

Jürgen stepped in front of her and blocked her. "Yes you do. I'm curious."

"Curious about what?"

"Why you had a change of heart. Actually, that you even had a heart at all. We have been at this for thousands of years, it isn't just something you can change overnight. You must have been wanting to run off for years." His eyes darkened.

She bit her lip, thinking of how she could answer the question to piss him off but not enough to hurt her. "I had been thinking about it for a while yes, but it didn't really hit me until then."

"And we were so close too."

"Yes, I know. I'm sorry." She gave him the most sarcastic 'I'm sorry' look she could. Jürgen glared at her.

"If we lose this war, just wait until we are in hell. I will make you pay," he threatened.

"Oh, so scared. What will you do? *Burn* me?" Gwen sarcastically replied.

"Among other things," he grunted. "Don't think just because James is there that he will be able to hold me back. He won't."

Her lips curved in a grin. "I wonder what he would say if he heard you threaten me like that."

Jürgen started moving again, and she followed. "I am serious, it will be your fault if we lose this war, and I'm not even sure I believe that you are back."

She glanced at him. "Oh? And why's that?"

"Because, only a couple days ago you were running from Paris with the enemy and now here you are, acting like you are your old self. James may be fooled but I'm no fool. I know a deceiving liar when I see one."

She placed her hand on her chest innocently. "I'm not lying. I saw what a fool I was to think they would trust me, to think they would help me run away from you. They are the same selfish bastards that threw us out of heaven."

"Ain't that a fact," he commented.

"Besides," she sighed. "I'm powerless without James. Going how long I did without him, I'm surprised I could even walk."

"That repulsive bond of yours."

"Repulsive? Now why is that? Are you just jealous?" she questioned with a smile.

"I am not jealous," he shot back. "It is just wrong. You

shouldn't make yourself dependent on each other, it isn't safe."

"Why? In case one of us runs off, the other is powerless?" she asked.

"Exactly. You have any idea how much James suffered while you ran off?"

She knew what he felt. The pain, the urge to destroy anything in her sight, the need she felt every moment, wanting to run back to him every second.

"Actually, I do," Gwen said.

"Yeah but that was your own damn fault. James didn't do anything wrong, and he had to pay for your stupidity."

"I'm sure he was fine."

Jürgen stopped. "No, you don't understand. He was heartbroken when you left him. You are a selfish bitch who doesn't understand how much you hurt him, Gwen. Then he found you with that human. What were you thinking? How could you do that to him? He loved you. He still does even though you don't deserve it. How could you ever have feelings for these low life beings in the first place?"

She raised her eyebrow. "What was that, Jürgen? About having feelings for a human?"

His eyes narrowed. "Don't even go there, Guinevere."

Gwen gave him a curious look. "Are you still mad at me for that? Jürgen, it has been centuries. Get over it."

"I'll get over it when you are burning in Hell," he replied cold-heartedly.

"But you'll be right there beside me," she commented.

"Anyway, I never had feelings for that human, I just thought I did. I made myself believe I could be human and have human feelings but in reality, I can't. It was just a mistake and James took it the wrong way."

"In the wrong way huh? Then why is Collin still alive?" he questioned.

"Because he shouldn't suffer for my mistake."

"Oh, that makes sense, you haven't ever made others suffer before. So making him immortal will undo all the horrible things you have done over the years?"

"No, I just brought him back to life. Only if I drink his blood, will he become immortal and awaken as a hybrid," she stated.

"You still committed a task that isn't looked too lightly on," he growled.

"And who's going to punish me?" she queried.

"I know Seth won't be happy," Jürgen said.

"Seth doesn't need to know about any of this now does he?" Gwen remarked.

"But if he did, he would punish you severely and I would really, really like to see that."

"I bet you would. Now." She turned and gestured to the tall building standing next to her. "This is my stop. Goodnight."

"Want me to walk you up?" He insisted more than asked.

She shook her head. "No, I think I can handle it."

He grabbed her wrist. "How do I know you won't run off?"

"Because I'm not that stupid. James would find me in

an instant," she smiled.

"I like how you said that instead of just saying you wouldn't run off again."

"Well, you just never know now, do you?"

Jürgen glared at her as she slipped out of his grip and stepped inside the lobby. She headed into the lift and went up the floors until she reached James' apartment. The higher she went, the more her ankle started to burn.

"Dumbass," she muttered under her breath. Only James would find a place to stay that would bring him pain like this. Such a masochist.

Using her spare key, she opened the door. It was dark and quite lonely without James. The only light came from the city below. Gwen turned on the light and collapsed on the couch. It had been a long day full of lies and things she didn't want to find herself doing again, like slipping into James' grasp. She loved him, but she didn't love who he made her become.

She had followed him down to Earth, blind of what she gave up for him. Now she was chained to this place, never to be free. But even to this day, she knew that if she could go back in time, she would still make the same choice. She would follow him anywhere.

She had made her last attempt to help the Gargoyles, sending the minion to tell Erik everything she knew about the attack for tomorrow. It was only a matter of time now. James and Jürgen shouldn't see it coming and the Gargoyles would stop them from turning Parliament. If they killed Jürgen, she would be happy. If they killed James, well, she would probably kill herself too. Life on earth would be torture without him, she'd rather serve in Hell with him. Either way, that was where she was going.

The door creaked open. Gwen didn't even look up to make sure it was James, she didn't need to. She could smell the perfume of those girls that had been hanging all over him. Perfume and blood.

James made his way to her and kissed her. She could still taste their blood on his lips.

Gwen opened her eyes to find his once fresh white shirt covered in lipstick. A few buttons had been ripped off. Typical. "You should wash up, I still taste blood on you."

"But you used to like it when I came home with blood on my lips," he whimpered.

"It's been a long century."

"I can tell you aren't as fun as you used to be," James commented.

She smiled. "I'm sorry to disappoint."

"You know." James clicked his stereo on. "I never got a dance with you."

Gwen laughed as he played her favorite song, a little poem from the 13th century. "Puis qu'en oubli".

"Where on earth did you find this?"

"Came across it one day in a coffee shop. They play the most random music in those places. Had to buy it, just for you." He pulled her up and wrapped his arms around her. "Just for you."

They danced slowly for hours, Gwen resting her head on his shoulder, letting James sway her back and forth to the music. The song only lasted a little over three minutes. The rest of the night was in silence.

CHAPTER 42

"She sent a what?" Collin questioned as Erik rubbed his face with his hands. He looked exasperated as he paced around the tiny room.

"Gwen sent a minion to tell us their next move." He sighed. "Then he stepped in front of a bus."

"Wait." Collin rushed to the window and peered through the blinds. Sure enough, there were ambulances and policemen scattered around the area. Blood smeared the pavement. He turned away, trying not to get sick at the sight of the body. Gore, so much gore witnessed through the past five years of his life. "What did he say?"

"He said that they're going after members of Parliament tomorrow morning." Erik sat down, folding his hands gently onto his lap. "Gwen wants us to use this information against them."

"You are trying to tell me that Gwen is still trying to help us?" Hugo asked.

"It appears so," Erik answered.

Collin's eyes widened. He tried not to show his excitement. He was right, she didn't go back. She was still good. He wanted to jump up in victory, but he had a feeling the three of them wouldn't appreciate such an action, especially since they hated her. But he was right, and they were wrong. He knew her better.

Elizabeth shook her head. "No. It's a setup, she's lying."

No, it's not, Collin thought, *she wants to help*. She has been trying to help this whole time.

Erik shrugged. "Or this could be our lucky break."

Elizabeth slammed her fist on the wooden table. Collin jumped from the sound. "Are you kidding me? You think she is actually trying to help? You can't be that foolish."

"You weren't there," Erik said. "You didn't see the things she did, Elizabeth."

"Oh, like what?" she sarcastically replied. Collin wondered what exactly Gwen had done to her. No one ever gave the exact details, he just knew it was bad. He wanted to know how bad.

"Like letting Erik dig a bullet out of her heart with a knife for starters," Hugo answered. "Not to mention killing minions and trying to help us find their headquarters."

"Did you find their headquarters?" Elizabeth

questioned.

"Well no, but..." Hugo started.

"She lied to you! If she knew where the others were in the city, you think she would tell you?" she said.

She was right, if Gwen could sense the minions, why couldn't she find the headquarters? If James was here, why couldn't she sense where he went? She could have been afraid of what James would do if they found him. That had to be it.

"She's using us! She's the most manipulative of them all," she argued.

"No, they're right Elizabeth, she *has* changed," Collin spoke up. It was his turn to stand up for her, like he should have done all along.

"You don't know her like we do, you don't know what she has done in her past."

Collin stood up and placed his hand on his chest. "And you don't know the life we lived together. You don't know all the kind things she did for others, you don't know all the things she has said to me."

"Did she ever once tell you what she really was?" she asked calmly. "Or did you find out the hard way?"

It was his turn to become silent just as the others did. No, she never did tell him what she was, but he could understand why. She was afraid he would reject her, she was afraid of rejection. Whether or not he would have left her, he didn't know but at this moment he wasn't ready to give up on her.

"She saved my life," he said. "That has to count for something."

"One nice thing out of millions of wrongs doesn't make her a good person," she countered.

"No, but it shows she can change," Collin replied. It was a valid argument, he thought, that if a demon was capable of doing one good thing, they were capable of doing more. She can change. She did change, they just couldn't see it like he could.

"If she did change, how do you know she didn't change back? How do you know she didn't go back to her old self? Thanks to Erik's stupidity, we can't hurt her. If she sets a trap, we are done. Finished."

"Collin's right though," Hugo said. "There is some hope that she has changed and is trying to help."

Elizabeth turned sharply to Hugo. "I'm surprised to hear you say those words, Hugo. She has tortured you many times and yet you still will believe her lies?"

"She's not lying. Not this time," Hugo answered. Collin didn't know what it was that made him change his mind about her, but he was happy to have another person on his side.

She shook her head. "I don't believe it."

Collin pondered on everything that happened. She sent a minion to them. It was probably the only way she could get information to them without James noticing.

"How did she find us?" Collin asked.

"Good question," Erik said. "She shouldn't have been able to know our location."

"Followed Collin or Hugo?" Elizabeth pointed out.

"If that were the case, then why didn't they just attack? Why don't they just wait for us at the door," Collin countered.

"Because she likes playing games," she retorted.

"No." Erik pointed his finger at him. "Collin has a point. If they wanted to easily set us up, she knows our location. The moment we step outside they could kill us."

"You are trying to justify her actions because she hasn't tried killing us yet. That doesn't mean it isn't a trap!" Elizabeth asked.

"Yes. She wouldn't send a trap this easy for all three of us to fall into. If she was back to her old self, then she would play it out as slowly as possible, not to mention playing with Collin. If she was back to her old self, she would want the time to torture him as slowly and painfully as possible," Hugo explained.

"That's not comforting," Collin mumbled.

"It's true, she said it herself," he said. "When have you known her to want to get killing us all over with as quickly as possible? That's not her style."

Elizabeth kept shaking her head. "I can't believe you two, you are justifying this to not be a setup because it's a setup that isn't her usual style."

"But it's true, if she was catch us in a trap, it would be a lot sneakier and a lot more planned out. This seems more like her attempt to help us the only way she knew how without getting caught," Erik said.

"I can't believe you think this is a good idea, you two are nuts."

"This could be our lucky break, Elizabeth, just think about." Hugo jumped up. "A demon down, it will be four against four. We could bring the odds to our favor."

She just stared at them. "But what if it is a trap?"

"Then you can say I told you so and we will all run for our lives. We will go early, see if anything is fishy. Two hours, we can go two hours before nine and see. Collin can sort of sense them. He can tell us if anything is wrong," Hugo said.

Elizabeth frowned. "Fine, but don't come crawling to me if this blows up in your face."

Hugo grinned. "I knew I could get her to agree."

"We will get things ready then. Silver, ash, salt. All of it," she said.

"How do you make holy water?" Collin questioned.

"Boil the hell out of it," Hugo snickered.

Erik shot him a look. "Have a vicar or someone part of a church bless it. Why?"

"I think I have an idea."

CHAPTER 43

Today was the day. James stretched, admiring the view of the sun rising from his apartment windows. Gwen was still snuggled up next to him, sleeping peacefully. They needed to meet Jürgen in an hour, so he knew he should wake her, but he always hated waking her. He kissed her gently on the cheek. Her eyes flickered open.

"Good morning, have a long night?" he smiled as he stroked her cheek with his fingers.

"Funny." She stretched and looked over at the clock. "What time is it?"

"About six."

"Six?" she rubbed her eyes. "So we were asleep for an hour?"

He shrugged. "All we really need."

"True." Gwen pulled him in close and kissed him. "Now we have time to have a little more fun."

"Even though I would really like to take you up on the offer…" He traced her bare legs that lay on top of the sheets. "We should get ready. We have to meet Jürgen soon."

She gave him a funny look. "Why? I thought we were attacking at nine."

He shrugged. "Plans change. Attack's at seven."

Gwen jolted up. "What?"

"Yeah, did Jürgen not tell you?"

Gwen got out of the bed, hesitant to reply. "Are you just playing with me? Because I was gone so long?"

"No, I'm not joking." He knew he had been right about her telling the Gargoyles. "Why? What does it matter to you?"

She shook her head. "It doesn't. It's fine. I just don't like it when plans change."

He raised an eyebrow. "You're one to talk."

Gwen stuck her tongue out at him.

"Nothing else?" He wondered if she would tell him the truth.

"No."

He had given her the chance to come clean. She didn't take it. What happened next wouldn't be his fault. "Well then, get ready," he said as he got up out of the bed. "And wear something that doesn't stand out. We want to blend in today."

"I know the drill."

"True, I guess you've been trying to blend in for some

time," he commented. "Then you met that human."

"I thought we weren't discussing him anymore." She gave him a look.

He grabbed her and held her close. "Sorry, I just can't stop thinking about what you saw in him, when you had me."

"I slipped, okay?" She gave him a quick kiss, escaped his grip, and started for the shower. "Now I'm back."

She closed the door behind her. *Well*, he thought, *I was right*. She had told them the attack was at nine. James rubbed his forehead out of frustration. He had known it would be a pain to turn her back to their side, but he really had hoped just one night with him would change her mind entirely. Guess not.

At least this way, they could hopefully take down a Gargoyle or two. Maybe even three. Wouldn't that be a treat, he thought. He knew it wouldn't happen, but the thought, nonetheless, brought a little more excitement to his mind. What he didn't want to do was go to great lengths to effectively bring Gwen back to her old self. Except he knew he'd have to bring her a lot of pain in the process. It would be well worth it, but it still hurt him to consider doing such a thing. Jürgen and Seth will be happy at least, seeing that he finally gave her the punishment she deserved for abandoning their cause so long ago. They didn't understand love, all they knew was power.

He got ready and headed out of the condo with Gwen tagging along close behind him They could take the bike which he admitted he did sorely miss. Modern motorcycles never felt the same. This time around, Gwen let him drive and they flew down the road toward 10 Downing Street.

As they approached the gates of the Parliament building, the bells of Big Ben began ringing. He counted the clanging of the bells. One. Two. Three. Four. Five. Six. Seven. It was time. Jürgen was already waiting. James parked the bike right in front of where he stood.

"Right on time. Surprise," Jürgen grunted.

"What's that supposed to mean?" James narrowed his eyes.

"You two are always late. I don't like to think about why."

"Oh, you know why." Gwen nudged him.

"I didn't say I didn't *know*, I said I didn't want to think about it."

"But enough about that. Shall we get this over with?" Gwen changed the subject.

"We shall." James put his arm around her.

Right on cue, the five guards they had turned into minions came to the gate and unlocked it. Their emotionless faces made them stand out from others, but no human in the area seemed to notice anything unusual about them. The guards led them toward where the Prime Minister awaited. It was all too easy.

It wasn't a busy morning for the Prime Minister, which was good for them. They didn't want more commotion than what there already was going to be. They just had to be careful to make sure they turned all the witnesses. They didn't need people warning others about what was going on, not that they would believe them after all this was over.

As they approached the house, one of the guards they hadn't turned gave them a suspicious look.

"Are you authorized to be here?" One of the guards in the building tried to stop them. Jürgen grabbed him and bit his neck. The man collapsed. Jürgen gestured chivalrously.

"After you," he said, blood dripping from his lip. It was the little things that made these operations fun.

James and Gwen stepped over the body as they entered the house. The smell of sausages and toast filled the hallway. Ironically it would be breakfast for them too. No one tried to stop them, once inside. He glanced over to Gwen. She didn't suspect a thing. Jürgen had turned more than the two they had told Gwen about. If she tried to run, there would be many to stop her, not to mention help take down the Gargoyles if they showed up.

Coming upon the room that held the meeting the Prime Minister was scheduled to be in, James kicked the door open. It could have been unlocked but he did love dramatics.

"Good morning, Prime Minister." He smiled as he stepped on the door he just kicked down. "I am hoping your day has been going by smoothly."

There were a good handful of the members of Parliament there, which made him happy. Now they didn't need to hunt them down as well. These really were the last ones they needed. It was always nice when plans went this well.

"Who are you? What's going on? Guards!" the Prime Minister called out.

James shook his head. "Oh, no need to call for them, they will only help us."

"What do you mean?" He started backing away. "What do you want from me?"

"For you not to scream," James said as his eyes turned yellow.

James appeared at his side and placed his hand over his mouth to muffle the Prime Minister's screaming and bit into his neck. He let go of him and he fell to the ground. The few other members of Parliament that were there started screaming. Gwen grabbed the one closest to her and bit his neck. Jürgen did the same. Soon all five of them were on the floor. Now they just had to wait for them to awaken as minions.

"Well." James wiped his mouth with his sleeve. "That went nicely. No unsuspecting guests. This is exactly what we needed."

"I'd say," Jürgen commented as he looked over the bodies.

James looked around but found no clock. "What time is it?"

Jürgen looked at his watch. "Seven-fifteen."

He clapped his hands together. "So we have roughly forty-five minutes to prepare for the Gargoyles."

Gwen stopped and stared at him. "What?"

"Oh, sweetie, you know. The Gargoyles you warned that we would be here at nine, and since they can't trust you—with good reason—they'll be early. It was a set up.

Thank you for helping us."

She shook her head and started backing away from him. "No, I won't let you."

"Do you really think you could stop us?" James snapped at her.

"I can try," Gwen said.

"Stop being a fool. Just give up and come back to us before you get yourself hurt," James warned.

"I can't, James. I already told you."

Gwen started for the door but Jürgen grabbed her. "Where do you think you're going?"

"Away from you two." Gwen punched him. She had regained all of her strength. Jürgen hit the ground, and she ran off toward the street.

"Damn it, James! Why did you have to let her regain her strength?" Jürgen glared at him as he got up and started for her.

"What was I supposed to do? We had to make it look like we trusted her." James followed behind.

They ran after her down the streets in the compound. She may have been able to run, but he could sense where she was. Their bond had been strengthened, she couldn't hide from him. Not this time. He had warned her enough times now, she was asking for whatever punishment he had planned at this point. James just hoped Jürgen wouldn't tell Seth about this. He didn't need more crap than what he was already given.

They hurried down the streets. He sensed her nearby. James motioned to Jürgen to go around the buildings the other way to cut her off. He nodded and left.

"Oh, Guinevere!" James called. "Please come back. We don't want to repeat history now, do we?"

He could sense she was just around the corner. He saw her heading down that street. As she got to the next crossroads, Jürgen was already waiting for her.

"Damn it." She turned around to find him standing behind her. She tried to run past him, but he wasn't about to let her get past. Not this time. He grabbed her and held her tightly.

"You are really going to regret doing that," James growled as he bit into her neck. It was the only way to slow her down, he had to deplete her of her energy. She struggled but as the seconds went by, she became weaker and weaker. Finally, he felt her body go limp.

CHAPTER 44

Erik jumped over the fence that surrounded the Prime Minister's house. Hugo and Elizabeth followed, Hugo carrying Collin. Their feet hit the ground, the soft clatter echoing around them. It was quiet. Too quiet. Not a movement was seen, not a noise to be heard. Nothing. Erik cursed under his breath.

"Erik, there is no one here," Hugo whispered.

"I can see that," he sighed. "Collin, do you sense anything?"

"No." He hesitated. "Wait, I think I sense something," he pointed down the street. "That way, I think it's blood. Gwen's…"

"Blood?" Erik questioned. Why, he thought, would he smell her blood?

"Yeah, she's bleeding. A lot." He started for where he could sense it. "This way!"

Erik hurried after him. If Collin just waited a moment, they would have been able to think this through. If he really did sense Gwen, and she was in trouble, they should have backed away slowly. They should have left right then and there. But they couldn't let Collin run off by himself. Humans. Never took the time to think things through.

Collin rounded the corner and Erik followed close behind. He could hear Elizabeth and Hugo's footsteps behind him. As he rounded the corner, Erik found Collin standing in the middle of the street, staring up at him with a worried expression. He looked at where his attention had been held. That's when he saw her. Gwen. Erik placed his hand over his nose and mouth. The smell and taste didn't go away, but the stench of blood lingered on everything around him. It masked any other scent there was in the surrounding area.

She hung six meters up, nailed to a fire escape, at least that's what it once was. The steel frames that once made up the ladder had been ripped away and now pierced through Gwen's body. Their jagged edges had been forced through her. It had to have taken a large amount of force since most looked to be pretty blunt. She looked like a pin cushion hanging there, metal stakes coming out of every which way. Blood trickled down from each piece, drops echoing as they hit the ground beneath her. Her clothes were drenched. This view was hidden from the public streets, which Erik was thankful for. At least he wouldn't have to deal with panic, especially when they realized she was still alive.

Gwen's head drooped down, her red-crusted hair masking her face. Her chest moved slowly, still breathing even though a good handful of the metal had pierced her lungs. Incredible what their bodies could endure. Erik noted bite marks on the base of her neck. James must have figured out she had tipped them off, which could mean only one thing.

Gwen didn't set them up, but the demons did.

Hugo and Elizabeth came around the corner, gasping at what they saw.

"What the?" Hugo examined Gwen's mutilated body. "No, they set her up."

"You think?" Erik commented.

"Or maybe she is in on it. Wouldn't put it past her," Elizabeth said. He didn't think so, no demon would put themselves through what he was seeing with his own eyes. Not even Gwen.

"Well well, what do we have here?" A voice called out behind them. Erik spun around to find James and Jürgen standing behind him with arrogant smiles covering their faces.

"I can't believe you would do such a thing to your own kind," Erik commented.

James looked as if he was weighing the options of other things he could have done in his mind. "Well, to be fair, I can't believe one of our kind would try to help yours. She had to be punished."

Erik shook his head, not believing the man who went

through so much to get her back would stoop so low using her to get to them. "I thought you cared for her more than that, James."

"And I thought she cared enough not to go behind my back again," he snapped back. "I guess I was wrong."

Erik nodded to Hugo. "Get her down from there."

Hugo nodded and flew up to where Gwen hung and balanced on what was left of the stairwell. He grabbed one of the pieces of metal and yanked it out. The pain jolted Gwen awake. Her yellow eyes widened as she felt every shard piercing through her.

She let out an ear-piercing scream.

"You should have heard her when we stuck them in. At least there's no name-calling this time." James watched as Hugo pulled out another piece. Gwen screamed again but this time it wasn't as loud, it was almost a broken cry.

"You are cold," Erik growled.

He simply laughed. "I thought you wanted me to get her to turn that poor human over there. She will only do it once she hits rock bottom."

Erik turned his attention back to Gwen. She let out one more whimper as Hugo pulled out the last piece. Hugo carried her down to the ground, her blood staining his clothes. Ribs stuck out of the wound in her back and chest, flesh barely clinging on. He could see parts of her lung that had been exposed. Pieces of skin had ripped away from her arms and legs to reveal more bone. Even with all that, only one thing occupied her attention. James. She kept a cold glare at him as Hugo landed on the ground and set her down.

"You bastard! You fucking bastard!" she yelled. She was breathing heavily and Erik didn't know if it was because of the pain or due to her hatred for James. He figured it was a mixture of both.

"There's the name-calling," James sighed. "If you didn't betray me again, you wouldn't be in this pain."

"Gwen." Hugo bent down next to her and put his wrist in front of her mouth. There was no hesitation as she bit into his wrist. Her eyes fixated on James. He just smiled back at her. Slowly, her skin grew back, and she looked normal again, other than being totally blood-stained. Erik glanced over at Collin who looked as if he was going to be sick.

"Drink up Gwen, you are going to need all the energy you can get," James jeered.

Gwen shoved Hugo's arm away and tried to attack James, her eyes a piercing yellow. Erik grabbed her before she could do anything stupid.

"No, he will just do the same thing to you again. You can't go after him alone." Erik pulled her back.

She fought to get out of his grip. "Oh, yes I can!"

"No, you won't," Erik's voice darkened. She finally stopped.

"So she *is* trainable," James joked. "You will have to teach me, Erik. Nothing I have done has seemed to work. But maybe another time, you are going to be preoccupied in a second." He clapped his hands.

Dozens of minions came out of the shadows, hungry for blood. Erik scanned around looking at them all. There had to be at least a hundred of them. It was all part of the plan, they had known Gwen would betray them. Erik backed up toward the others, ready to fend them off as a team.

James stepped forward. "Now, shall we get down to business?"

CHAPTER 45

Gwen peered around the area, taking in how many minions surrounded her. Damn him. Damn him to Hell. He had set her up to get to them. He had used her.

She was sick of being used. She was sick of being used by everyone. Gwen bolted away from Erik and the others, pounding her fist into the chest of a minion. She had to get her anger out somehow and Erik was right; she was no match for James or Jürgen in this weakened state. Letting her hands slip around its heart, its beating rhythm pulsated against her palm, Gwen kicked the minion away. She held its bleeding heart still in her hands, breathing heavily, letting herself take it all in. Her anger controlled her, and she didn't want the feeling to go away anytime soon. She needed it; she needed it to keep going, otherwise she might curl up into a whimpering mess of a demon and that was exactly what she didn't need right now. She dropped the heart to the ground, receiving the satisfaction of its death. A hundred more and Gwen thought she might feel a little better.

Turning her attention back to her surroundings, Gwen saw the Gargoyles had come prepared. Silver knives, sacks of ash, and what appeared to be a water gun.

"What the hell?" Gwen whispered under her breath. She had no clue what the water gun was for. Her curiosity had done her in again. While she had been staring, she felt claws slice into her back.

She whirled around to find a minion trying to kill her. Like it could kill her. Maybe, if it got really lucky with a torch or a sword of some kind. With a swift move of the hand, she dug her nails into its jugular and ripped its throat right out. Such weak beings, really. But still, they came in handy. And in vast numbers like this, they distracted the Gargoyles very well.

Gwen ran back to where the demons and the Gargoyles fought one another. And Collin. Why did they have to bring Collin? This wasn't the safest place to bring a human. They must really want her to turn him.

James and Jürgen were smart, they were trying to split the Gargoyles up. James had Hugo, while Jürgen tried to distract Erik and Elizabeth. She had to admit, they had this plan thought through. They knew she was going to betray them again. Gwen hadn't expected this many minions. They surrounded the Gargoyles, weakening them so that the demons could attack the Gargoyles more effectively.

She started after James to help Hugo in the fight, or at least stop James before he did anything irreversible. She couldn't hurt James, or actually she couldn't kill him. She wanted to hurt him plenty, in retaliation for what he had done to her. Jürgen saw her as she ran toward them.

"Not so fast, Gwen," he stepped out in front of her. Twenty minions had stepped in to occupy Erik and Elizabeth in the meantime.

"You can't do anything to stop me, Jürgen," she warned.

"You really don't want to start with me," he said "You never know how things like this will end up."

"Afraid of a little fight?" she coaxed him, hoping that maybe she could distract him enough so Erik and Elizabeth could defeat the minions and go help Hugo.

"I could kill you, but then I would be in a lot of trouble with James and I don't particularly want to piss him off right now. You did a good enough job of that already."

"And here I thought you didn't fear anything," she smiled. Pissing him off was always a good distraction. She could do it so well too.

He threw a punch at her which she tried to dodge, but wasn't quick enough to avoid. His rough knuckles impacted with her jaw. She heard the crack. Landing on the stone ground, she felt the wound heal. She was glad Hugo had given her more than what she needed to heal the first injuries inflicted on her by James earlier.

"See, you aren't even worth it," he gestured to some of the minions nearby. "You all deal with her. Don't kill her but make sure she suffers."

Gwen quickly stood up from the ground, but they were on top of her in a second. Minions never fought fairly. They ripped at her skin, causing her to lose more blood and more energy. She shoved them off of her and looked for the closest weapon she could find. She didn't see anything. There never was anything handy when you truly needed it.

"I guess we will have to do this the old-fashioned way then, eh?" she turned to them and rammed her hand into the closest minion's chest yet again, grasping its heart and pulling it out of its chest. Such an interesting way to go, she had to admit. She didn't know if she would pick it out of the three ways of killing a minion, though. Or four, counting the triduanum. It definitely wasn't a way she wanted to die herself. The minion fell to the ground.

"Who's next?" she called out.

It had been a while since she had engaged in real hand-to-hand combat. All six charged at her at once. Now she had to plan a real strategy in order to help Hugo.

The minions clawed at her. Damn those claws. Grotesque features really. Their bodies transformed into a mixture of that of a human and that of the demonic spirits that possessed them. *Goody, is that what I look like when I transform to my true self?* She sure hoped not. It had been so long ago that she couldn't remember. Grabbing another heart, she ripped it out. That left five of them now to defeat.

Turning down the street, she figured it would be best

to try to outrun them. Not all of them had the same speed. She could separate them. Bring them down one by one. Rounding a corner, she jumped up to a ledge and waited for one to approach her.

Gwen watched as they came around the corner, clueless where she had gone to. Such stupid beings. There was a reason the Twelve were in charge, not them. They were minions for a reason. She pounced on the last one in the group and sliced her nails along its throat, like a cat with its prey. That left four angry minions to go.

They realized what happened and darted after her.

"Oh crap." Gwen spun around and bolted after them. That's when she ran into Collin.

"Collin, run!" She shoved him forward.

He pulled out the water gun and shot at the four minions that followed behind. The water burned their skin, eating away at their flesh all the way down to their now exposed bone. Disgusting, really.

She looked at the water gun. Holy water. Incredible. She wondered why she didn't think of that earlier, not that she could use it. Any spilt water would burn her skin as well.

"Did you fill that with holy water?" she questioned, amazed at the idea.

Collin looked down at his invention, proud. "Yeah, pretty nifty, eh? I thought it up last night."

"You're a genius." She laughed as they ran. Although the holy water slowed them down, they didn't lose them for good. Collin put away the gun and pulled out the sword. "You don't happen to have another one of those do you?"

He pulled out a knife and handed it to her.

"Thanks." She turned and plunged the blade into the closest minion's heart and twisted. It yelled out in anguish, its beady little eyes confused by the sudden pain. It grabbed at her, but it was no use. It fell to the ground just like the rest of them did.

The street would be littered with bodies this morning. She wondered if James and Jürgen had planned for that. They could make it easily look like an assassination attempt on the Prime Minister. Name a country and presto, war. They had it very well thought out, even without her help, which actually made her a little sad. They didn't need her.

Collin sliced through the throat of a minion, cutting all the way through the vertebrae. The neck snapped in two and its head plummeted to the pavement before its body even collapsed. She had to hand it to Hugo, he had trained him well.

"Two more," she said as they stood back to back, ready for their next attackers. Strange, really, for her to be fighting side-by-side with a human. Surprises still come every day when you live forever.

"I'll take the ginger, you get the blonde?" He held up his sword, waiting for her word.

"Sounds fair." She swung her knife forward straight into its chest, pinning the minion to the wall. Slowly she inched the knife closer and closer to its heart, piercing it carefully. She listened to its scream. Music to her ears.

She needed some more energy. Confident that Collin had her back, she could take it from this minion without having to worry about another attack. Gwen sank her fangs into its throat and let the energy consume her. Although minion's energy was less filling than a human's, and far below that of James', it still felt good to gain more energy in the midst of battle.

"Gwen." Collin came up behind her. He had already finished off the ginger. "Just kill him."

She took her mouth off of its neck. "All right." She pushed the knife all the way in and took it out. The minion collapsed to the ground.

She turned around and smiled. "Now, on to more pressing matters." She started for where James was when Collin grabbed her wrist.

"Wait," he said.

She turned to him, puzzled. "Collin, I have to hurry."

"Turn me now."

She just looked at him. "What?"

"We can win this if you just turn me. I will be stronger," he argued.

Gwen shook her head. "No, not now. This isn't the time."

"Gwen, I have to help. I can only do that if you turn me."

Her eyes turned yellow. "Don't you dare tell me what to do! When I say this isn't the time, it isn't the time. Now, let go of my wrist."

He slowly let go of her wrist and she hurried to get to Hugo before it was too late.

CHAPTER 46

Collin watched as Gwen ran off in the direction James was in. He had tried to get her to turn him, but it was no use. She was as stubborn as she always had been. And he liked that about her.

Turning his attention to Erik and Elizabeth, he watched as Jürgen sent minion after minion at them. He was keeping them away from Hugo. James had him all to himself along with the minions that helped him. Divide and conquer, always the best war tactic.

He had to distract Jürgen so that they could help Hugo. Jürgen was a lot bigger, stronger, and more ruthless than he was. But Collin knew he had an advantage. They couldn't kill him. Not until Gwen turned him, anyway. So this was his chance to make a difference. This was his chance to really help the Gargoyles.

Before he could do it, though, he had to get through the wall of minions that Jürgen had set up around him. To protect him. They, Collin figured, could hurt him. He didn't know if they knew they weren't supposed to kill him. He didn't want to have to find out the hard way. He picked up a pebble. Throwing it at one of their heads, it bounced off and landed next to it. The minion slowly looked down, its dark eyes studying what had just hit him. It turned, its otherwise unemotional face now expressing utter annoyance. He had successfully gotten their attention. Six minions charged after him.

Collin pulled out his Holy Gun. It's what he named it. It was better than "a water gun full of Holy Water," as Hugo boringly call it. The liquid burnt their skin, dissolving through their flesh. He was a genius, as Gwen had said. The invention came in quite handy for these types of battles, even though it left a vulgar stench in the air.

The minions tried to make the stinging pain go away by wiping away the excess water, but that only burnt their hands. It was really useless. The smell of burnt flesh filled Collin's nostrils. He hated the heightened senses, especially when the smells being heightened were unsavory.

Collin pulled out his sword. Now that they were distracted, he could take them down. He swiped at their necks. Their vertebrae cracked as the blade hit it. A clean cut. Three heads fell to the ground, rolling away into the gutters. Collin swallowed, trying not to lose his breakfast from that morning. He knew he should have eaten lighter. The gore never got better, but he didn't actually throw up. Anymore.

Three more to go.

They ran at him with pure rage. The rage wasn't because he had killed their colleagues, but he figured because they were always like that. He hadn't seen a minion that didn't seem to be full of rage. They always wanted to tear him limb from limb. Strange creatures, really.

Or maybe it was because he burnt them with the holy water. Either way, they were always like that.

He plunged his sword into one, pulling up and slicing through the chest. Collin could see its exposed ribs as he pulled out the sword. Ribs tangled with innards. Images from high school anatomy popped into his head. He'd hated that class, especially when they had to visit a morgue. He threw up his lunch that day. He vowed to never see those things again. Now he did. All the time. Life was funny that way.

Two left. He turned his attention back to them. Their razor-sharp nails dug into his skin. Damn them. That was his last clean shirt. Now he would have to ask Erik to run by the store to get him a new one. Such a pain. He stabbed it between the eyes. Right through the glabella. Something else he remembered from anatomy class. Blood ran down its face. Collin pulled out the sword, and the minion fell, blood and grey matter all around him.

Last one.

This one used to be a brown-haired man, in his thirties. Same age as him actually. To look at them as humans was quite frightening. To think of what they once were was a depressing notion. Collin tried his hardest not to think of them as former human beings, but every once in a while, he wondered about it. Did they have a family? Were they good men or women? Did someone depend on them? All questions he never wanted to know the conclusive answer to because it'd make the task of killing them more difficult than it could be otherwise.

Collin swung his sword one final time. Straight through the stomach. The hilt hit the skin. He could see the blade behind it, dripping with blood. He pulled it out. The minion fell, lying next to the others. It was done. The task was finished.

Taking in a breath, he released it slowly. The bodies of fallen men surrounded him. They were minions, he told himself. Not humans. It wasn't wrong. Deep breaths. In and out. Not humans.

Back to Jürgen.

He stood a little distance from Erik and Elizabeth, watching as they struggled against the many minions he had ordered to fight against them. He kept a smirk on his face as he folded his arms across his chest.

"Jürgen!" Collin called out, still holding his sword in his hands. Jürgen turned to face him, irritated that he had distracted him from the show. He looked surprised to find Collin behind him. He probably thought it was

Gwen bugging him.

He looked at his sword and grunted. "What do *you* want?"

"I've come here to fight," Collin brought his sword up higher.

Jürgen just laughed. "Go home kid, and let the real warriors fight."

He shook his head. "No."

"Beat it, before you annoy me further," Jürgen turned back to Erik and Elizabeth.

Collin pulled out his holy gun and shot Jürgen in the back with water.

The water splashed against his skin. Collin watched as it ate away at his flesh. Jürgen grabbed at the wound and spun around, his eyes turning a piercing yellow. "You are going to pay for that kid!"

"Oh, shit!" Collin spun around on his heels and ran as fast as he could.

CHAPTER 47

"Hugo, Hugo, Hugo. When are you going to learn that it is not a good idea to go up against me in a fight?" James jeered as he circled the Gargoyle. Hugo watched closely, cautious of his next move. "It never ends well for you."

"Actually, it was Gwen who always got me, not you. You were but a formality, really." He was out of breath already. The minions had already worn him down a bit. He still needed to be stronger than him, though. He needed to make that possible in order to survive.

"True, and you still trusted her. Interesting really," he said. It was actually, after the things she had done to him.

He shrugged. "What can I say, I'm a trusting sort of guy."

"Yeah, well, I'm not." James moved to him in a flash.

He pulled out his knife and stabbed Hugo in the back, the blade cracking a couple of ribs in the process.

It didn't even stun Hugo. He spun around and pulled out a knife of his own. The triduanum. James jumped back as he slashed toward him. That was a blade he didn't want to see the edge of. Ever.

He made distance between the two of them. "The triduanum. I should have seen that coming."

"Your girl gave it to me," Hugo jeered.

"So very nice of her, I will be sure to return it to her after I rip your heart out." James motioned toward a group of minions. He needed to weaken him more. "But first, I will have my men deal with you. They are new and I have to show them what it's like to be in a war. A real war."

The minions attacked him. One after another, after another. Hugo held them off though, he was used to their attacks through the years. As he killed the third one, James flashed next to him, driving his knife into his side once more. Hugo let out a quick moan in pain.

"Have to hand it to you James." Hugo wiped away the blood. The wound healed in a flash. Still too strong for him. He needed more minions. Or more knives. Either one. "You are quick to learn."

He swung the triduanum at him again but James dodged it again. Demons were faster than Gargoyles. It was only fair. Gargoyles could fly.

Speaking of which, Hugo leapt straight up into the air, invisible wings keeping him suspended in the air. James watched carefully, pulling out his .45 caliber. He would have to time it just right.

Hugo dove down at him. James jumped to the side just as Hugo would have made impact with him. He shot right into where his wings would meet in his back. Hugo let out a scream and fell. James stepped on his back and shot the base of the other wing.

Now he would be incapable of flying, at least for fifteen minutes or so. They could heal themselves with time, just like their bodies. The bullets would make sure of that. Like clipping the wings of a bird.

James smiled. "Come on Hugo, you should have known better."

"You're right, I should have." Hugo spun around, plunging the triduanum into the side of James' leg. "But so should you."

James fell back, grasping his leg. The dark tendrils of poison shot through his body. He wouldn't be able to move fast, not as fast as he wanted to, anyway.

"Now." Hugo stood up and walked over to where James laid. He tried to back away, but it was no use. He held out the knife "Shall we finish this?"

James watched as three minions attacked Hugo from behind. Good 'ol minions, coming to the rescue in just the nick of time. They knew their master needed them. James took this lucky chance to get in a better position to fight.

He could barely put weight on the leg. Damn that knife. He limped around the corner and leaned against the building, taking in deep breaths as the poison ate away at him. The sound of Hugo dealing with the three minions filled his ears. After a loud crash, the sound stopped. Hugo had bested the minions. James peered around the corner. Hugo was talking to Gwen.

He was distracted by her and she didn't see James. He crept closer, trying not to make a sound. She had Hugo's attention fully.

"Gwen, what are you doing? You need to get out of here." Hugo tried to push her away, but she wouldn't budge. She was stubborn that way.

Slowly James stepped closer, listening to their conversation.

"I can't let you fight alone, not when all of this is my fault," she exclaimed. James rolled his eyes. Such theatrics coming from the girl that had tricked them so many times.

They still didn't notice him.

Hugo placed his bloody hand on her cheek. "No, listen to me. You are worth it. I believe in you."

A few more steps.

"Do not give up in this war."

Almost there.

Hugo was right in front of him. "Don't ever give up in what you bel..." James jammed his hand into Hugo's back. He grasped his heart.

"Hugo?" Gwen questioned.

James ripped the heart out of his body. Hugo turned into a pile of dust in an instant. He glanced down at it. "He was right, I couldn't beat him without your help." He looked up at her and smiled. "Thanks partner."

"No!" she screamed. She knelt down to the pile of ash.

He was long gone. "You monster!"

"Monsters? Really? Look who's talking." He grabbed her and pulled her up.

"Get away from me!" She tried to resist his grip but it was no use. She was weaker than him, even though he had been stabbed with the triduanum.

"Hey, I'm not done with you yet." He pulled her closer to him. "I need a drink. That friend of yours stabbed me."

James bit into her neck. She didn't even try to escape his grasp anymore. She knew there was no use.

"You deserved it," she stated coldly as he finished taking the blood he needed. At last he could put weight on his leg.

"Speaking of what people deserve," he bent down and picked up the triduanum. Without hesitation, he plunged it straight into Gwen's stomach. She gasped. "This is for everything."

"Was that... really necessary?" she whimpered as she shut her eyes.

"It is. I need you to be as weak as possible to turn that stupid human I bargained for you with." He took the knife out and plunged it into her again, this time a little harder.

"I won't do it. There's nothing you can do to make me do it." She shook her head, tears of pain rolling down her face.

"We will see about that." He nodded to Jürgen who had an unconscious Collin flung over his shoulder.

"Collin," she whispered as she fainted. James flung her

over his own shoulder.

He motioned to Jürgen. "Well, this went well."

CHAPTER 48

Erik felt it. It was like something inside of him had been ripped out. Snapped away. Like a piece of his heart had been torn. There was no denying what had just happened.

Hugo was gone.

Elizabeth noticed it too, her gasp surprising even him. He turned to her. Horror filled her face. They both knew they needed to get out of there fast. They needed to get out of there before James and Jürgen came for them.

He pounded his sword into the nearest minion and grabbed Elizabeth by the arm. They had to run. They couldn't lose another life to the demons. The minions ran after them, but it was no use. They weren't about to stop and fight them. Time was going by and each second mattered. Jumping over the fence that encircled the area, the minions tried to reach for them. They scraped their claws against the metal, unable to get over the fence.

Erik pulled Elizabeth down the streets of London. He didn't know how far would be far enough to go so he kept on, never looking back. They had lost Hugo to the demons, he would never forgive himself for that. He should have made sure they didn't get split up. It had all happened so fast. The demons knew what to do, and they did it well.

They traveled as fast as they could, bumping into a few pedestrians along the way. Erik never looked back at Elizabeth. He didn't want to see her face. He didn't want to see her sadness. She knew this was going to be a failure and now they'd lost one of their own. He didn't want to hear it, he already knew it was a mistake. A mistake that cost Hugo his life.

Elizabeth tugged at him to stop. He turned to find her with tears falling from her eyes. He hated it when she cried. It made him want to cry, but he held it in. He had to be strong for her.

"How did this happen? How could he have..." she started crying. Erik grabbed her and embraced her. He was surprised she could pull her away from the fight, but she knew there was no hope. They couldn't keep going.

"Shh, it's okay. Everything will be okay," he whispered as he stroked her back. People around them walked by and gave them looks for the scene they were making, standing in the middle of the street and being covered in blood. It didn't matter, if anyone said anything he could erase what they saw.

She shook her head. "No, no it won't Erik. Not this time."

He just held her in silence. She was right, it did not look good to those passing by where they were standing. Everything had been slowly falling apart for them. It could still end up differently than they predicted, though. They could still win this war in the end.

Erik had seen Jürgen take Collin. They had to finish the pact, no matter what. James may be mad at Gwen, but he wasn't going to risk her life. He would make her finish it. They would change Collin soon and it would be back to three against five. They would still be fighting against the odds, but it didn't matter. They would find a way and win this war. They had to.

Elizabeth backed away from him. "What are we going to do next?"

Erik shook his head. "I don't know."

"You said they would be going to Germany," she sniffed. "We should head there." It was true, that would be their next stop but there was more they still had to do, more they had to wait for than just trying to get ahead.

He nodded. "Yes, but we have to wait to see how this will play out. We have to wait for Collin."

She looked at him. "You think he can handle it? You think he can handle the change?"

"I am willing to bet on it," he said. He wasn't sure but really hoped Collin could. So far his heart had been in the right place, hopefully it would stay that way after the change. And Gwen didn't change that about him.

"If not, there's little hope for us, is there!" she claimed. Erik was surprised by how negative she was being. She usually was confident, not giving into doubts. She was always someone who could keep her head up high and have faith that all would turn out for the best. Her sudden change made him fear the end even more.

Erik put his hands on her shoulders and looked deep into her eyes. "Don't say that. We will find a way. Our kind always does."

Elizabeth shook her head. "Erik, there are only two of us left."

"Two of the best." He tried to smile but he didn't have it in him. Too much had happened. She was right, there were only two of them. He was beginning to lose faith in winning this war as well. He had to keep a positive outlook though, for the sake of doing what Hugh would have wished for them to do. He never knew what could happen in the end.

"But there are five of them," she replied.

"So? We can win. We will win," he tried to be positive. It was the only thing they could do now. "We will win."

"Do you really believe that?" Elizabeth asked, wiping away the last of her tears.

"I do."

Elizabeth took a deep breath to calm herself down. "Then what should we do now?"

"We will wait."

CHAPTER 49

Gwen slowly opened her eyes to see James' shoes right by her face. She looked up to find him grinning down at her, as he always did. Pain echoed through her body as she twisted on the concrete floor. The triduanum. Hugo.

James rolled her over, kicking her in the stomach. She glared up at him.

"Wake up Sleeping Beauty, your prince is worried about you," James said as he nodded toward the other side of the room.

Gwen looked over at Collin. He sat against the wall, his face full of worry.

"Collin?" she whispered as James kicked her again. He drove his foot right in the knife wound. She gasped.

"Stop it! You're hurting her!" Collin exclaimed.

James turned to him. "I gave her plenty of warning. I told her if she betrayed me I would rip her heart out. I'm being nice."

He pulled her up by the collar and shoved her against the wall. Gwen felt her spine snap from the impact. She shifted her body and popped the vertebrae back in place. Damn, she hated these bodies. Too fragile.

"Is this all you have James? You're weakening." She spat out blood at his feet. The liquid freckled his shoes. "You need someone to teach you how to torture someone."

James tightened his grip around her throat, nails digging into her skin. "You really love pain, don't you?"

"It's the only time you meet someone's real self," she croaked out.

"Funny you say that." He pulled out a revolver. "Because I miss my old Gwen."

"Hey, aren't those illegal here?" she jeered. It was the only way she dealt with the inevitable. Joke about it.

He smiled as he put the barrel against her temple. "Shall we play a little Russian roulette?"

Gwen's eyes widened as he started to slowly pull the trigger. He wasn't joking. A bullet through the brain wouldn't kill her but it would hurt it like hell. The impact of the bullet, the radiating fracture of the skull, the large exit wound it would create. The barrel would also burn her skin where the burst of flame came out, not to mention all the unburnt gunpowder that would stick into her skin. She grimaced. She didn't want to go through that, not again.

She glanced at Collin. He just stared at them, not sure if he should do something but knowing there wasn't anything he could do. Not against James. So he just sat there and watched the show.

The sound of the trigger clicking made her twitch. There was no bullet in the chamber. She let out the breath she had been holding.

James pulled back the revolver and let her collapse to the ground. "Funny, I thought all the chambers were full." He pointed the gun down at her and unloaded the rest of the gun into her. Five bullets scattered across her body. Gwen yelped, cursing at James for being such an ass, even though she knew she deserved it in the end. It didn't mean it didn't hurt, both physically and emotionally.

"Stop it! You'll kill her!" Collin jumped up. James only laughed.

"Oh I am far from killing her. Ain't that right Gwen? We can never die! Not truly. After this world is just another pit of darkness. Forever!" James stomped on her left hand. The bones cracked under the weight of his foot. She cried out in pain. "There is no forgiveness for us! There is no turning back! There is no redemption, no sorry, no returning!" He pushed down harder. "Yet you still helped those who cast us down here! Those who kicked us out of heaven. Why?!"

"I don't know!" she yelped.

He took his foot off of her hand. She held it. She didn't have enough energy to heal it. Not after the bullets and the knife.

"You're lucky I don't let Jürgen in here, he would kill you in an instant. I'm letting up since we have a little history."

"Exactly why he didn't want you dealing with me," she commented.

"That's my decision not his." He pulled her up by her hair. "Besides, I want to hear you scream for mercy."

He bit into her throat. She tried to scream but couldn't—his fangs pierced her throat and she couldn't speak. He dug in as if was going to rip her throat right out. Tears rolled down her face. Tighter and tighter he closed his jaw. Any more and he might snap her neck in half. Releasing his grip, James let her fall to the ground, blood oozing everywhere. He turned to Collin.

"Talk to her now, Collin. You think you can still find that good girl to treat you kindly? Be my guest." James took a few steps back. "I won't stop you. Prove to me she is good and I will let you two go."

Gwen lay on the floor, blood from her wounds soaking her clothes and the surrounding floor. Her heart hurt, and it wasn't because of the bullet. No, it was because James was right. There was nothing for her to gain. There was no going back.

Collin bent down slowly beside her. "Gwen," he whispered as he looked at her wounds, most likely disgusted with the gore.

She closed her eyes. "Collin, you should get out of here."

He shook his head. "I'm not leaving you."

Gwen let the pain engulf her. She could feel everything

her body was telling her. The pain of each wound. Gwen began to think of what that pain was for. Helping the same beings who gave her a body that could feel pain. The same beings that threw her out of the heavens and onto earth where she suffered day after day in this form. The same beings who had used her to get a creature she created. Collin.

She looked over at him. He just sat there, watching her suffer. He was just another worthless human being. She was crazy for thinking otherwise. Why she had brought him back was beyond her.

Pulling herself up, she collapsed a little from the pain.

"Let me help you." Collin reached out to her. She shoved him away.

"Run," she whispered.

"What?"

She looked up at him with her yellow eyes. "I said run."

There was no turning back now, she finally regained the hatred that filled her heart so many years ago. Hatred at herself for thinking she could better her wrongs, hatred for those who tried to help her, hatred for this man who showed her how to love and caused her all of this pain.

There was no forgiveness.

He didn't move two steps before Gwen grabbed him and dug her fangs into his neck. His blood filled her mouth, the sweet taste she had been longing for since she had given him hers. The connection was complete, he was hers. She breathed it in like the air around her. Such power, such control. It was all hers.

The deed was done. She dropped him to the floor, like waste. His blood added to the puddles that stained the ground. He was for the Gargoyles to deal with now. Gwen would just have to wait for him to start crawling back to her. He would need her blood. He would crave it like a drug addict, except there was no coming down from this high. It was marvelous.

James started clapping.

"You make such a show, my darling, no matter what you do." He stepped to her. She slapped him.

"Don't ever do that to me again." Her voice was dark.

He simply smiled as he rubbed his cheek. "Don't put me in a position to do so again."

"I admit it, you were successful." Gwen licked the blood on her hands. "You ripped my heart out."

"You shouldn't have underestimated me. I know what buttons of yours to push." He pulled her close and kissed her lips.

"That's true," she looked down at Collin's body, admiring his humanity one last time. It would be gone when he woke. That's when something on Collin's hand caught her eyes. "That can't be."

She bent down and looked at the ring. It was. It was James' garnet ring. She pulled it off his finger and put it on her thumb.

"Is that my ring?" James examined it on her hand.

"It is, how on earth he found it, I don't know. Didn't you lose it to some pirate?"

"I did." He pulled it off and placed it on his. "Now

everything is back where it belongs."

She grinned as she wrapped her arms around him and bit him. The poison from the knife disappeared from her body.

"I will contact the Gargoyles and let them know the deed has been done." He eyed her after she finished drinking his blood. "You know, they can't kill you twenty-four hours after you turn him. We could set up a trap. There's nothing they can do to stop you, not without risking Erik's life."

"As tempting as that sounds." She traced her finger along his chest. "I want to spread the fun out a little more. There are only two of them left and we already got one today. Anymore and it will all come to an end."

He kissed her forehead. "There's my Guinevere."

She smiled as she dipped her finger into the pool of blood on the floor. "Speaking of which." Gwen started writing on the wall with the blood that covered her. "I have a little game to play."

CHAPTER 55

Back at the flat, Erik and Elizabeth got another telegram from Gwen. This one was a young girl. She didn't step in front of a bus though, she just walked away, back into the crowd. Blending in.

They ran. Gwen had finally turned Collin, and he needed to be there when he woke up. There was no telling what he might do or where he might go.

"Over here." Erik motioned to Elizabeth. The place looked abandoned, but Erik knew better. It had been their base. They were long gone now, off to Germany probably. They made their mess and converted whom they needed. Just as always.

Erik kicked down the door. The sound echoed through the deserted hallways. They entered slowly, making sure it wasn't a trap. It would have been low of them to try, but they were low creatures.

Pulling out his flashlight, Erik shined it down the hallway that they entered. It was eerily quiet. The only sound that they heard was that of the street. Elizabeth followed closely behind.

They found him in one of the torn-out rooms. Blood covered the concrete floor and walls. It looked as if there had been a massacre. It was probably all Gwen's—her punishment for what she had done. Whatever it was, it had caused her to give in and turn Collin. James knew what he was doing.

"Collin!" Elizabeth exclaimed, as she hurried to his side. She placed her fingers on the side of his neck that wasn't covered in blood. "He still has a pulse."

Suddenly his eyes shot open. Both Elizabeth and Erik jumped. Collin was breathing heavily and twitching like mad. He looked up at them. His eyes glowed yellow.

Just like a demon.

"My head," he grasped it. "It hurts so much."

Elizabeth knelt down beside him. "Collin, it's okay. We are going to help you." She grabbed him and placed his mouth against her wrist. He sank his fangs into her wrist. Elizabeth knew it was what he needed to calm down.

Erik started to glance around the room. That was when he realized that some of the blood on the wall spelled out words.

Three little Gargoyles who hadn't a clue. We killed one more and now there are two.

It was the warning Gwen used to leave with the Gargoyles she had killed. Her little game. Erik kicked the chair out of frustration.

She was back.

CHAPTER 51

"What beautiful place shall we corrupt next?" Gwen questioned as she sat down on the train seat next to James. He had done it. She was herself again. She was all his.

"What is a war without Germany, my love?" James wrapped his arm around her and kissed her firmly on the mouth. Her dark lips tasted oh so sweet.

Jürgen eyed the both of them suspiciously.

Gwen laughed. "Sehr Gut! Deutschland ist es!" Gwen noted that Jürgen was still staring at her. "What is it, Jürgen? Don't you love Germany?"

"I just don't get why she is free to roam around. I think we should have just put her in with the luggage," he growled.

"But if it weren't for her, we wouldn't be down one Gargoyle, now would we?" James explained with a smile.

"And besides Jürgen." She pulled out her knife and threw it at the map that hung in their first-class cabin. It hit Berlin dead center. "I'm back."

CHAPTER 52

Collin kept to himself as he and the Gargoyles made their way through Rome. He didn't quite understand why they were there but went along with it. Why wouldn't he?

He had given the deed to the pub to Hywel and said his last farewell to him. Hywel tried to ask questions, but Collin didn't even have an answer to them. He just said goodbye and walked away.

Collin kept thinking of the last memory he had of Gwen. Her fierce eyes looking at him hungrily, her sharp fangs piercing into his neck. No resentment, no hesitation. She went straight for him.

She was a monster.

Now here he was, a soul trapped in what he deemed

was a "vampire's" body. He wasn't a demon, he wasn't a Gargoyle, he wasn't a minion. He was what all the stories talked about, a vampire.

The idea seemed cool, but the reality of his new circumstances was not. His blood felt hot. His body ached. His heart longed. All for one thing.

Blood.

He wanted it. Every person he saw, every girl, every boy. All of them. That's why he kept his head down while he walked, to get the thought out of his mind. It didn't work, he still wanted it. Bad.

They came upon the Vatican, and Collin followed Erik and Elizabeth up the steps. He knew he shouldn't have been surprised that that was where they were going, but it did. Collin watched as Erik talked to one of the Fathers.

"What is he saying?" Collin asked Elizabeth.

"He is asking to talk to the keeper of the candles," she said.

"The what?"

"For every Gargoyle there is a candle to let the Church know if the end is coming. When a Gargoyle is destroyed, there is a ceremony to un-light the candle," she explained.

"Ah, I see." He really didn't but that was okay. He would figure it out as time went on.

They followed Erik through the corridor and down the stairs into the basement of the Vatican. Coming upon a door, Erik pulled out the key the bishop had given him and opened it to reveal a tall man standing by the candles. His balding white hair was messy, and he appeared to Collin to look the slightest bit crazed.

"Good to see you again, even though it is under these circumstances," the man greeted.

Erik nodded, and they watched as he put out one of the candles, the one that stood for Hugo. The candle-keeper recited a Medieval Latin prayer as they held their heads down and listened. Collin didn't understand what he was saying, but knew that Erik and Elizabeth did. They had been there when Latin was a commonly spoken language. They had lived through it all. Collin felt sorry for all the friends they had to see die throughout the years. Now he would have to do the same.

Once the ceremony was over, Collin followed Erik and Elizabeth out of the Vatican. "Is that all he does, guard those candles?" he questioned them.

"Yes. It is important for the Church to know when the end is coming. If those candles don't stay lit, then they won't know how many of us are left," Erik explained.

Collin nodded. It made sense to him. Personally, he would just keep a tally on a board, but he knew how the Church liked their tradition. That way they could have the ceremony as well.

"Then what is next if the end is coming?" Collin asked.

Erik turned to face Collin and smiled. "We stop it, of course."

Thank you so much for reading! Readers like you make it possible for authors like me to write stories! If you could spare a moment and leave a review on Amazon, Goodreads, BookBub, and wherever you like to buy books, that would mean the world to me! It really helps authors like me to succeed in the publishing world.

Book 2: The Turned coming March 2021!

Acknowledgements

This novel has been many years in the making and am so excited to finally get it out for readers to enjoy. There are many people who helped make this possible, including my mentors Mike, Joe, Betty, Paul, and many more over the years. I also want to give a big thank you to my editors Chantelle and Justin who have been encouraging me to keep writing since we first met, and to my new editor and friend Hilary who found interest in my story and wanted to be involved. I also want to say thank you to my writing group, Bernie, Traci, Rebecca, Stacy, and Christi who have been so helpful and great readers, editors, and listeners. To my friends, including Earlene, Veronica, Faye, Dave, and Amelia who helped edit and give feedback, thank you as well! Thank you Biserka Designs for the wonderful cover! To my parents who have helped through the years to keep on going. And lastly, to my husband who has stuck by my side, helping me through it all.

About the Author

Dani Hoots is a science fiction, fantasy, romance, and young adult author who loves anything with a story. She has a B.S. in Anthropology, a Masters of Urban and Environmental Planning, a Certificate in Novel Writing from Arizona State University, and a BS in Herbal Science from Bastyr University.

Currently she is working on a YA urban fantasy series called Daughter of Hades, a YA urban fantasy series called The Wonderland Chronicles, a historic fantasy vampire series called A World of Vampires, and a YA sci-fi series called Sanshlian Series. She has also started up an indie publishing company called FoxTales Press. She also works with Anthill Studios in creating comics through Antik Comics.

Her hobbies include reading, watching anime, cooking,

studying different languages, wire walking, hula hoop, and working with plants. She is also an herbalist and sells her concoctions on FoxCraft Apothecary. She lives in Phoenix with her husband and visits Seattle often. Feel free to email her with any questions you might have! danihootsauthor@gmail.com

Printed in Great Britain
by Amazon